MURDER OF A REAL BAD BOY

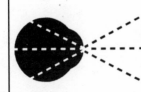

This Large Print Book carries the
Seal of Approval of N.A.V.H.

A SCUMBLE RIVER MYSTERY

MURDER OF A
REAL BAD BOY

DENISE SWANSON

THORNDIKE PRESS

An imprint of Thomson Gale, a part of The Thomson Corporation

THOMSON

GALE

Detroit • New York • San Francisco • New Haven, Conn. • Waterville, Maine • London

THOMSON

GALE

Thorndike Press® Large Print Mystery.

The text of this Large Print edition is unabridged.

Other aspects of the book may vary from the original edition.

Set in 16 pt. Plantin.

LIBRARY OF CONGRESS CATALOGING-IN-PUBLICATION DATA

Swanson, Denise.
    Murder of a real bad boy : a Scumble River mystery / by Denise Swanson.
        p. cm. — (Thorndike Press large print mystery)
    ISBN-13: 978-0-7862-9282-0 (lg. print : alk. paper)
    ISBN-10: 0-7862-9282-2 (lg. print : alk. paper) 1. Denison, Skye (Fictitious character) — Fiction. 2. School psychologists — Fiction. 3. Women psychologists — Fiction. 4. Large type books. I. Title.
PS3619.W36M856 2007
813'.6—dc22   2006033330

Published in 2007 by arrangement with NAL Signet,
a member of Penguin Group (USA) Inc.

Printed in the United States of America on permanent paper
10 9 8 7 6 5 4 3 2 1

To my wonderfully supportive husband, who performs every role from therapist to copy editor with love and generosity. There would be no Scumble River mysteries without you.

ACKNOWLEDGMENTS

Thanks to all the folks who told me their stories about bad, awful, and worst contractors.

AUTHOR'S NOTE

In July of 2000, when the first book in my Scumble River series, *Murder of a Small-Town Honey,* was published, it was written in "real time." It was the year 2000 in Skye's life as well as mine, but after several books in a series, time becomes a problem. It takes me seven months to a year to write a book, and then it is usually another year from the time I turn that book in to my editor until the reader sees it on a bookstore shelf. This can make the timeline confusing. Different authors handle this matter in different ways. After a great deal of deliberation, I decided that Skye and her friends and family will age more slowly than those of us who don't live in Scumble River. Although I made this decision while writing the fourth book in the series, *Murder of a Snake in the Grass,* I didn't realize until recently that I needed to share this information with my readers. So, to catch everyone up, the following is when the books take place.

Murder of a Small-Town Honey — August 2000

Murder of a Sweet Old Lady — March 2001

Murder of a Sleeping Beauty — April 2002

Murder of a Snake in the Grass — August 2002

✓ Murder of a Barbie and Ken — November 2002

Murder of a Pink Elephant — February 2003

✓Murder of a Smart Cookie — June 2003

✓Murder of a Real Bad Boy — September 2003

The Scumble River short story and novella take place:

"Not a Monster of a Chance" — June 2001

"Dead Blondes Tell No Tales" — March 2003

Although there is a painting named *Frida and the Miscarriage*, the one referred to in this book by the same artist exists only in my imagination.

Scumble River is not a real town. The characters and events portrayed in these pages are entirely fictional, and any resemblance to living persons is pure coincidence.

Chapter 1
One Fell Swoop

"Dude?"

"Just five more minutes," Skye Denison mumbled, still half asleep.

"Dude, are you okay?"

Skye slowly lifted her head from the desktop and swiped at the damp spot on the blotter. She turned toward the door of her tiny office, wondering if there was a rule somewhere in the cosmos that stated the smallest space in any school building was automatically assigned to the school psychologist.

Granted, she'd only worked in two places — New Orleans, Louisiana, and her present job in Scumble River, Illinois — but from what she had heard from others in her profession, the fortunate few school psychs who were actually given an office of their own usually described it as being the size of a refrigerator box.

Before she could contemplate this complex issue further, the tall, thin young man standing at her door repeated his question, and it dawned on her that she had just been caught by the custodian not only asleep, but also drooling. She might as well get the L tattooed on her forehead, since she was now officially a Loser.

Skye swept the hair out of her eyes. "I'm fine, Cameron. I was just resting my eyes. I haven't been getting much sleep lately because . . ." She heard herself babbling and trailed off.

Cameron nervously fingered the three whiskers on his chin that made up his goatee, and said, "Whoa, dude. TMI." He backed up, pulled a set of headphones from around his neck, and plunked them on his ears before escaping down the hall.

TMI. Too much information. The story of her life. Skye leaned back against the orange molded-plastic chair and scanned the drab green walls. The bright posters with positive sayings she had hung at the beginning of the year mocked her depressed mood.

She searched her mind for some task that she could accomplish in her present state, something that wouldn't suffer from her distracted condition. Even though it was only the end of September, her to-do list was already several pages long. Already there were reevaluations to arrange, committees to organize, and the never-ending paperwork that was a major part of any school psychologist's job.

Without a doubt, she had plenty of work waiting to get done — her appointment book should have a warning label on its cover stating DATES ON CALENDAR ARE CLOSER THAN THEY APPEAR — just nothing she felt able to undertake with everything that was already occupying her thoughts.

Too bad there was no one around to talk to. Discussing her problems would probably make her feel better, but her best friend, Trixie Frayne, had left yesterday for a romantic Lake Tahoe getaway with her husband, and the rest of the staff had poured out of the building a half hour ago when the elementary school's final bell had rung, eager to get an early start on their weekend.

Skye briefly considered walking over to the high school, but then remembered that Alana Lowe, the art teacher, whom Skye could usually count on for an after-school chat, wasn't available. Alana's boyfriend was visiting from New York, and that morning she had mentioned meeting him right after school to go into Chicago for a big night on the town.

Who else would be around that Skye could kill some time talking to? No one. No one hung around on a Friday afternoon who didn't have to. No one, that is, except Skye, who, unlike her colleagues, didn't want to go home.

Skye watched another ten minutes tick by on the wall clock before concluding that if she stayed any longer she would probably fall asleep again, and being awakened by the janitor on a second occasion did not bear contemplating. With her luck, this time she would be snoring.

She reluctantly stood, retrieved her tote bag, and edged from behind her desk — there was just enough room to squeeze past as long as she didn't add any inches to her already generous curves. It took her less than two full steps to cross the small room. Then after locking the office door behind her, she walked listlessly out to the deserted parking lot and climbed slowly into her car.

The bright aqua 1957 Chevy Bel Air had been a gift from her father and godfather. On good days she appreciated the effort they had put into restoring it for her. On bad days she cursed the difficulty she had parking it, and its unquenchable thirst for gasoline.

Today was a bad day. When Skye started the engine, she noticed that the needle on the fuel gauge pointed to E. Cursing the Bel Air's gluttony, she headed to the cheapest place in town to fill up its tank.

The station with the best prices was on the same street as her brother Vince's hair salon. As Skye drove past his shop, she noticed that his Jeep was in its usual spot, even though the CLOSED sign was in the front window. She considered stopping to say hi, but then remembered that when she had talked to him a couple of days ago, Vince had mentioned a big date he had planned for Friday night.

Sighing in envy of Vince's uncomplicated love life, Skye pulled up to the pump, hopped out, and unscrewed the Bel Air's gas cap. As she turned to grab the nozzle, she caught sight of a red Mercedes with a license plate that read CRMPAYS parked by the side of the building.

Skye wrinkled her brow. What was Loretta Steiner doing in Scumble River? Loretta lived in Chicago and claimed the only reason she ever left the city was if someone paid her to do so. And since Loretta was one of the best criminal attorneys in Illinois, when Loretta got paid it was usually because someone was under arrest for murder.

Skye and Loretta had both belonged to Alpha Sigma Alpha at the University of Illinois, but after college they had lost touch. A few years ago when Skye's brother was charged with killing an ex-girlfriend, Skye had remembered reading about Loretta's spectacular law career in *The Phoenix,* their sorority magazine, and called Loretta to represent Vince.

From that time on, they had renewed their friendship, getting together for lunches and girls' nights out — but only in the city since Loretta claimed she was allergic to small towns.

Had something happened in Scumble River that Skye didn't know about? Was someone under arrest and Skye hadn't heard about it? She'd been wrapped up in her own problems, but surely anything big enough to bring Loretta to town would have penetrated her preoccupation.

Skye was still trying to figure out why her friend was there when Loretta came out of the gas station's mini-mart. At six feet tall, with coal black hair and mahogany skin, she looked like royalty from some exotic land, a queen wearing Manolo Blahnik suede boots and carrying a Louis Vuitton purse.

As Loretta approached her car, she turned her head and her gaze met Skye's. For a second, a strange expression seemed to flit across the lawyer's face, but it smoothed out so quickly, Skye wasn't sure it had ever been there. Abandoning the gas pump, Skye dashed toward Loretta at the same time Loretta started toward Skye. They met between the building and the fuel area, hugging and talking at the same time.

"What are you doing here? Is someone in trouble?" Skye demanded.

"Girl, how are you doing? It seems like months since I've heard from you. Why haven't you returned my calls?"

Silence. Skye chewed her lip, trying to come up with a good explanation.

It appeared Loretta was in no hurry to answer Skye's question either, but finally she said, "I had to see a client downstate, and I remembered Scrimshaw River had the best gas prices along I-55."

"Why didn't you call me if you were going to be in *Scumble* River?" Skye asked. Loretta frequently pretended she couldn't remember the town's name; it was a familiar game.

"Sorry. I wasn't planning on stopping." Loretta's gaze slipped from Skye's. "Anyway. What's up with the silent treatment?"

"Sorry about that. I've been pretty depressed lately — hiding out and not wanting to talk to anyone." Skye hugged her friend. "Hey, let's get some supper and I'll tell you all about it."

"Sorry, sweet cheeks, I'm booked for dinner. How about a quick cup of coffee? I need to be back on the road no later than five."

"Sure." Abruptly Skye realized that a heart-to-heart with a non–Scumble River friend was exactly what she needed. She checked her watch. It was already four thirty, so she'd have to talk fast if she wanted Loretta's perspective on everything that was going on. "But I'm not sure where we can get coffee close by."

Loretta frowned, then pointed to the mini-mart. "I'll get us a couple of cups in there and we can sit in my car and talk. You finish filling up."

When Skye walked out after paying for her gas, Loretta was already settled in her Mercedes.

Skye moved the Bel Air next to the sleek red car, and after sliding into the luxury sedan and thanking Loretta for the coffee, she said, "You won't believe all that's happened since the last time I talked to you."

"So tell me." Loretta gave Skye her full attention.

"Would you believe I now have to plot my drive home from work every day as if I'm avoiding enemy land mines?"

"Say what?"

"I can no longer simply go the quickest way." Skye took a sip of coffee, wincing as she burned her tongue.

"Why?"

"Because the best route takes me past the bowling alley."

"And this is bad why?" Loretta asked. "Have you suddenly developed a phobia about smelly rental shoes or shiny black balls?"

"No, but Simon owns it and his mother Bunny manages it."

"Simon Reid, the town undertaker and county coroner, owns a bowling alley?"

Skye frowned. "Remember, last December I told you Simon bought the alley for his mother to manage? Bunny needed a steady job in order to fulfill the terms of her probation for using a fake prescription to get pain pills. You helped her when she lost the paperwork, remember?"

"Right. Sorry, I did know that." Loretta scowled. "So why can't you drive past the bowling alley your boyfriend owns?"

"He's not my boyfriend anymore."

"What?" Loretta's scream hurt Skye's ears. "What happened? Why didn't you call and tell me this?"

"I didn't want to talk about it." Skye took a deep breath. It still hurt to say it out loud. "He cheated on me. When he went to California in August, he told me he was staying with a college friend. This 'friend' turned out to be female." Skye gazed out the window. "Everyone keeps telling me that staying with her doesn't mean they were, ah, you know . . ."

"Screwing?" Loretta supplied.

Skye nodded. "But if they weren't, then why didn't he tell me his friend was a woman?"

"Good question. What was his answer?"

"He refuses to explain himself. Says that if I trusted him, I wouldn't need an explanation."

"That's just man talk for 'you caught me with my pants down and I don't have any reasonable excuse.' " Loretta hugged Skye, then said, "I still don't understand why breaking up with Simon means you can't drive past the bowling alley."

"Because Bunny is way too anxious to chat about why Simon and I broke up."

"And?" Loretta still looked puzzled.

"And, unfortunately, Bunny refuses to believe that I don't want to talk to her. She's taken to trying to ambush me by dashing into the road and waving her arms as I approach. The speed limit in town is only twenty miles per hour, and for a woman in her late fifties wearing stiletto heels, Bunny is a surprisingly fast runner. She nearly caught me the last time I tried going home that way."

Loretta's eyebrows had disappeared into her hairline and she was shaking with laughter.

Skye closed her eyes. This was not funny to her. The image of Bunny, long, curly red hair flying behind her and surgically enhanced breasts bouncing up and down as she pursued Skye's car, made Skye cringe. No way was she driving past the bowling alley until Bunny's interest had waned.

Loretta got herself under control and asked, "Isn't there another way home?"

"The next best road is Kinsman, but it's off-limits, too. It goes past the police station where my mother works." May, a dispatcher, worked the three-to-eleven shift.

"And May wants to talk to you about your breakup, too, right?" Loretta guessed. "I'll bet she could almost feel those grandbabies in her arms."

"She was practically knitting baby booties."

"Does she chase you down the road, too?"

"No, but Mom watches for me out the station's big front window. As soon as she sees me going past, she counts to one hundred, then punches in my home number. The phone is ringing when I walk through the front door. If I don't answer it, she sends a county deputy to make sure I haven't died or had an accident in the five minutes that've passed since she saw me drive by the station."

Loretta snorted. "I'm guessing you're about as eager to talk to May as you are to talk to Bunny about your love life."

"Right." Skye grimaced.

"Speaking of the police station, what about that cute chief? Now that you and Simon are broken up, I'd expect him to step right in. Every time I've see you together, the sexual tension between you two could make a virgin swoon."

"I'm thinking about swearing off men."

"That's silly." Loretta shook her head. "A man is like a hammer. It hasn't evolved much over the past hundred years, but it's still handy to have around."

"Yeah, and if you don't watch what you're doing with them every second, you end up

24

hitting your thumb and hurting yourself really badly." Skye forestalled Loretta's next comment by returning to her original problem. "Anyway, the last reasonably short route home is the worst by far. It puts me directly in front of Simon's funeral home. And the last thing I want to do is see that double-dealing jerk."

"Why? Does Simon run after your car, or send the cops if you don't answer your telephone?"

"No." Skye answered grudgingly, deep in her heart a little disappointed that he didn't. "But even the sight of him ruins my night." She swallowed a lump in her throat. The hurt of his betrayal was still as sharp as it had been the day she discovered it. "I've been hanging up on him since we had it out about his 'old friend' being female."

"So, how do you get home?"

"I have to drive way out of my way, circle the town and come back in from the north." Skye sighed. "Playing hide-and-seek in order to get home is one of the reasons I dread quitting time, but sadly, it's not the main one."

"You mean there's something worse?"

"Believe it or not, the main reason I don't want to go home is even more of a headache than my love life. The main reason I don't want to go home is Beau Hamilton, my building contractor. He's a thorn in my side bigger than a redwood tree."

"Why do you have a building contractor?" Loretta asked. "You live in a rental cottage."

"Not anymore." Skye blew out a tired breath. "I guess I haven't talked to you since I found out I was Alma Griggs's sole heir."

"No. I've been a little absentminded lately, but I would have remembered that. Who is Mrs. Griggs and why did she leave you her estate?"

"It's a long story." Skye leaned back against the Mercedes's comfy leather seat. "Mrs. Griggs was an elderly woman who was murdered in August during the Route 66 Yard Sale. Earlier in the summer, I helped her when an unscrupulous antique dealer tried to take advantage of her, and after that we became friends. Since Mrs. Griggs had no relatives, and she sort of decided I was her reincarnated daughter, she changed her will and left everything to me, asking that I fix up her house and live there."

"Reincarnated daughter?" Loretta choked on the coffee she had just sipped. "You're kidding me."

Skye shook her head and went on. It felt good to finally put it all into words. "I was surprised that the whole business of inheriting Mrs. Griggs's estate was taken care of so quickly, but now I suspect the attorney rushed it through to get it off his hands. After all, this is Stanley County, and if you know the right people and are part of the good old boy system, anything is possible."

"So I've heard," Loretta observed.

"To be fair, the lawyer did warn me about the unpaid back taxes, and the lack of liquid assets. But who knew being an heiress would be so complicated?"

"Anyone who has ever been one."

"I paid off the taxes with the money I earned during the summer as the Route 66 Yard Sale coordinator, and I got a home equity loan for the renovations. With those two problems settled, I thought the rest wouldn't be too bad." Skye took a deep breath and shook her head. "Boy, was I wrong."

"Why did you do everything so fast? You're not usually so impulsive."

"Maybe I should have waited before starting to fix up Mrs. Griggs's house, but since my rental cottage had been sold out from under me, and I only had a month to vacate the premises, it seemed silly to waste time. I had to live somewhere, and after my last experience staying at my parents' house, I wasn't going back there again no matter what."

"I'm with you there. I'd live in my car before I'd move in with my parents." Loretta took a sip of her now-cold coffee. "So what's the problem with the contractor?"

"I wish I knew. He came with wonderful recommendations — it seemed like everyone in town had used him to remodel their houses or add rooms. Plus I'm friendly with his sister. She's the art teacher at my high school." Skye took a breath. "I checked his references, got an estimate in writing, and made sure he had insurance and was bonded."

"But?"

"But he rarely finishes anything, and when he does, the work is terrible." Skye tried to think of where she'd gone wrong, and like always, the problem came back to hiring Beau Hamilton in the first place. "I should have known anyone who looked that good would be trouble."

"Okay, now we're getting somewhere."

"I remember the day Beau came out to the house to give me an estimate. When he zoomed up on his shiny black motorcycle, he was so gorgeous I could barely catch my breath."

Skye closed her eyes and pictured him.

Molded bronze muscles strained the smooth white fabric of his T-shirt, and worn denim jeans emphasized his powerful thighs and slim hips. His thick red-gold hair rippled in the breeze as he walked toward where she sat on the porch. As he got closer, he took off his expensive Oakley sunglasses, and his compelling blue eyes nearly mesmerized her. When he smiled, dimples bracketing his sexy lips, Skye all but forgot her own name.

Loretta broke into Skye's pleasant daydream. "What happened?"

"He was this massive, self-confident presence, and I was swept away by his charm."

"You signed on the spot, didn't you?"

Skye defended herself. "He had glowing references, his estimate was reasonable, and . . ." She trailed off.

Loretta shook her head. "You should have trusted your instincts. Anyone that good has to have a flaw. Never hire a hottie."

"You're right. I gave in to hormones and haste. He's amazingly handsome, and I was in a hurry to get the renovations started." Skye paused, then confessed, "You know, what amazes me the most is that every day I go home intending to fire him and I can't seem to do it, even though when I get there, I find he hasn't finished anything, or worse, has done work so sloppy it looks as if a five-year-old was playing with his dad's tools."

"So, why can't you fire him?"

Skye felt herself blush. "First he looks so darned yummy, with his shirt off and his muscles all golden tan, my mouth goes dry."

"And?"

"And then he starts talking, and he's so charming. He always has a really good excuse, and then he asks how my day went and how the kids I'm working with are doing and . . ." Skye trailed off. She knew it sounded lame, but it was hard to explain the enthralling effect Beau had on women.

Loretta narrowed her eyes. "So he's a real bad boy."

"Exactly, but he looks deep into your eyes and makes you feel as if he could be real good to you."

"Girlfriend, I know you've had bad luck with men, but being taken in by a bad boy isn't like you." Suddenly Loretta grinned and snapped her fingers. "How long has it been since you broke up with Simon — a month? Obviously, you need to get laid before you do something else stupid."

"I told you, I'm swearing off men." Skye frowned.

"Yeah, it sure sounds that way," Loretta retorted, then asked, "How much money have you given him?"

"He said he needed a third up front." Skye couldn't quite bring herself to name the actual amount. "But I did make him give me copies of receipts for his suppliers."

"That's good. At least you don't have to worry about the suppliers coming after you. But never hire a contractor who can't work without getting paid first."

"Why?" Skye asked. "Everybody requires a deposit."

"Because now, if you fire him, he has your money and you have what? A hole in your roof?"

Skye groaned. Loretta had hit the nail on the head — which was more than Beau ever seemed to do. "You mean I can't get my money back?"

"Legally? Probably, yes. But practically, good luck." Loretta looked at her Rolex and grimaced. "Sorry, sweetie, but I've got to run. Call me Sunday and we'll talk some more." As Skye fumbled for the door handle Loretta added, "Fax me a copy of your contract. At least I can send this SOB a scary lawyer letter."

"Thanks." Skye kissed her friend on the cheek and got out of the car. "Drive carefully."

Skye watched Loretta turn out of the gas station, then got into her own car and started her indirect route home. As she made her final turn onto Brook Lane, she sat up straighter and took a calming breath. Soon she'd have to face him.

She exhaled slowly, willing herself to remain composed. She had made up her mind. No matter how much she hated doing it, she had to get rid of Beau. She had no choice.

Chapter 2
Two Sides to
Every Question

The Griggs house, as Skye still thought of the dilapidated two-story white edifice that she now called home, was a mile north of the city limits, along the west branch of the Scumble River.

There were no other buildings along Brook Lane, and very few vehicles ventured down the narrow, twisting road. Her new residence was even more secluded than her cottage had been, and Skye's sense of isolation increased as she maneuvered her car through the brick columns at the end of the driveway.

She turned her face away when she went by the old wrought iron gates that lay rusting in the weeds. The ornate double Gs entwined in the center were unwelcome reminders that Mrs. Griggs had begun her life in this house as an affluent wife, and died there a poverty-stricken widow. Skye hoped the gates weren't also portents of her own bleak future.

At the end of the long driveway, Skye steered the Bel Air first to the right, then spun the wheel around and pulled into the left side of the detached two-car garage. Mrs. Griggs's ancient Lincoln Continental occupied the other half. Its keys, along with those to the house's back door, hung on a hook in the kitchen, untouched since the old woman's death. Getting rid of the Continental was another task Skye had yet to deal with.

According to the date inscribed in the concrete floor, the garage had been built in 1964. With its good roof, thick insulation, and reliable electric heater, Skye had begun to believe she should have moved into it, rather than its seventy-year-old neighbor.

As she walked toward the house, Skye wondered for the umpteenth time what form of architecture it represented. The design seemed to have Colonial, Tudor, and even Victorian features.

The closest she had come to identifying the style was a picture of a house labeled an American Foursquare, but it hadn't had a wraparound porch like hers did, and the description of the interior had been wrong. A Foursquare was named for the four nearly equal-sized rooms per floor, forming a square, whereas Skye's house had an uneven number of rooms on each floor and they varied in dimensions.

Shrugging away the mystery of the house's architectural lineage, Skye examined the building for any sign of progress in its renovation.

Her exasperation grew when her gaze fell on the section of Tyvek-encased wall where Beau had begun to remove the old siding. As usual, he had totally ignored her instructions.

He had begun that project while Skye was at work, conveniently forgetting that she had told him she had decided *not* to replace the clapboard. He stopped when she came home and threw a hissy fit, but by then half of her front wall was stripped. Now she had to have the whole house re-sided. But Beau Hamilton would *not* be doing it.

A line formed between Skye's eyebrows as she continued her inspection. The number of gaping holes covered in plastic where the new windows were supposed to go had not decreased, nor had the number of enormous tarps swathing the partially torn-off roof.

Her fury peaked when she realized that not only had nothing been accomplished, but there was also no sign of Beau or his crew. She stood still and listened: no sounds of saws or hammers or men swearing. She sniffed: no trace of cigarette or cigar smoke. She looked around: no indication of his motorcycle, or the truck and van of his workers.

How could she fire the jerk if he wasn't there? Skye felt as if the top of her head would blow off. Now she'd have to hunt him down to get rid of him. Trying to telephone him was useless. He never answered his phone or returned her calls.

She climbed the wide front steps, dropped her tote bag by the door, and followed the porch along the left side of the house. No hint of any work having been done there either.

The porch ended three-quarters of the way around, and Skye carefully picked her way down the narrow broken steps and along the cracked sidewalk that wound to the back. As she rounded the corner, she paused. The yard emanated a sense of abandonment.

At one time it had contained a formal garden, but the geometrical plots had long since merged into the general mess of the lawn. In the growing dusk bits of litter and tin cans gleamed bleakly among overgrown weeds.

She hated seeing it like this, but the

landscaping would have to wait until she got the house itself in shape. And at the rate Beau was going, that would be as soon as they had a blue moon on Leap Day.

Nothing on the outside had been touched since Skye had left ten hours ago. It looked as if the contractor hadn't even been there while she was gone, though to be fair she should check inside before drawing that conclusion.

The adrenaline rush from her initial anger was dying down and depression was setting in as Skye started down the remaining wall of the building. She felt as if she had been on a roller-coaster, slightly nauseous and a little dizzy. Her footsteps dragged, and the weight of her situation settled on her shoulders. Loretta's prediction about the contractor echoed in Skye's thoughts, making her feel hopeless and discouraged.

Skye was halfway along the last side when she heard a noise. She stopped, slowly turning toward where she thought the sound had come from. Her auditory directional skills were poor, but it seemed as if the noise had come from the backyard. That couldn't be right. When she had been there a few seconds ago it had been empty. Suddenly she stiffened. She had thought she was alone out here. Was that assumption wrong?

She retraced her steps, her instinct to investigate stronger than her unease. She scanned the lawn, but it looked exactly as it had a few minutes ago. All that had changed was the breeze, which had become stronger and now blew from a different direction.

Skye scrubbed her eyes. Was the stress starting to get to her? Was she imagining things?

No. There it was again, a faint sound carried on the wind. It seemed to come from her left, maybe from the woods that stood between the house and the river. She could hear the noise a little louder now, though it was still indistinct — clunking, then a few creaks, and finally a sort of moaning that died away.

Wait a minute. Maybe it was Bingo. She felt a surge of hope. Her beloved cat had gone missing on Wednesday, and she'd had no luck in her search for him since then.

The large trees that grew at the southwest border of the property stood limb to limb, draping that section of the backyard in darkness. Skye squinted into the gloom. Was there a shadow near the ground that was moving? Bingo was black, thus hard to spot in the twilight.

Raising her voice, she called, "Here, kitty, kitty. Here, Bingo."

There was no response, and Skye rubbed the goose bumps on her arms. What had been a crisp day was turning into a cold evening. The thin cotton sweater she wore with lightweight twill slacks was not enough to protect her from the chill.

She took a step toward the trees, calling, "Kitty, kitty. Bingo."

Abruptly she stopped. What if it wasn't Bingo? What if something less domesticated was making that noise? Should she call someone? She couldn't simply forget it and go inside, not with the least chance it might be her much-loved pet trying to find his way home.

This was the trouble with living alone — no one had your back and there was no one around to give you a second opinion.

Skye considered whom she could ask to come over. Trixie was out of town, Vince was on a big date, it was her godfather Charlie Patukas's poker night, and her father was unavailable — he never answered the telephone and her mother wasn't home to pass on messages.

Simon briefly crossed her mind, but he and Skye would inevitably end up arguing about his female friend in California. He would insist that if she trusted him, he didn't have to explain, and if she didn't trust him, he refused to explain. Skye couldn't convince him that when a woman answers a phone that a man is expected to answer, an explanation is the very least a girlfriend is owed.

That left Wally Boyd, the chief of police and an applicant for the newly open position of Skye's boyfriend. Although they had never dated, Skye and Wally shared an emotionally charged past. There had been chemistry between them since she was a teenager and he was a rookie cop. Given that back then she was underage, nothing had happened. When she returned to Scumble River as an adult, he was married, and by the time his wife left him several months later, Skye had already become involved with Simon.

Now that she and Wally were both free, Skye wasn't sure she wanted to get involved with him. Her track record with men was terrible. Maybe she should just resign herself to being alone for the rest of her life.

Skye hadn't heard anything while she had been deliberating, but now the noise sounded again and this time it didn't seem as eerie. She shook her head. What had made her think she needed someone to protect her?

She could imagine the way Vince would

tease her if she called for help and the sound turned out to be a broken branch scraping against a tree. Plus, any sign of vulnerability would convince May that Skye *did* need a man around the house.

Skye squared her shoulders. She was a capable adult. She wasn't afraid of every little noise and she wouldn't let this old house spook her. She could certainly rescue her cat without the assistance of a big, strong male.

Before she could change her mind, Skye grabbed the closest weapon available — a garden shovel — just in case, and calling "Kitty, kitty," she marched toward what appeared to be an overgrown path.

When she entered the cluster of trees, her sweater snagged on a branch. She heard the rip, but it took a moment for her eyes to adjust before she could assess the damage. Threads from the sleeve were tangled in the bark and there was a puckered spot in the knit. Terrific. A wardrobe fatality this early in her search was not a good omen.

She sighed and moved forward calling, "Kitty, kitty" every few steps. The air was heavy with the scent of pine. She sniffed, then pinched the bridge of her nose, hoping she wouldn't start sneezing.

Once she was well into the woods, she

stood still, listening for the noise again. When it occurred, she realized a new element had been added — water lapping at the shore. Damn. Could Bingo have fallen in the river? Gripping the shovel, she moved along the path, which seemed to lead toward the sound.

After walking for what felt like quite a distance, she saw that there was an old wooden dock with a modern-looking green motorboat tied to a post. The wind had produced swells in the river, which were causing the boat to thud against the dock.

As she watched the boat hit the pier, she heard a familiar clunk, then a few recognizable creaks, and finally as the boat drifted backward, a moaning sound coming from the bottom of the boat. Her call of "Kitty, kitty" brought no black furred head with pointy ears popping over the boat's side.

Laying the shovel down, she edged forward onto the dock, conscious of the rotten wood and the fact that she was not a lightweight. With every screech of a board, she held her breath, but kept inching forward, hoping the dock would hold her.

Finally she was close enough. When the boat floated toward her, she grabbed on and looked down into it. Screaming, she staggered backward, windmilling her arms in an attempt to regain her equilibrium. Her left foot smashed through a decayed board and she fell hard onto her rear.

The dock groaned, and Skye felt wood splintering as she crashed through the pier and plunged rump first into the river. At first shock from the fall and the cold water closing around her immobilized her, but she quickly gathered her wits and half swam, half crawled back to shore.

Trailing weeds and covered in muck, she got to her feet and turned to check on the motorboat. It was gone. The post it had been tied to had come loose when Skye had fallen, and the boat was drifting out into the river.

In an instant she shed her shoes, pants, and sweater and waded back into the water. She couldn't let that boat get away. Not with Beau Hamilton sprawled bleeding in the bottom.

CHAPTER 3
THREE SHEETS
TO THE WIND

Swimming was the only exercise Skye enjoyed and the only athletic activity she was good at. Although she did laps nearly every day, either at the high school's indoor pool or at the Scumble River Recreational Club where she worked as a lifeguard during the summer, neither experience had prepared her for attempting to rescue a bleeding man in a skipperless boat.

Within minutes, Skye was struggling to keep afloat and move forward. The water temperature dropped sharply as she swam farther away from shore, and soon she realized the undertow was much stronger than anything she had ever experienced.

Almost immediately, she began to tire. Her arms grew heavy and her kicks barely moved the water. Her teeth chattered and she fought a rising panic. No one knew she was out there. If she drowned, no one would know what had happened to her. It might be days before some fisherman discovered her body; by then they'd only be able to identify her from her dental work.

Mmm, dental work. Was it time for her six-month checkup? Let's see, six months from now would be the end of March. Hey, that was spring break. Maybe this year she'd go on vacation to Florida. No, darn, what was she thinking? She couldn't afford a vacation; she'd poured all the cash she could beg, borrow, or steal into her new house. And that jerk Beau Hamilton was spending her renovation money like it was water.

Water! Beau Hamilton! Oh, my God! She was supposed to be catching the boat in which he was bleeding to death, not making dental appointments and vacation plans. What was wrong with her? Why was her mind wandering? Could she already be experiencing hypothermia?

Skye forced herself to concentrate. She could still see the motorboat, but it was getting farther and farther away, and her strokes were growing weaker and weaker. She turned her head. The shore was also receding. It was time to decide. Should she keep trying to catch the boat or should she do the sensible thing and turn back?

At that moment, Beau let out another groan. His life was at stake. How could she even think of giving up? Skye saw that the boat had become snagged in a floating jumble of tree limbs, fishnets, and other litter. Knowing that it could break free at any minute, she summoned a burst of energy and darted forward.

The motorboat bobbed enticingly, wedged against a tangle of rotten logs. As Skye reached out to grab the side, one of the logs broke free and drifted away. When the boat floated after it, she screamed in frustration. With a flurry of mighty kicks she shot ahead and snatched a rope trailing from the stern.

Panting, she clung to the line, waiting for her heart to regain its normal rhythm and her breathing to even out. After a long moment, she pulled herself closer to the boat, moving hand over hand up the rope, her uncontrollable shivering making the task more difficult.

When she finally reached the side, she peered over the edge. Beau Hamilton was still lying on his back in a pool of blood, but he no longer appeared to be breathing. Skye clutched the rim. Was she too late? Could she still save him?

She had to get into the boat. There was no way she could push it all the way back to shore. It was too big. For most people climbing into a boat from the water wouldn't be a problem, but four years running in high school, Skye had been voted Most Likely Never To Do A Single Chin-Up.

Chin-ups were impossible, hanging from the parallel bars unimaginable. Heck, she couldn't even get out of the pool without using the ladder. The sad truth was she had no upper body strength. She was a weakling, and not a ninety-eight-pound one either.

Skye shivered in the cold water. How would she get up and over the side of the boat without a ladder? There was no giving up. She couldn't quit and take the bad grade. This time she had no choice. She had to, so she would. It was literally a matter of life and death. At least, unlike PE classes, no one was here to witness her inelegant attempts.

Before her first try, she shoved the boat back into the logjam and used the rope to tie it to the debris. Then she attempted to scale the side. She was halfway up when she slid back into the water.

For her second go-round, she tried to use a log as a step and quickly discovered she would never be the logrolling champ of Scumble River.

It was river two, Skye zero when her gaze fell on the outboard motor. It had lots of nooks and crannies. Could she somehow use it to climb aboard?

She looked over the motor, using her hands to feel for what lay below the water-line. There were a couple of toeholds and the boat seemed big enough not to tip over as she attempted to mount it from the rear. Luckily the bow held all of Beau's weight, which would counterbalance her own.

Fearing that the outboard motor would turn on by itself and shred her leg, but determined to get on board, Skye fitted her foot in the first space and heaved herself upward. The boat lurched and she clung to the motor's housing like it was a bucking bronco.

The second toehold was smaller and more difficult to locate with her foot, but this time she was prepared for the boat's sudden movement.

Skye's waist was now nearly even with the edge of the boat. She steadied herself and swung her left leg over. Success! She sat astride the rim for half a second before swinging her right leg over and toppling into the boat's interior.

She got to her knees and edged toward the bench seat separating her from Beau. He hadn't moved since the last time she had looked at him.

"Beau, are you okay?" Skye crawled up on the bench and reached for his wrist. She concentrated. Did she feel something or was that her own pulse beating in her ears?

"Speak to me, Beau." Inching closer, she put her cheek near his mouth. Yes! She definitely felt a faint breath.

"You're going to be fine." Okay, now what should she do? The blood seemed to be coming from the back of his head. Should she try to stop the flow? Skye looked around the boat's interior. There was nothing. No oars, no life jackets, not even a seat cushion. All she had on were a soaked bra and panties, which would be of no help, and Beau wore only jeans and a T-shirt. Getting either of those off of him would probably do more harm than good.

"I'll get you to the hospital." Since attending to his injuries was out, she needed to get him help fast. "Stay with me, Beau."

The last time she had been in a boat like this one, she had been twelve and fishing with her dad. They had been out on the water less than ten minutes when she vomited. Her father had silently driven her home and never suggested another trip.

Skye made her way aft and looked at the motor, trying to figure out how to turn it on. She vaguely remembered that there was some sort of cord with a wooden handle that had to be yanked, sort of like a lawn mower, but she didn't see anything of that sort.

Wait a minute, what did this switch do? She flipped it and the motor roared to life. Grabbing the bar sticking out of the motor, she was ready to steer. So, why weren't they moving?

Shit! She had tied the rope to a log. After she unfastened it, the boat started forward at a crawl and Skye shouted up to Beau, "Here we go. Hang in there."

There had to be a way to make the boat go faster. What had her father done? Ah, there was a rubber grip circling the handle — maybe it was like a motorcycle, and you twisted it to accelerate.

Yes. The boat sped up and Skye tried to ignore how cold she was. Instead, she examined the banks of the river, attempting to figure out where they were. The current flowed northwest and the banks were getting higher, which meant they were headed out of town. She needed to go the other way, get back to where there were houses and people.

After awkwardly making the turn, she tried to keep the boat in the center of the channel, fearing she might run it aground if she got too close to shore.

The river was dark, and Skye was wondering how she would recognize her own dock when she saw a glow on the east bank. As she drew closer, she realized it was coming from her property. It looked warm and inviting.

Skye yelled to Beau, "We're almost there. I can see the lights." She turned the boat toward shore, planning on beaching the vessel, as she had no idea how to dock it and didn't think there was much dock left to tie it to anyway.

Then she frowned. Why were there lights on her property? She hadn't noticed any halogen lamps that would have come on automatically after dark. She didn't know if Beau had slipped and hit his head accidentally or if he had been attacked. If it were the latter, maybe whoever had hurt Beau was waiting on shore to finish the job.

CHAPTER 4
FOUR CORNERS
OF THE EARTH

The glow had turned into a blinding light, and Skye squinted as she maneuvered the boat closer to shore. Were they friend or foe? Should she turn back, go farther down the river into town? Mmm, that option had a serious drawback. If she docked in town, she'd have to walk down Basin Street dressed in nothing but her soaked, transparent underwear. That was a picture she'd hate to see on the front page of Scumble River's weekly newspaper.

Nevertheless, she couldn't think of an alternative. How could she be sure it was safe to land, if she couldn't tell who would be there to greet her? If it was Beau's attacker, he'd probably kill them both.

Survival won out over vanity hands down, and Skye was on the verge of steering back out into the river when she became aware of voices yelling her name. She looked back to the shoreline and saw a swarm of people waving their arms, pointing, and shouting at her. She could hear only an occasional isolated word over the noise of the outboard motor.

For a split second it appeared the cast from the old TV program *Gilligan's Island* had decided to film a reunion show on the banks of Scumble River, but then she recognized the figures lined up near her destroyed dock.

Looking very much like the Skipper, six feet tall with muscles starting to soften and a head full of thick white hair, was her Uncle Charlie. Next to him stood Justin Boward, the coeditor of the school newspaper that Skye sponsored. Tall, skinny, and going through an awkward stage full of knees and elbows, Justin fit the role of Gilligan to a T.

Clinging together like the millionaire and his wife, but otherwise nothing like them, were Skye's parents. May resembled the perky cheerleader she had been forty-some years ago, and anyone even glancing at Jed knew he was a farmer.

Rounding out the group were the Professor and Ginger, AKA Skye's ex-boyfriend Simon and his mother, Bunny. Simon stood apart from the group, dressed in an Armani suit and expensive silk tie, not an auburn hair out of place. His arms were crossed and he was frowning.

Bunny, on the other hand, bounced around the edge of the assemblage precariously balanced on four-inch heels, her red curls swirling in the wind, her face alive with inquisitiveness.

Briefly Skye wondered where Mary Ann was, but then Frannie Ryan, Justin's coeditor and girlfriend, stepped from the shadows. She had the wholesome good looks for the role of a Kansas farm girl, but was built on a slightly larger scale than the TV version.

Abruptly Skye came out of her flight of fancy and became aware of two things at once: She was freezing, and her surroundings seemed to be spinning in a dizzying spiral. As the world turned black, she wondered who had turned off the television.

"Skye, sugar, are you okay?" Someone was holding her in their arms and wrapping a coat around her.

"Did you call an ambulance?" a familiar male voice demanded close to her ear.

"Of course I did. Do you think I'm an idiot?" the person holding her barked.

As she fought to come around, someone else grabbed her in a bear hug and said,

"You two had better do something about the guy in the boat. By the look of him, the services of both the coroner and the police are needed. I'll take care of Skye. Come on, sweet pea, open your eyes."

She struggled to do as the voice asked, but her lids seemed too heavy for her to budge. She was so tired. If she could only sleep a little longer, the bad dream she'd been having would go away, and everything would be okay again.

Skye sank back into a semidoze, but came instantly awake when she felt a light slap on both cheeks. Her mother's face hovered above her, a scowl darkening the green eyes that were an exact match for Skye's own.

Strong fingers grabbed Skye's chin and May demanded, "What in the world were you doing out on the river in the middle of the night, in the dead of winter, in your underwear?"

"It's not the middle of night, and it's only fall," Skye babbled, breaking off when she remembered all that had happened. She looked around. Charlie was standing by her demolished dock holding her in his arms.

"Where's the boat? Beau Hamilton is in the bottom of it and he's hurt really bad."

"Wally and Simon are taking care of him," May answered, then said to Charlie, "We need to get her in the house. She's turning blue."

"I can walk." Skye made an effort to stand, clutching the jacket around her. "I'm fine." She knew she was too heavy for her seventy-four-year-old godfather to carry.

Charlie started to insist, but Skye's father stepped forward, silently put his arm around her waist, and started up the path toward the house. Not to be outdone, Charlie took her other side.

Trailing them were May, Justin, Frannie, and Bunny. All were shouting questions that Skye disregarded, concentrating on putting one foot in front of the other.

When it became apparent that Skye would remain silent, May turned to Justin and Frannie and commanded, "You two run ahead and start a hot bath."

"But Mrs. Denison, warm water is better for hypothermia," Justin protested.

"We learned that in health class," Frannie explained.

Bunny slapped Skye's mother on the shoulder. "These kids are sure smarter than we were at their age, aren't they, May?"

May shooed the teenagers away, saying, "Fine, then start a *warm* bath." She ignored Bunny, who was on May's bad list for several reasons, not the least of which was trying to seduce May's husband, Jed, and having a son who cheated on May's daughter.

As they rounded the corner of the house, Skye saw an ambulance skid to a stop in front of the sidewalk where Wally and Simon stood. Wally said something, and the EMTs ran with him and Simon toward the river. Skye stared at the paramedic trailing the small group. He didn't look old enough to start a car, let alone a heart.

Skye's thoughts were interrupted as she was hustled into the house and up the stairs to the second-floor bathroom — the only one with a tub, and luckily the one under a portion of the roof that was still intact. May ordered everyone else out, firmly shutting the heavy oak door in their protesting faces.

May tried to strip the jacket from Skye, but she clung to it. The navy nylon had a replica of a police badge sewn to the right breast pocket and above it CHIEF BOYD was stitched in gold. Skye traced the letters, touched that Wally had been the one to give up his coat to warm her.

Finally, taking notice of her mother's mutters, Skye shrugged off the garment and hung it on the back of the door. Then she removed her soggy undergarments and got into the tub. The warm water felt like heaven against her cold skin, and she relaxed back with her head against the rim.

May dragged a stool over to the tub's edge and demanded, "What on earth happened?"

Skye countered her mother's question by asking, "How's Beau?"

"Uh." May's gaze fastened on a bottle of bath gel. "I don't know." She glanced up; then in a rush, before Skye could ask, she said, "Simon and Wally didn't say how he was."

"Oh." Skye thought she remembered something being said while she was semi-comatose that meant her mother was not telling her the whole truth — May never lied outright. Skye strove for several seconds to recall the information before giving up. Too many other questions crowded her brain, so instead she asked, "Why were you all down at the river? Where did the lights come from? What's going on? Shouldn't you still be at work?" She didn't know what time it was, but it couldn't be past eleven p.m., the official end of May's shift.

May started to ask her own question again, but the look on her daughter's face must have changed her mind and instead she said, "It's a long story."

Why does everyone always say that? Skye wondered for a split second before suggesting, "Give me the *Reader's Digest* version."

May sighed. "I tried to call you after the time you should have been home from work, but I kept getting your answering machine, so I got worried."

Skye blew an exasperated breath. "Maybe I had a date or went shopping, or visited a friend."

"You always tell me if you're not going to be home." May shrugged away Skye's protestations. "Anyway, I waited until nearly six, then I decided to have your father go check on you."

"No, I don't always tell you where I'll be."

May shrugged again, a stubborn look on her face.

Abruptly a thought occurred to Skye. "But Dad doesn't answer the phone. How did you get ahold of him?"

"I called Charlie to go tell Jed to go look for you."

"But it's Uncle Charlie's poker night."

"I caught him before he left for the game," May explained. "He went and got Jed and they came over here."

"Okay, that explains you three, but what about the rest of the seven dwarfs?"

"Justin and Frannie arrived about the same time as Jed and Charlie. The kids were looking for you to tell you their big news."

"Oh, my God." Skye felt the room start to spin. Maybe she shouldn't have played matchmaker. Justin and Frannie were only sixteen and seventeen, respectively, and had only been dating a little over a month. "They're not getting married, are they?" *Shit!* Frannie's father would kill them all.

"What? Of course not. That newspaper of yours at school won some award." May brushed the honor aside with a sweep of her hand.

"Phew." Skye sank deeper into the soothing water. "So how about Simon and Bunny?"

"*They* were not my fault." May frowned. "When Jed and Charlie got here, they saw your car in the garage and your purse on the front steps. When they went around back they noticed that the weeds were flattened heading down to the old path. Then they saw threads from your sweater caught on the tree."

"And?"

"And they followed the path, found your dock destroyed, and your clothes on shore." May's voice rose with each horrible fact.

"So?"

"So, Jed called me, and I called Wally at home."

"That does not explain my ex and his

mother." Skye crossed her arms.

"That's entirely your father's fault." May pursed her lips. "He called Simon's cell phone, and Simon was at the bowling alley when he got the call. I guess that trollop insisted on coming with him, like she had some claim to be worried about you." May shook her head in disgust. "I know everyone has a right to be stupid sometimes, but that woman abuses the privilege."

Skye ignored her mother's aside. "How did Dad get Simon's cell phone number?" She was curious how a man who was so phone-phobic that he made his wife call up and order tractor parts happened to know her ex-boyfriend's number. "How did he even know Simon had a cell phone?"

"That's a good question." May's eyebrows rose. "And the answer better not have anything to do with The Tramp." "The Tramp" was May's not-so-affectionate nickname for Bunny. "Now you know how we all got here."

"Where did the lights come from?" Skye was sure they hadn't been there when she started on her little adventure.

"Wally had the fire department put them up."

That was interesting. Wally must really have been worried to call in a favor like that.

In a small town, favors were the currency that everyone lived by, and they weren't spent recklessly.

May's patience was very nearly exhausted and she demanded, "So, how *did* you end up in a boat, half naked, with your contractor?"

"I want to tell everyone what happened when we're all together." Skye figured none of her rescuers would go home without hearing her story.

"After everything you've put me through, you're going to make me wait?" May's face turned red and she stamped her foot. "Someday you'll be sorry you treated me like this. I won't live forever, you know."

May had been threatening her early demise for as long as Skye could remember, and Skye was firmly convinced her mother would outlive them all. "Sorry, Mom, but I'm just too exhausted to say it over and over again." Skye gave a convincing cough and weakly reached for the drain plug — the water was getting cold, and it was time to face the music. "Could you get me some clothes?" she asked meekly, knowing the best way to keep her mother happy was to give her something to do.

May harrumphed, but left and returned several minutes later with fresh underwear, a black jogging suit, and a hot pink T-shirt. Skye had used the time to scrape her unruly curls into a French braid.

As Skye started to dress, May said, "I'll go down and make you some hot tea." She turned to leave, then stepped back and rested her hand on Skye's upper right arm near the site of a bullet wound Skye had sustained in August. The scar was still red and shiny. "Why can't you act like a normal daughter?"

"Mom, normal is a setting on the washing machine."

May was not amused by Skye's attempt to divert her. "Why do you keep getting mixed up in this kind of stuff?" May did not like commotion, and saw life as something to hide from.

Skye was silent, not knowing how to answer her mother. When she had first returned to Scumble River after being gone for twelve years, she had tried to keep to herself and not become involved with the local people or their troubles. Her plan had been to keep her head down, do her job, save some money, and leave town before most of its citizens had noticed she'd been back.

But what they say about the best-laid plans is true. Skye hadn't been home a week before she discovered a dead body and became deeply involved in the subsequent murder investigation. After solving that mystery, Skye had attempted to get back on track and to return to her solitary life, but then she met a man — make that two — was co-opted by a couple of teenagers, and was pressed into service by several more people who needed her help. Her plans for a hermitlike existence had fizzled like a mosquito in an electric bug zapper.

Still, she didn't know why she did what she did. The best reason she could come up with was something her Grandma Denison had said, and now Skye repeated it to her mother. "I think I just have a strong streak of justice running through me. I want things to be right, and people to get what they deserve. I hate seeing someone hurt someone else, and I hate seeing them get away with it even more. When that happens, I feel compelled to get involved."

May shook her head and declared on her way out the door, "You don't get that from my side of the family."

Skye smiled and followed her mother into the hallway. May's view of life and her own were as far apart as a Frank Capra movie was from a Francis Ford Coppola flick.

May continued down the stairs while Skye

ducked into her room to finish dressing. When Skye had moved into the house, she had been reluctant to use Mrs. Griggs's bedroom, but now she felt a sense of rightness about being there and had even taken to having conversations with the deceased woman. This worried Skye a little, but since she didn't hear Mrs. Griggs answering back, she figured she was still on the safe side of sanity.

Tonight, sitting in front of the vanity, tying her tennis shoes, she said out loud, "What I have gotten myself into this time?"

To her semirelief, there was no answer. She took a peek in the mirror and shuddered. Her normally chestnut hair was dark and oily-looking from her swim, her skin was dead white, and there were deep circles under her eyes.

This wasn't exactly the appearance she wanted to present when she spoke to her ex-boyfriend for the first time since their breakup fight. As a bonus, a man she was really attracted to would also be in the room.

Skye considered putting on makeup but realized no amount of Estée Lauder could help her at this stage. She was only postponing the inevitable. She had to go down and face them all.

As she descended the stairs, she heard raised voices and paused to see if she could figure out who was speaking and what they were arguing about.

At first she couldn't make out enough to know who or what, but then a voice she couldn't quite identify boomed loud and clear: "This is my jurisdiction and you're not stealing another case from me."

Skye recognized Wally's voice when he thundered, "That's bullshit. Half of that dock is in Scumble River, which is my jurisdiction. How do you know whatever happened didn't happen on my half?"

Shit! Shit! Shit! She had briefly forgotten that her house was not within the city limits and the county sheriff would have authority out here. But who had notified him? It definitely hadn't been Wally.

Skye felt her stomach knot. Sheriff Peterson was an incompetent good old boy, and he hated Skye and her family.

Peterson's snarl snapped Skye's attention back to what was being said. "My techs are sweeping the woods, the shore, the boat, and what's left of the dock with a fine-tooth comb even as we speak. And if they can pin down exactly where the incident occurred, and it's in my half, you're off the case."

Even filtered through a wall, the loathing

in Peterson's voice was evident. Skye hugged herself. If the sheriff handled the investigation alone, he would make the situation a hundred times worse and enjoy himself in the process. The sheriff had made his feelings clear many times in the past. If he was in charge of the world, he'd not only keep the death penalty, he'd add an express lane.

CHAPTER 5
TAKING THE FIFTH

When Skye reached the bottom of the staircase, she saw through the archway that everyone was gathered in the parlor. She quietly entered and glanced around, immediately noting her mother's absence and chalking it up to May's declaration that she was going to make tea.

The picture of her mother trying to bring order to the chaos currently occupying the kitchen brought a grin to Skye's face. Simply figuring out how to turn on the faucet — it required a wrench, a hammer, and a goodly amount of determination — might take May the rest of the evening.

Skye noticed that Simon was also gone, which was a relief. She wasn't sure why he had shown up to begin with. His refusal to explain his behavior undeniably proved he no longer cared for her.

Too bad Simon hadn't taken his mother with him. Skye liked the older woman, but too often Bunny wasn't smelling what the rest of the world was cooking.

Right now she was clinging to Charlie like the paper liner on a cupcake, and that could only mean one thing: trouble. Their on-again, off-again relationship worried both Skye and her mother. Charlie seemed to lose all common sense around the redhead.

Frannie and Justin were whispering in the far corner, undoubtedly hoping the adults would forget they were there. Skye caught their attention and gave them a look that informed them she was well aware of their presence. Frannie giggled, not the least bit intimidated by Skye's message. Justin pushed up his glasses and sighed loudly, indicating his opinion of the whole matter.

Turning slightly, Skye spotted her father sitting in a lounge chair, one of the few pieces of furniture she had brought over from her cottage. It seemed out of place among Mrs. Griggs's delicate antiques, but Jed looked right at home stretched out with his feet up. His mild brown eyes met Skye's and he raised an eyebrow. She nodded that she was fine, and he went back to observing the others.

In the center of the small room, Wally Boyd and Buck Peterson stood nose to nose, snarls on both their faces.

Sheriff Peterson was the first to notice Skye. "So the princess has finally decided to make an appearance," he snapped.

Skye didn't respond. Suddenly she felt dizzy again, and the situation took on a surreal quality.

"Are you okay?" Wally pushed past the sheriff and put an arm around her. His warm brown eyes studied her for a long moment. "Your mother said you refused to go to the hospital or see a doctor."

"I'm fine." She fought the urge to collapse against him and let him take care of her. "Just cold and tired and confused." She reluctantly eased out of his embrace. "How's Beau?"

"Dead." Peterson cut off Wally's attempt to speak. "The hospital called for Reid while you were getting all prettied up."

Skye took a step backward, her hand going to her throat. "Dead," she repeated dully. Even though the news of his death numbed her, her mind continued to process mundane information: *So that's why Simon's gone.* He'd been called away because of his duties as the Stanley County coroner.

"Don't act so surprised." Without warning, Peterson stepped close to Skye and thrust his face into hers. "Why'd you shoot him?"

As she was battered by shock after shock, Skye kept on having tangential thoughts. *So Beau was shot. Damn, I was really hoping it was an accident, that he fell and hit the back of his head.*

Before she could speak, Wally swept past her, grabbed the other lawman by the front of his jacket, and growled, "That's not how this is going to go. Right?"

Wally had a couple of inches on the sheriff, and a lot more muscles, not to mention the little matter of being twenty years younger. "Fine, fine." Buck Peterson immediately backpedaled. "Didn't mean to step on any toes."

Wally released him. "So we agree to let Skye tell us what happened before jumping to any more conclusions." When the sheriff didn't answer, Wally demanded, "Right, Peterson?"

"Right." Buck nodded, but his gray eyes were flat and hard — a snake ready to strike.

Wally turned to the others and announced, "You'll all have to step out of the room. We'll call you back in if we need you."

Charlie, leaning against a wall, narrowed his eyes. "I don't think that's a good idea." He motioned to the sheriff. "I've known Bucky here since he used to steal penny candy from the dime store. His mind's as

71

narrow as a possum's tail and he's about half as trustworthy."

Bunny hung on to Charlie's arm and nodded vigorously.

Wally's face remained expressionless as he strode over to Charlie and whispered something in his ear.

The older man thought for a moment, then straightened and said, "Okay, but it's on your shoulders if anything happens to her." He patted Bunny's hand. "Come on, my dear, let's see what's taking May so long in the kitchen."

After Charlie and Bunny left, Wally turned to the teenagers. "Time to go home. It's nearly curfew."

They got reluctantly to their feet.

Frannie frowned. "What time is it?" Neither teen wore a watch.

Wally looked at his wrist. "Eight forty-five."

"I thought curfew was ten o'clock," Justin objected.

"It was changed when school started. It's nine on weekdays now."

Skye wondered if she had missed that news, or if Wally was stretching the truth.

Justin and Frannie shuffled toward the parlor's archway, but Justin turned before leaving and said, "Ms. D, you really okay?"

"I'm fine." Skye waved. "I'll talk to you two tomorrow. Congratulations on winning the newspaper prize."

That left only Jed. He had straightened the back of his chair and put down the footrest, but not gotten up.

Wally said to him, "You'll need to leave, too."

Skye's father nodded, but took his time standing. As he walked toward the door, he stopped near Skye and advised, "Remember what I told you when you started to date."

Before she could respond, he was gone. What had her dad told her eighteen years ago? Skye wrinkled her forehead trying to remember. Something about boys being like weathermen. What they promise and what actually happens are two different things, and if you depend on their promises you could get seriously hurt.

Skye smiled to herself. Jed had nothing to worry about. Considering her recent dealings with ex-boyfriends and contractors, her trust quotient was at an all-time low.

"Is that it?" the sheriff growled after Jed's exit. "Can we get on with this?"

Wally ignored him and guided Skye to a delicate Queen Anne armchair. "Tell me what happened when you got home from work." He squatted in front of her, keeping his body between her and Peterson. "Be as detailed as you can."

Skye took a deep breath and closed her eyes, trying to remember everything. After a moment she began to speak. "The first thing I noticed after I parked my car in the garage and started to walk toward the house was that no work had been done."

Peterson ran a hand over his bald head. "I'll bet that made you madder than a wet hen."

Skye chose her next words carefully, knowing that her problems with the contractor might make her look guilty. "I was definitely displeased, but it certainly didn't make me want to kill Beau."

Wally shot the sheriff an irritated glance, then took her hand and squeezed. "Keep going. What happened next?"

Skye described searching, then hearing the noise and thinking it might be her lost cat. In conclusion she said, "So I followed the sound into the trees."

Peterson snorted. "That doesn't make any sense. Why would you go into the woods alone in the dark? If you really thought it might be your cat, why didn't you call for help?"

Skye knew the sheriff would never understand her need for independence, but she tried to explain anyway. "Because I didn't *need* any help. Bingo is my pet and I can take care of him."

Wally scooted closer. "Then what?"

"Then I saw the boat tied to my dock." She continued describing her actions after discovering Beau injured in the bottom of the vessel and the boat breaking free.

"How did you manage to get the boat back? The current is pretty strong along this part of the river and the water's mighty cold to be swimming in." The sheriff's tone was skeptical.

"I don't know." Skye's voice quivered. Recent events were all starting to crash down on her and she felt herself unraveling at the edges. "I knew Beau needed help, and there wasn't much chance of anyone else being on the river this time of year, so I just did it." She pressed a knuckle to her eye to stem the threatening tears. "But it didn't do any good, did it? He died anyway, didn't he?"

There was a moment's silence; then Buck Peterson started to applaud. "That was a mighty fine performance, girl. You even had me going for a minute there." He hitched up his pants and moved closer. "I might even buy your story, if there wasn't a dead body hanging around every time I see you.

Not to mention I find it mighty odd that you're now living in a deceased woman's house."

"You know I didn't kill Mrs. Griggs. The guilty party confessed." Skye sagged against the chair's back, too tired to fight.

"With a little help from you."

Wally stood and faced the sheriff. "She's told us what happened, and she's obviously exhausted, so unless you have another relevant question, I suggest we let Skye get some rest and finish this in the morning."

Peterson didn't blink. "Was there anyone else here when you got home?"

Skye shook her head.

"Did you see any vehicles on the road while you were driving home?"

"No, the road was deserted."

"How convenient." Peterson's grin was derisive. "No witnesses."

As he took a step closer to Skye and Wally, a voice exploded from the doorway. "Buck Peterson, you stop right there!" May bustled into the room. "If you don't want to have all your dispatchers call in sick tomorrow, you better back off and think about what you're doing."

The sheriff froze and without turning around said, "Now, May, you know you can't do that. You're a city dispatcher, not a county one."

May darted up to the sheriff. He had ten inches on her, but she had the righteousness of a mother protecting her young. She poked him in the bicep with her index finger and demanded, "Care to try me? Betty and I formed all the dispatchers in the surrounding area into a little union."

Skye caught Wally's eye and tilted her head questioningly. Betty was the head county dispatcher.

Wally shrugged, but he was grinning.

Buck hadn't answered May's original question, so she went on, "You might also want to consider the election coming up. Do you have any idea how many friends and relatives I have in Stanley County?"

The sheriff took a step back and met May's eyes. "I don't know why you're so riled up, May. I'm not accusing Skye of nothing."

"Right." May looked him up and down. "And I'm not saying that if brains were water, you wouldn't have enough to baptize a flea."

Skye watched as Buck slowly processed the insult, and a scowl formed on his face as he realized what May had said. Skye closed her eyes for a moment. She knew her mother had only been trying to help, but calling the sheriff a nitwit was not the way to win his cooperation and goodwill.

"Son of a bitch!" Buck's bellow made the glass knickknacks in the étagère rattle. He turned on Wally. "You have her in my office tomorrow at nine a.m. sharp, or I'll put out an APB."

Wally's expression was implacable. "No. Skye will be at the Scumble River police station tomorrow at nine. I'll be happy to have you sit in when she makes her statement."

Buck's face turned the color of a ripe eggplant. He sputtered, grabbed his hat, and flung open the front door. "This ain't over, not by a long shot." He stomped out, slamming the door behind him.

May turned to Wally and nodded. "That was good. But you remember, if you hurt my daughter, you'll be without dispatchers, too." With that, she turned on her heel and marched out of the room.

Wally said goodbye to Skye and followed May out. There was a low conversation on the front porch that Skye couldn't quite hear; then a car drove away.

Seconds later Charlie, Bunny, and Jed came back into the parlor and she repeated what she had told Buck and Wally about what had happened. After extensive reassurances that she was fine, Skye persuaded them all to leave.

Charlie and Jed had come together, May had driven her own car, and Bunny had come with Simon. This left Charlie giving Bunny a ride home, and Jed driving May's Oldsmobile.

As Jed backed up and turned the car around, May shouted out the passenger window, "I'll have your bed at home ready in case you change your mind and decide to stay with us. Even if it's late, just use your key and come on in."

"Thanks, everyone." Skye waved her parents off and went inside.

For a minute she leaned against the closed door; then she made her way to the back of the house where, at some point, a sunroom had been added. This was the only place, besides her bedroom, where she felt she could relax — she really missed her homey little cottage. The parlor and dining room were too formal, and with the renovations, the kitchen was a mess.

A space heater provided the only warmth, so a couple days ago Skye had brought out an old afghan. She snuggled under it as she nestled into the cozy cushions on the wicker furniture. Like everything else, they were threadbare, but she didn't care how they looked as long as they were comfy. With a sigh of relief, she relaxed.

She must have dozed off, because the next thing she knew the doorbell was ringing and she had a crick in her neck from lying on the too-short settee.

She considered ignoring the bell, but it was probably her mom or Uncle Charlie, either of whom would assume she was dead if she didn't respond.

Reluctantly, Skye stood up, but kept the afghan draped around her as she trudged through the kitchen and hall to the foyer. When she looked through the peephole, her heart skipped a beat and she felt light-headed again.

She fumbled to unlock the door. As soon as she got it open Wally stepped inside and wordlessly swept her into his arms.

Skye squinted, peering over his shoulder. Was that a car pulling out of her driveway? Before she could decide, Wally gently cupped her chin with his right hand, turned her head to face him, and claimed her lips.

As the afghan fell to the floor, Skye realized that the decision as to whether she should give up on men, or at least not start dating someone new so soon, was being taken out of her hands. Wally had plainly decided that he'd waited long enough.

CHAPTER 6
SIX OF ONE,
HALF A DOZEN
OF THE OTHER

Wally's mouth covered Skye's hungrily, and she returned his kiss with a reckless abandon that surprised her. Even as he roused her passion, it was clear that his own was growing stronger, too. He gathered her more closely, her soft curves molding to the contours of his lean body. Blood pounded in her brain and her knees trembled. She had never felt this way before.

As Skye's world spun out of control, a thunderous whooshing sound exploded around them.

"What the hell?" Wally lifted his head.

The first noise was followed almost immediately by a loud pop.

Wally froze, but kept Skye protectively in his arms.

A booming whistle like Old Faithful erupting caused Skye to break out of Wally's embrace and dart toward the kitchen. He followed immediately at her heels. As she skidded to a stop on the wet linoleum, Wally barreled into her and they both went down in a heap.

Skye was already fighting her way out from under him when he levered himself upright and demanded, "Where's your main water shutoff valve?"

"The basement." Skye pointed to a door at the back of the kitchen. "Bottom of the stairs near the water heater."

Wally nodded as he wrenched open the door, pulled the string to turn on the light, and disappeared down the rickety wooden stairs.

Skye scrambled up, staring in dismay as water shot upward from where her kitchen faucet had been. A few minutes later it stopped and she hurried forward, flinging open the cabinet door beneath the sink and twisting both of the sink's shutoff valves. She yelled down the basement stairs to Wally that he could turn the main valve back on.

When Wally reappeared, Skye was already mopping up the water. He shrugged off his leather jacket and placed it on the back of the one chair that had remained dry, then joined her in cleaning up the mess.

"Do you have any idea what caused your faucet to erupt?" Wally asked as he wrung out a sopping wet rag into the sink.

"It could be anything." Skye shrugged. "Beau has been promising to get his plumber in here for a month. Maybe Mom did something earlier this evening when she was trying to make me some tea."

Wally paused and took a tiny notebook from his shirt pocket. After jotting down a few words, he replaced the pad and went back to work.

A half hour later the kitchen floor was dry, as were the table, chairs, and counters that had also been soaked. Skye and Wally stood in the small downstairs bathroom sharing the last clean towel to wipe off their hands and faces. Their clothes had remained surprisingly dry.

When Wally took a corner of the towel and dabbed at Skye's cheek, following up that gesture with a light kiss on her lips, she suddenly felt shy. She knew it was silly after their earlier uninhibited embrace, but her mind had had a chance to click back on, and now she chided herself. *Where was my self-control? It's too soon after Simon for this.*

She had been caught off guard by Wally's sudden appearance; still, there was no excuse for throwing herself at him. Feeling self-conscious, she eased out of his reach and stepped out of the bathroom. He followed her into the foyer, a puzzled expression on his handsome face.

When he tried to take her hand, she turned away and attempted to divert his attention by posing the question she should have asked when he first arrived. "So, what are you doing here? I wasn't expecting you to come back."

He gave her a faintly amused look before answering, "I wanted to make sure you were really okay."

"Oh. I'm fine." Skye looked at her wrist. "What time is it, anyway?" Her watch had not survived her earlier swim.

"Nearly midnight."

Skye backed a little farther away. "Would you like something to drink?"

"No, thank you."

"How about something to eat?"

"No."

It appeared that Wally planned on staying a while, so she picked up the afghan she had dropped earlier and started to lead him into the parlor.

He stopped her by placing his hands on her shoulders and turning her around. "Where do you sit when you don't have company? Somewhere comfortable."

She took a quick peek at him, then looked back down at her fingers, which were nervously playing cat's cradle with the yarn of the afghan. "In here." She led him into the sunroom, aware of both its shabbiness and its intimacy.

Skye watched warily as Wally unbuckled his leather utility belt and placed it on the wicker coffee table. Next he loosened his collar and took off his tie.

Oh, my God! Is he undressing? Skye held her breath, not sure if she was dismayed or excited by the possibility.

When he made no move to remove anything further and had settled on the settee, she told herself she felt relieved and attempted to edge past him to the armchair. But he captured her hand and pulled her down next to him, nestling her against his side.

Confused, Skye wasn't sure what to do or even what she wanted to do. Sitting this close to him set her pulse racing, but she wasn't used to his forceful approach. Simon had always let her take the lead and stepped back if she was uneasy.

As Wally started to free her curls from their French braid, Skye tried to mask her inner turmoil by asking, "So, what's happened since you left here?"

A suggestion of annoyance flickered in Wally's eyes, but he shrugged and continued to unbraid her hair, massaging her scalp as he proceeded. "Not much."

"Could I have done anything differently to save Beau?" Skye asked the question that had been gnawing at her since she heard the contractor had died.

"No. Beau was declared dead once he reached the hospital. The EMTs said he never had a chance. He was shot at close range in the back of the head. There was too much brain damage and blood loss for him to survive."

Skye slumped. All her efforts had been for nothing. "I thought if a person was shot in the head they died instantly."

"Only on TV. A person can live for hours or even days. It depends on the injury."

Skye was silent for a moment, then asked, "Have you found out anything else? Any idea who murdered him?"

"Nothing much. We notified his sister and she formally identified the body. His mother's dead, and the sister told us they don't know the whereabouts of his father."

"Shoot. I forgot about Beau's sister. She's the high school art teacher. I'll have to go see her. I only hope she doesn't blame me for Beau's death." Skye paused, abruptly recalling what Alana had said earlier that day. After a moment she asked, "Did you have any trouble finding her? Alana told me she and her boyfriend were going into Chicago for the evening."

"No. She mentioned they'd had to cancel their plans due to some business emergency her boyfriend had to deal with. He's some big shot."

"Right." Skye nodded. "I met him when school started. He's really classy. Even his name makes you think of money. Neville Jeffreys — doesn't that remind you of yachts and mansions?"

Wally gave a noncommittal shrug.

Suddenly, Skye felt close to tears. "I feel so sorry for poor Alana. She must be completely alone now, with both her parents and brother gone." Skye tried to smile, but without success. "At least her boyfriend is visiting so she has someone to help her through this awful time. He flew in a few weeks ago from New York. He has some kind of important deal going on in Chicago and he's been staying with Alana."

Wally had finished freeing Skye's hair and started to rub her shoulders, but he stopped and said, "She didn't have much to say tonight, but we'll be talking to her again tomorrow, so don't go over there until Sunday. We don't want Peterson accusing you of trying to influence her."

"Okay." Skye was both confused by and grateful for Wally's attitude — grateful that he believed she was innocent, but confused because he hadn't ordered her to keep her nose out of the investigation.

"Good." Wally relaxed and started massaging her neck. "Your fingerprints will be all over the boat, and we don't want him to have any more ammo against you."

Skye, having started to relax under Wally's ministrations, stiffened at his last comment. "Sheriff Peterson really does want to pin Beau's murder on me, doesn't he?"

"Let's just say he wants the case solved, and he wants to be the one to do it. He doesn't care who he puts in jail. To him a scapegoat is almost as good as a solution."

"So, if we give him someone else . . ." Skye trailed off, inviting Wally's response.

"Peterson won't care, as long as he gets credit." Wally bent his head to nibble at her earlobe.

"Then we need to find the sheriff some other suspects." Skye tried to stifle the dizzying current racing through her. "Do you have any idea who might have had it in for Beau?"

"No. Only thing I heard was that he's popular with the ladies." Wally's lips seared a path down her neck as he peeled off the jacket of her sweat suit and pushed away her T-shirt to gain access to her shoulder.

For a long moment she felt as if she were floating, then she wrenched her thoughts back to the problem at hand. "How about his business practice? He was sure doing a lousy job for me."

"Can't we talk about this later?"

"No. How can I think of anything else when the sheriff wants to put my butt in the electric chair?"

He sighed, then kissed the tip of her nose. "Okay, there is some rumbling around town that Hamilton's customers haven't all been happy with his work, but so far no one has made a formal complaint."

"That's odd. Everyone I talked to gave him a good reference." Skye drummed her fingers on Wally's thigh. "Why would they lie?"

"Good question." Wally stretched his legs and put his arms behind his head. They sat in silence for a few seconds, neither one having an answer or able to think of anything else they knew about Beau.

Skye picked up a yellow fuzzy mouse and absently tossed it from hand to hand.

Wally watched her play with the cat toy, then asked, "So, how did Bingo get lost?"

"Beau let him get out." Skye's expression

clouded with anger. "When I got home from work Wednesday afternoon, he was gone."

Wally put his arm around her shoulders and gave a sympathetic squeeze.

"I looked all over for him. I called animal control and put up posters around town, but it's so deserted out here I'm afraid a coyote got him."

"Has he ever been out before?" Wally put his other arm around her and held her.

"Only that time when Grandma was murdered." Skye snuggled in Wally's embrace. "I'm really careful not to let him out. His front paws are declawed so he has no defenses."

"How did it happen that Hamilton let him out?"

"That's the weird part. I had closed Bingo in my bedroom with his food, water, and litter box. Beau was not supposed to be doing anything in that part of the house. He had no reason to open my bedroom door. Yet when I got home, Bingo was gone."

"What did Hamilton say?" Wally pushed a curl behind Skye's ear and kissed her cheek.

"He claimed he didn't do it, and that none of his crew did either."

"But you didn't believe him?"

"No. Unless I have a ghost or Bingo grew opposable thumbs and can turn a doorknob, it had to be Beau or one of his guys."

Wally stiffened. "Have you mentioned to anyone that you blame Hamilton for Bingo's disappearance?"

"No. Why?"

"Don't. This would be exactly the kind of motive Peterson would love to get ahold of."

Wally was right; Skye's expression was sober. "Okay, but I'll still keep searching for Bingo."

"That's fine. Just don't say anything about Beau being the one who let him out."

"I won't." She swallowed the lump in her throat. "You know, when Grandma Leofanti died, everyone wanted her possessions, but I knew that of everything she had, she loved her cat best, so I wanted him. He's the last living connection I have with her."

"I'll tell my officers to keep an eye out for him, too." Wally brushed his thumb under her eye, wiping away the half-formed tear there.

"Thank you." She leaned back into Wally's arms, but returned to the question of who could have murdered Beau Hamilton. "Let's see, we know Beau was a ladies' man, which can certainly get a guy killed. People aren't happy with his work, but no one says anything. And he's a liar. Anything else?" Skye closed her eyes and thought, then answered herself. "The other day I heard him on his cell phone arguing with a supplier about overdue payments."

"That sounds like plenty to work on." Wally stretched back out, drawing Skye partially on top of him. "Tomorrow."

"Tomorrow," Skye agreed, suddenly tired of waiting for precisely the right time. She had wanted to make love to Wally for eighteen years. By now the prolonged anticipation was almost unbearable. She'd probably regret this later, but she was sick of always being a good girl.

She half turned so she could look into Wally's eyes, then ran her fingers through the silver strands at his temples. She liked the way the silver emphasized the midnight blackness of the rest of his hair. Next she traced the smooth olive skin that stretched over his high cheekbones.

Wally's brown eyes went from the color of milk chocolate to dark chocolate with each of her caresses. Finally, he captured her right hand and brought it to his lips, kissing and nibbling his way to her wrist.

She shivered as he nuzzled the sensitive skin there. She responded by burrowing her left hand under his shirt and kneading the muscles of his broad shoulders while kissing the strong column of his throat.

His hands moved under her T-shirt, skimming her waist and ribs as he eased the garment over her head.

She had started on the buttons of his shirt when the radio clipped to his utility belt squawked to life.

At first he ignored it, intent on the clasp of her bra, but Skye felt him stiffen when the words "Beau Hamilton" crackled from the little box.

Skye and Wally exchanged one long look, and then he gently moved her off his lap and onto the settee cushion before leaning forward and grabbing the radio. He pushed the button and said to the dispatcher, "Call me on my cell phone."

"Negative on that, Chief. You must be in a dead zone. All I get is your voice mail."

"Call me at this number." Wally recited the seven digits of Skye's phone, then turned to her. "Where's your phone?"

She finished putting her T-shirt back on, pointed him to the parlor, and trailed behind him, pondering the fact that Wally had her number memorized. The phone was ringing when they stepped through the archway. Skye listened as Wally talked.

When he hung up, he said to her, "Officer Quirk found Beau's truck at the Recreational Club. Someone tried to drive it into one of the lakes, but the one they picked was too shallow, and the truck was stuck half in and half out of the water."

"I'll bet the murderer arrived here in the boat that I found Beau's body in, and he must have left by stealing Beau's truck." Skye had been trying to figure out why there was no extra vehicle in her driveway.

"That's what I think, too, which is why I had Quirk call the county crime techs. They'll meet me at the truck. I want them to go over it with a fine-tooth comb." Wally suddenly frowned. "You've never been in Beau's pickup, right?"

Skye thought for a moment, then shook her head. "Nope. Never even touched the door. He usually rode his motorcycle here."

"Good. That's one less piece of evidence Peterson has against you."

"Yippee," Skye said, whirling her finger in the air like a New Year's Eve noisemaker.

Wally took her chin in his hand and tilted her face upward. "Trust me. I won't let Peterson hurt you."

"I know."

"And I know that you can take care of yourself, so I'll trust you to do that."

Skye smiled and cupped her hands over his. Wally had said exactly what she needed to hear. "I suppose you have to leave right away?"

He nodded. "I want to be there when the techs arrive."

"Can you wait one second while I run upstairs and get the jacket you loaned me?"

"Sure. Go ahead."

When she returned with the coat, he was standing by the front door wearing his leather jacket and utility belt.

His goodbye kiss was slow and thoughtful, and when she closed the door behind him, the reality of what she had been about to do with him sank in. What had she been thinking? It was too soon. She wasn't the kind of woman who flitted from man to man.

As Skye climbed the steps to her bedroom, she resolved to slow down their newly forming relationship. She needed time to get to know Wally as a boyfriend before becoming his lover.

CHAPTER 7
BE AT SIXES
AND SEVENS

Skye turned over, dragging the sheet and blanket with her. She reached out to stroke Bingo's warm fur, but encountered only a cold unoccupied pillow.

Puzzled, Skye pried open an eye. Bingo always slept next to her, and never left the bed until he was sure she was heading toward his food bowl.

Abruptly, Skye remembered that Bingo was gone. Her beautiful black cat was out on his own — cold, hungry, and in danger — all because of that jackass, Beau Hamilton.

Oops! Beau Hamilton was dead. For a moment Skye had forgotten yesterday's events. She closed her eyes and said a quick prayer for the contractor's soul. She had a feeling he might need it.

Next, the memory of what she had nearly done with Wally the night before popped into her mind. A small inner voice warned that she had to persuade him they needed to take things slowly — but more importantly, she had to convince herself she didn't want him to sweep her off her feet and have his way with her.

She closed her eyes again and prayed, "Lord, please don't lead me into temptation," then muttered, "I have a feeling I can find the way all by myself."

Now that she remembered Bingo's disappearance, Beau's death, and Wally's kisses, she also recalled that she was supposed to start her day being interrogated by the county sheriff. She hoped that being at the Scumble River PD versus his own office would keep Peterson under control.

Skye slumped back against her pillows. It was all too much. Depression washed over her and she wondered if murder suspects could call in sick. Her fondest wish was to claim she had the flu, pull the covers over her head, and stay in bed all day.

Her new clock radio clicked on at quarter to eight. She had thrown away her old alarm, a gift from Simon, when she moved. Instead of an annoying high-pitched beep, this one usually woke her to the soothing music played by a local station.

Today, however, the DJ's voice roused Skye from her thoughts. "Yesterday evening

Beau Hamilton, a successful local contractor, was transported from a Scumble River residence he was in the midst of renovating to Laurel Hospital, where he was pronounced dead on arrival. Details on the hour."

Skye put a pillow over her head. It hadn't taken long for news of Beau's death to get out. She reached to turn off the radio, then stopped. It would probably be a good idea to hear what was being said about the murder.

She showered in record time and ran back into her bedroom as the 5th Dimension sang the last few lyrics of "Going Out Of My Head." Skye skidded to a stop and plopped down on the vanity bench while still towel-drying her hair.

After giving traffic and weather updates, the newscaster finally said, "Scumble River contractor Beau Hamilton was pronounced dead yesterday evening at Laurel Hospital. Police chief Walter Boyd and Stanley County Sheriff Buck Peterson are jointly investigating the death, which is currently being termed suspicious. No other details have been released."

Skye blew out a relieved breath. She had been afraid her name and address would be mentioned.

After finishing her hair and makeup, Skye opened her closet and pondered her choices. What should she wear to be questioned by a hostile sheriff and to make the right impression on a sexy police chief whom she wanted to keep interested but wasn't ready to leap into bed with? Considering how bad she had looked last night, she needed a terrific outfit to redeem herself this morning.

Finally she selected a pair of black jeans, a black turtleneck, and a pale yellow cardigan with leopard print trim around the neckline and down the front plackets. She hesitated between short black boots and flat black loafers, deciding on the former when she remembered she also planned to go out to the Recreation Club and take a look at where Beau's truck had been abandoned.

It was already quarter to nine by the time she was ready, and cooking anything in her partially remodeled kitchen was out of the question, so Skye grabbed a brown sugar cinnamon Pop-Tart from her emergency stash on the way out the door. A can of Diet Coke completed her breakfast of champions. She generally drank caffeine-free, but she always kept a six-pack of regular for those mornings when she didn't have time for her usual cup of Earl Grey tea.

Skye pulled into the police station parking

lot at five to nine, noting the sheriff's car was already occupying the handicapped spot nearest the door. She wondered if she could persuade Wally to give Peterson a ticket.

Swallowing the last of the Pop-Tart, she got out of the Bel Air and headed toward the entrance. She only vaguely knew the part-time dispatcher who ushered her into the interrogation/coffee room; May generally worked Monday through Friday and wasn't on duty, a small blessing Skye duly noted.

Sheriff Peterson sat at the end of the table with a Styrofoam cup at his elbow, an unlit cigar clenched between his teeth, and a newspaper open in front of his face. Wally leaned against the far wall, his arms crossed and his eyes watchful.

Skye felt the tension in the room as soon as she entered, and glanced at Wally questioningly.

He gave her a reassuring wink, then said, "Have a seat. Would you like a cup of coffee?"

"No thanks." Skye sat as far from the sheriff as possible, reached into her tote bag, and produced the can of Diet Coke. "I brought my own."

Peterson threw his paper aside, scowling. "Are you sure you're all comfy?"

"I'm fine. Thank you." Skye wondered why the sheriff was acting so hostile toward her and her family. As far as she knew, they hadn't done anything to cause his enmity.

Wally settled into the chair across from Skye, smiled his encouragement, and looked down the table to the sheriff. "Then let's get started."

Peterson muttered, "It's about time."

Wally clicked on the tape recorder, listed those present in the room, gave the date and time, then asked, "Ms. Denison, are you aware you're being recorded?"

"Yes."

"Please state your full name and address." After Skye complied, Wally said, "We'd like you to tell us your whereabouts and actions from four thirty p.m. Friday until you arrived back at your dock with the victim in the boat."

Skye ignored the sheriff's grunts of disbelief as she retold her story. Instead she looked into Wally's steady gaze and recounted every detail she could remember.

After she had finished, Wally said to the sheriff, "Do you have any questions?"

Peterson rose slowly from his seat and walked over to Skye. As he leaned over her shoulder, she had to fight a surge of nausea as tobacco and alcohol fumes engulfed her.

His fingers dug into the flesh of her upper arms as he whispered, "Don't think because you're leading Boyd around by his dick, you're fooling me."

"What?" Skye squeaked. Had the sheriff lost his mind?

"Once we get the posh mortem results, your ass is grass."

Was the sheriff thinking about the death styles of the rich and famous? Skye suppressed a giggle. Or maybe Peterson was just plain crazy.

Without another word to Skye, Buck slammed out the door, saying to Wally, "I'll expect a copy of that statement by noon."

"What did he say to you?" Wally asked, getting up from his chair and moving around the table to Skye, his expression protective.

"That I'm not fooling him." Skye edited the sheriff's message.

Wally's look was skeptical, but he didn't press her. Instead he gave her a yellow legal pad and pen, and said, "Okay, write out your statement and we'll be done."

"But I thought you recorded it."

"The only dispatcher who could transcribe from tape quit about a month ago. The rest of them need a written page to type from."

"Then why did you record it?"

"Because the attorney wants all statements taped." Wally massaged his temple. "It's a vicious circle. The board won't vote the department any budget increases, but the needs of the town keep growing."

"Did the police department get any money from the Route 66 Yard Sale proceeds?"

"That money hasn't been voted on yet. The meeting is next week. But the library, school, roads, water, and sewer all want a piece of that pie."

"Should be an interesting meeting." Skye reached into her tote bag for a small notebook and made a note. "I think I'll have the school newspaper cover it."

Wally brushed a curl from her cheek and pushed the yellow legal pad closer. "Right now, let's just get the statement taken care of."

Skye was distracted by Wally's presence as she wrote. The attraction between them was even stronger than it had been last night. Every time her gaze met his, her heart turned over.

When she finished and handed him her statement, she asked, "Did they find anything in Beau's truck?"

He raised an eyebrow, clearly not fooled by her attempt to pretend there was nothing between them, but answered affably, "Nothing helpful. Just what you'd expect — tools, paperwork, and trash."

"Fingerprints?"

"Wiped clean." Wally frowned. "Too many damn TV programs like *CSI* and *NYPD Blue* are teaching criminals how to avoid getting caught."

Skye refrained from mentioning that those were a couple of her favorite shows, and instead asked, "How about the boat? Anything on it?"

"With the exception of your fingerprints, there's only one interesting one on the transom. It looks like it might have been made when the motor was attached, and whoever wiped the boat clean overlooked that spot because the motor covered it."

"Whose is it?" Skye brightened, hoping the print would belong to someone that the sheriff would consider a better suspect than herself.

"All we know for sure is it's not yours or Hamilton's." Wally shook his head. "It takes a lot longer to identify a print than TV would lead you to believe. Then there's always the chance that it's completely innocent — the print of the guy who sold the boat to the suspect, or someone like that."

Skye's shoulders slumped. Darn. A moment ago the fingerprint had seemed so promising.

"And if the person who made the print isn't in the system, we may never figure out whose it is."

"Oh, right." Skye felt completely deflated, then perked up at another possibility. "Did they find the gun?" she asked, hoping they had and it wasn't somewhere on her property. Even though the shore, woods, and yard had been searched, there were a lot of hiding places in the house, and it would have been easy for the murderer to get inside. Considering the state of disrepair, he or she could crawl through a hole that had once held a window.

"No."

"So, what's next?" Skye asked, struggling to keep upbeat. "Besides Sheriff Peterson trying to prove I'm guilty."

"Don't worry about Buck." Wally stroked her hand. "I've got Quirk out interviewing Hamilton's crew, suppliers, and customers, and another officer trying to track down the boat's origins. Plus I'll be talking to his sister this morning and any personal contacts this afternoon."

"Good." Skye got up and moved away from his touch, her pulse skittering. "It scares me that the sheriff seems to think it's me."

"Buck is like a hunting dog. He gets on one scent and can't see that there's a bear in back of him about to bite his butt." Wally opened the door for Skye. "Stop back in a couple of hours to sign this." He waved the sheets of yellow paper.

"Okay."

"What are you doing the rest of the day?" Wally asked as he walked her to her car.

"It sounds coldhearted, but I guess my first priority is finding a new contractor." Skye settled behind the wheel. "I can't live with gaping holes where windows should be, or a partially ripped off roof." She dropped her tote bag on the seat next to her. "I hope hiring someone right away won't make me look even more guilty to Sheriff Peterson."

"Buck is very political. I can't figure out why he's so antagonistic toward you, since you'd think the last thing he'd want to do is offend your family — which includes nearly everyone in the county. I'm sure that as soon as we find him another suspect he'll back down." Wally stood between the open door and the car's interior. "As to being coldhearted, one thing this job teaches you is that life goes on. You've got to do what you've got to do."

"Intellectually, I know that's true, but emotionally it feels funny. It's like saying people are interchangeable, and if one dies or leaves, there's another ready and willing to take his place."

"Sometimes that's exactly how it is, and how it's supposed to be." Wally cupped her face in his large hand. "You've got to grab happiness when you see it, before it gets away and you've lost that chance forever. You know opportunities are never lost. Someone else just takes the ones you miss."

Skye forced her hands to remain in her lap. She had an overwhelming urge to throw her arms around Wally's waist and rest her head against his chest. The sexual magnetism between them was thrumming like a taut rubber band, and she had a feeling they were no longer talking about hiring a new contractor.

When she didn't answer, Wally shrugged. "But I suppose there's no harm in taking things slowly." He leaned forward and lightly kissed her lips before asking, "How about dinner tonight?"

Skye took a relieved breath. "I'd really like that, but I have to warn you there won't be any dessert." She knew they had to slow down, but if Wally pressed the issue, she wasn't sure she could resist.

"What?"

"No repeat of last night," Skye explained. "I need to get to know you before we . . . ah . . . you know."

"We've known each other for nearly eighteen years," Wally protested.

"Not really. We sure didn't really know each other when I was a teenager. Then when I was gone for twelve years we didn't keep in touch. And in the past four years, how much time have we spent together, alone?"

"Can we talk more about this tonight?" Wally asked. When she nodded, he said, "Good. I'll pick you up at six."

Skye nodded again and motioned for him to let her close the car door.

Before getting out of the way, he leaned down, brushed a velvety kiss across her forehead, and said softly, "See you tonight."

As she drove off, she could still feel the imprint of his lips on her skin. She needed to break his spell so she could concentrate. She deliberately pictured herself in jail — no electric curlers, no choice of clothes, no Earl Grey tea or Diet Coke. She shivered. Wally might not be worried about Buck Peterson, but Skye wasn't about to leave her fate in that good old boy's dirty hands.

CHAPTER 8
CRAZY EIGHTS

Skye drove slowly toward the Scumble River
Recreation Club, her mind still on Wally
and the morning's events. She probably
should have told him she was going out to
look at the place where Beau's truck had
been dumped.

Wally had been open with her, and unlike
in the past, he hadn't fussed about her
investigating. So, why hadn't she told him?
Maybe it was that their new relationship felt
so iffy. It was too recent to rely on. It took a
while to build trust, and they hadn't had
that time yet.

Yes, that was exactly it, and it was also
exactly why they shouldn't sleep together.
She'd tell him so tonight.

As Skye made the turn into the club's
entrance, she reached into the inside zipper
pocket of her tote bag for the key to the
gate. From Memorial Day until Labor Day
a guard was employed to check identifica-

tion cards and determine who was allowed in. But during the rest of the year, members had to get out of their cars, unlock the gate, drive their vehicles through, and get back out to close the gate behind them. It was a tedious process unless you had a passenger along to help.

Climbing back into the Bel Air the second time, it dawned on her that whoever drove Beau's truck here must have had a key to get in. She'd have to mention that to Wally and see if the police had already realized that little clue.

From what Wally had said when he got the call about the truck the night before, she was pretty sure she knew where it had been abandoned. After driving through the entrance, she took a left turn, then followed the road as it kept forking right.

She drove slowly to avoid the many puddles on the dirt lane. Autumn had been wet, and it had rained hard again Thursday night, leaving the unpaved roads a muddy mess. Trees that lined the edge of the road were starting to turn colors, their leaves glowing red and gold.

Suddenly the lake loomed in front of her. In reality, it was a bit to her left, but the way the terrain dipped, it appeared that the road ran right into it.

Why had the killer picked this particular place to dump Beau's truck? It was one of the shallowest bodies of water in the whole recreation area. There were several deeper lakes a little farther into the club's interior. If the murderer had submerged the pickup in any one of those, it would probably never have been found. So, why this one?

Skye turned this question over and over as she parked the Bel Air and hiked down the short incline toward the water. She was careful to stick to the grassy edge, not wanting to add her footprints to the hodgepodge of tire tracks and shoe prints on the path in front of her.

She noticed that some of the foot tracks contained the residue of the plaster casting material used by the county crime techs to take molds. On some level, this evidence of the techs' work reassured her more than anything Wally had said. Skye knew that unlike the sheriff, the county crime techs were competent and fair, and since she was innocent, any evidence they found would point toward someone else.

At the lake's edge, Skye peered at the tire tracks as they abruptly ended, half in and half out of the water. Her best guess was that the killer had somehow put the truck into gear, gotten out of the cab, held the brake down while he wedged the accelerator to the floor, and then let up on the brake while jumping back.

Skye walked along the shore in both directions but saw nothing other than rusty beer cans and crumpled snack bags. The temperature was back up into the fifties, the sun was shining, and it was a pleasant morning for a stroll, but the techs had obviously found anything there was to find, and after an hour or so, she gave up.

Sitting behind the wheel of her car, she listed in her notebook the three questions she wanted to bring up to Wally that evening.

1. How did the killer get past the locked gate?
2. Why did the killer choose that particular lake?
3. Was there any evidence of how the killer left the recreation club — was he picked up, did he walk, have a bike stowed in the back of the truck or what?

After stopping by the police station and signing her statement, Skye drove home, intent on finding another contractor ASAP. She still had her notes from the first search, and this time she would choose whoever seemed the most honest and competent. No hometown points or extra credit for being a hunk.

When she turned into her driveway, Skye was surprised to see a bright purple truck parked off to the side. Which one of her many cousins, uncles, aunts, or relatives twice removed drove a purple pickup?

She couldn't come up with anyone. The women she knew didn't drive trucks, and the men would never drive one the color of a pansy.

Skye hesitated, unsure what to do. Her house was too isolated for people to casually drop by — plus there was the bothersome little fact that Beau's killer was still at large.

Skye decided to err on the side of caution and parked the Bel Air near the front steps rather than in the garage. This way she'd have a quick means of escape if worse came to worst. She also decided to stay inside the car until she saw who had come to call.

As soon as she stopped the Bel Air, Skye saw someone get up from the porch swing and start toward her. She couldn't tell her visitor's gender, or much else about the person. Dressed in overalls over a hooded sweatshirt, her guest wore a purple baseball cap and a pair of sunglasses with dark lenses.

Skye rolled down her window as her mysterious caller walked up to the side of the Bel Air. A hand was held out and a low, smooth voice said, "Skye Denison? I'm Dulci Smallwood. Your friend Loretta Steiner sent me."

"Why?" Skye shook hands with the woman — at least she was pretty sure "Dulci" was a female name. "Why did Loretta send you, I mean?"

"She said you needed a good contractor, and by the looks of this place, she wasn't exaggerating."

"But how . . . I mean when . . . why would she . . ." Skye stuttered to a stop, unsure which question to ask.

Dulci didn't appear rattled by Skye's less-than-warm welcome. Instead she explained, "Loretta called me yesterday and said you were having trouble with your present contractor and asked if I could come out and give you an appraisal sometime this coming week. Then she called me back this morning and asked if I could come out today. Said your previous contractor was dead, and you needed someone right away."

"How did Loretta hear about Beau?" Skye was more confused than ever.

"She didn't say and I didn't ask." Dulci took a small notepad from her back pocket. "I don't like getting involved." She started walking toward the backyard. "Let's look at the outside first."

It took Skye a moment to decide to get out of the car and follow. That, along with the contractor's long legs and quick strides, kept Dulci a couple of steps ahead of Skye, who felt like a pudgy puppy chasing a racehorse.

When Dulci paused at the side steps and whipped out a tape measure from her front pocket, Skye caught up and asked breathlessly, "So, how do you know Loretta?"

Dulci took her time making notes from her measurement, then said, "She's my attorney."

Skye started to nod, then realized what the contractor had said. Loretta only handled criminal cases, and of those, only the most severe. If you weren't charged with murder, rape, or kidnapping, Loretta wasn't interested. On rare occasions she handled white-collar crime, but only if it was something really big and juicy and guaranteed to make the front page of both the *Chicago Tribune* and *Sun-Times*. Somehow the woman kneeling in the mud with a pencil clenched between her teeth didn't look like a stock trader, so what in heaven's name had she been charged with?

Dulci didn't wait for Skye's reaction to her last statement; she had already turned the corner of the house by the time Skye had figured out what to say.

Skye hurried after her and verified, "Loretta is your attorney right now? Currently?"

"Yes."

Skye waited for Dulci to elaborate, but she didn't appear to feel the need to explain. She continued to measure, make notes, and crumble parts of the house between her fingertips. She answered Skye's questions about the house, but artfully evaded the disclosure of any personal information.

Finally they completed the circuit, ending up where they had started, at the bottom of the front steps. Skye was torn. She was confident that Loretta wouldn't send her a dishonest or incompetent contractor; on the other hand, Loretta didn't represent clients accused of jaywalking. What to do? Should she thank Dulci and send her on her way? Did she feel comfortable letting the woman inside her house? She needed to talk to Loretta, but couldn't figure out what to do with Dulci while she made the call.

Again, Dulci was several steps in front of Skye. As she opened the front door, she turned and spoke over her shoulder. "You really should keep this locked."

"I do." Skye dashed up the steps and skidded to a stop behind the contractor, who was standing in the middle of the foyer gazing at the stairway. "In fact, I made double sure it was locked this morning before I left."

Dulci turned, frowning, then walked around Skye and squatted in front of the open door. "No marks or scratches, doesn't look like it's been forced." She straightened. "Does anyone else have a key?"

Skye was aware she was reddening. The question should have been who didn't have one. "Ah, actually quite a few people have keys. My mom, Uncle Charlie, my brother, my best friend . . ." She trailed off, then said, "But none of them would let themselves in without a good reason, and they certainly wouldn't forget to lock up on their way out."

Dulci seemed unimpressed with Skye's justification. "How about your dead contractor and his crew? Did they have a key?"

"Shit!" Skye felt like a fool. "Only him, not his crew." But whoever killed Beau could have taken his key ring. "I couldn't be here all the time and he was bonded." She knew her explanation sounded lame.

Why did this woman make her feel so inept? "We probably should get out of here and call the police." When Dulci didn't move, Skye continued, "You know, in case whoever left the door unlocked is still here."

"Do what you need to do, but there's no one here."

"How do you know?"

"I was here a half hour before you showed up, and I sat on your porch swing the whole time without hearing a thing." Dulci shrugged. "There's no vehicle on the premises. Very few criminals walk to the scene of the crime. But if you're afraid . . ."

Skye shook her head, knowing she was being silly to let Dulci make this a contest of who was the bravest, but unable to give in. "No. That's fine. I'll call them later to report the incident."

"How many doors did your contractor's key open?" Dulci asked.

"Only this one. The kitchen door and the French doors up in my bedroom use different keys."

"Good. I'll replace this one lock right now, so you won't have to worry. It's not a top-of-the-line mechanism, but it will do for the present."

"Thanks. That would be great. How much will that be?"

"Consider it a sample of my work."

"Thanks again."

"You're welcome, but what you really need are new locks with an extremely restricted key distribution." She took out her pad and made another note. "You should spring for a security system, too."

Skye nodded. She should, but could she afford it? That would depend on if she got her deposit back from Beau Hamilton's estate.

While Dulci put in the new front lock, Skye checked her messages. There was one from Trixie saying she was having a great time in Tahoe, another from Frannie and Justin wanting to know when they could talk to her about the award, one from the local newspaper wanting to discuss Beau's death, and the last from May wanting to know if Skye was dead.

Skye tried calling Loretta and the teens first; neither answered, so she left messages for both saying she'd try to get hold of them that afternoon or the next day. She didn't return the reporter's call, having no intention of being interviewed. Skye debated whether to call her mother back, then realized she'd better wait until she had more time. May required a half hour minimum.

When Skye returned to the front hall,

Dulci had already finished the lock installation and was looking over the stairway. She ran a caressing hand along the banister. "This is beautiful work. Hand-done. One of a kind."

Skye smiled. "It's my favorite part of the house." When she walked down those stairs she felt like Scarlett O'Hara about to meet Rhett Butler for the first time.

Dulci hadn't removed her sunglasses when she entered the house, but now she took them off and folded them into her breast pocket. When she turned, Skye was dazzled by her extraordinary eyes. They were amber, flecked and ringed with a lighter shade of gold.

Skye forced herself to stop staring and get back to the business at hand. "Upstairs or downstairs first?"

"What needs to be done?"

"Besides the windows, roof, siding, outside steps and sidewalks, in here the only things that can't wait are the kitchen and bathroom plumbing." Skye described last night's geyser. "I'm only fixing what's broken. I can't afford cosmetic upgrades at this time."

After a comprehensive inspection of the rest of the house, with Dulci silently assessing and making notes, they ended up at the kitchen table.

Skye asked, "Would you like something to drink? Coffee, tea, or a soft drink?"

"Coffee would be great, if it's not instant." Dulci smiled for the first time. "I'm addicted to the stuff, but it's got to be good."

"My friend Monika who lives in Hawaii sent me some Kona. How's that sound?"

"Great."

Skye went to fill the pot with water from the guest bathroom, the kitchen faucet currently being shut off. When she returned and started the coffee brewing, she put some chocolate chip cookies her mother had baked on a dish, and got out a box of artificial sweetener and a bottle of vanilla-flavored creamer from the fridge.

After arranging everything on the table and pouring two cups of coffee, she sat down opposite Dulci and asked, "So, what do you think?"

Dulci had pushed back the bill of her cap while she was working, and Skye could see a few strands of strawberry blond hair. The color was almost apricot, and Skye marveled that anyone would hide such beautiful hair, but then she realized that a woman working in a mostly male occupation would probably want to draw as little attention to her physical attractiveness as possible.

Skye brought her focus back to the matter at hand as Dulci started to speak. "This is tough since someone else already screwed around." She paused to take a sip of coffee. "Plus, I don't want to steer you wrong. I promised Loretta I'd come within a hundred dollars of my estimate."

"Which is?"

Dulci slid a notebook page across to Skye and pointed at the first column. "This is what the materials will cost, unless your dead guy already has some of these stored somewhere. Do you know if he has?"

"I saw receipts for materials, so my best guess is maybe." Skye shrugged. "I'll try to find out this afternoon."

"Good." As Skye put two packets of Sweet'n Low and a healthy dollop of creamer in her coffee, Dulci's nose wrinkled, her expression unmistakably stating, *How can you ruin good coffee that way?*

"What's this column?" Skye asked, ignoring the contractor's disapproval of her drinking habits.

"That's labor." Dulci indicated the last three numbers and said, "And this is time bonuses."

"What are they?" There hadn't been anything like that in the estimate Beau gave her.

"I've broken it into three separate tasks." Dulci underlined the first amount with her pencil. "This is what you pay us if we get your windows in within a week of hiring us. The next figure is what you owe us if we get your roof done within three days after that. And the last fee is if we are totally finished with the job within six weeks of beginning."

Skye approved of the incentive system. It reminded her of the positive reinforcement she used with the students she worked with. Also, even with the bonuses, the amount was less than Beau's estimate. She opened her mouth to say, "You're hired," but at the last moment bit back the words. This time she would be more cautious.

Even though Skye liked the quiet confidence that the other woman displayed, and felt an instant trust, she told herself she shouldn't hire Dulci until she had thoroughly checked out her references.

Dulci sipped her coffee, seemingly comfortable to let Skye think without continuing her sales pitch. She doodled on her notebook as she waited, and when Skye finally spoke, she had nearly finished a sketch of how the Griggs house could look if it were fixed up properly.

"Your estimate seems fine," Skye said, folding the paper in half and putting it

123

aside. "But I do need to check a few things out. Can I call you on Monday with either an answer or more questions?"

"Sure." Dulci finished her coffee and stood up. She dug out a business card from one of her numerous pockets and handed it to Skye. "Here are my numbers."

Skye walked her to the door. As Dulci started down the outside steps, she turned and said, "I'll do a good job for you. You have my word."

"Thanks. That means a lot. And thanks again for the new lock."

When Dulci reached the sidewalk, she turned again and said, "Remember, innocent until proven guilty."

Skye nodded automatically, but she wasn't quick enough to keep the alarmed look off her face. What in blue blazes had Loretta gotten her into?

CHAPTER 9
WHOLE NINE YARDS

After Dulci left, Skye paced up and down the parlor, trying to think of all she had to do. *Call the police about my door being open. Call Mom to reassure her I'm okay. Continue to search for Bingo. Make a condolence call on Beau's sister.*

She stopped after coming up with the last item and mentally erased it. The visit to Beau's sister was the first thing on Sunday's list. She had promised Wally she'd wait until then so the sheriff couldn't accuse her of anything sneaky and put another black mark in her column.

But what about the other items on her list? Which should be first? She thought for a moment, then decided that informing the police about her door was a top priority.

She should tell the sheriff's department, since the house was in that jurisdiction, but the Scumble River police wouldn't be mean to her. And she had no doubt that whoever had been inside her house was involved in the murder. And since the PD was investigating Beau's death, they were the ones she should tell.

After punching in the police department's nonemergency number on her cordless phone, Skye went into the kitchen and opened the refrigerator. It was after one and she was starving. Before she could figure out what to eat for lunch, the dispatcher answered and said that Wally wasn't at the station. Skye left a message explaining about the open door and Beau having a key, then hung up.

Next Skye tapped in her parents' number. She wedged the receiver between her ear and shoulder and reached for a package of boiled ham.

Her mother answered before the first ring had finished trilling. "It's about time. I've been worried all morning. I thought maybe that fool Buck Peterson put you in jail." May didn't need anything as newfangled as caller ID; she had mother ID. It was rarely wrong.

"Believe me, I'd have called you if he had." Skye attempted to inject a little humor into the situation. "Do you think Dad would have sold a few acres to raise the money to bail me out?"

"This isn't funny, missy. I've had a bad morning. First I don't hear from you, then your brother goes missing."

"What? Vince is missing?" Skye told herself to calm down. She knew her mother tended to make things sound worse than they actually were.

"Not now," May grudgingly admitted, "but this morning he was nearly an hour late opening up his shop. Aunt Kitty had a seven o'clock appointment and when he didn't show up, she came over and got me. We looked all over.

"His Jeep was at his apartment, but he didn't answer the door. I tried my key, but it didn't work. Why would he have changed the lock?"

"Are you sure you had the right key? Or maybe you were so shook up the key stuck." Skye couldn't imagine someone as laid-back as her brother changing the lock on his apartment door.

May ignored Skye's questions. "He wasn't at the Feed Bag having breakfast, or anywhere else we tried. Finally we went back to the hair salon, and he was just pulling into the parking lot."

"Where had he been?"

"He wouldn't tell us." May's voice held the outrage of a two-year-old being denied the last piece of candy. "I want you to go talk to him and find out."

"Mom. He's nearly thirty-eight years old. He doesn't have to account for his every movement." Skye couldn't quite bring herself to mention the S word to May. Somehow discussing her brother's sex life with her mother was way too embarrassing, so she tried to be subtle. "Maybe he spent the night at a friend's house."

May snorted. "He broke up with that skanky little slut he's been dating a couple of weeks ago, and no one's told me he's started seeing anyone else."

Skanky little slut! Skye nearly dropped the receiver into her open sandwich. May's vocabulary was expanding, and not in a good way. Nevertheless, her mother was right about knowing if Vince was going out with a new woman. In Scumble River, someone would have told her.

"So, you have to find out what he's hiding," May finished saying. "I've been so worried, I couldn't get a thing done today."

"Mom, worry is like a rocking chair; it gives you something to do, but doesn't get you anywhere."

"Don't try that counseling baloney on me. Just find out what's going on with your brother."

"I'll talk to him, but no promises." Skye grabbed the mustard bottle and squeezed. "Listen, Mom, I've got to go. I've got a lot of other calls to make."

"Whoa Nelly, not so fast." May was only winding up; she apparently hadn't thrown her final pitch yet. "A little bird told me that Wally came back out to your house late last night."

Skye took a deep breath before answering, since she was pretty sure screaming at her mother was one of the top ten big sins that would get her a one-way ticket on the express train to hell, and she didn't have time to go to confession. "Does this little stool pigeon work as a police dispatcher?" Wally should never have had them call him back at Skye's number. May was bound to be immediately informed.

"Who told me isn't important," May sputtered. "The fact of the matter is that even though I like Wally, he's not the one for you."

Skye silently counted to ten. "Why not? He's a sweet, decent man with an important job."

"He's also divorced, six years older than you, and not Catholic."

Skye put the top slice of bread on her sandwich and cut the whole thing in half as

129

she tried to figure out how to respond to May without admitting anything. Finally, she said, "The divorce wasn't his fault, six years is not that many, and his religion is his own business."

"You and Simon will patch things up." May's voice took on a wheedling tone. "He's the best catch in town. He's good-looking, well-off, never been married, has a lot of money, Catholic, did I mention he's loaded?"

"Yes, Mother, you did." Skye took a savage bite of her sandwich, chewed and swallowed. "What you failed to mention was that he's a lying scumbag who won't even apologize for cheating on me."

"Everyone makes mistakes. Look at the poor example he's had with that trollop for a mother."

"Another reason not to be involved with Simon." Skye popped open a Diet Coke and took a gulp. "How could I marry someone whose mother you hate?"

"Well, I mean she's not, um . . ." May had talked herself into a corner, but rallied. "You can't hold a man's mother against him."

"Mom, leave it alone." Skye sank into a kitchen chair. "I'm not marrying anyone right now, maybe never." Her mother's shriek was loud enough to shatter an eardrum; luckily Skye had moved the receiver away from her ear, prepared for May's maternal wrath. "I really have to go. We'll talk about my love life some other time — say February thirtieth." Skye didn't wait for her mother to realize what she had said. "Love you. Love to Dad. Bye."

Skye kept her finger on the phone's disconnect button until she was ready to make her next call, sure that May would call back as fast as she could dial the phone. Skye didn't want to talk about Wally or Simon with her mother anymore today, and a busy signal was the only thing that would stop May.

After locating Loretta's numbers, Skye tried to call her at her home, office, and even on her cell phone, but she didn't answer any of them. Skye left messages on all three, saying she urgently needed to discuss Dulci Smallwood.

Having hung up on her mother and left messages for Wally and Loretta, Skye was unsure of her next move. There was plenty to do around the house. The task of sorting out Mrs. Griggs's vast accumulation of possessions and figuring out what was valuable and what was trash could take years all by itself.

Another chore her mother had just added

to Skye's list was to talk to Vince. She could go to his salon and try to get him to tell her why he had been late that morning, but that was probably best left until she could run into her brother casually — say at church.

Although she usually attended nine o'clock Mass, she'd attend the eleven thirty service tomorrow, which was Vince's favorite. Afterward, she'd suggest they get a cup of coffee and see if she couldn't get him to tell her what was going on.

If not clearing out junk or talking to her brother, then what? She had a nagging feeling there was something she was supposed to be doing. What was it? Bingo! Of course, what she really needed to do was look for Bingo.

Skye checked her watch. Nearly three. If she hurried she could look for the cat for a couple hours before she had to get ready for her date with Wally.

She ran upstairs and changed into old jeans, a hooded navy sweatshirt, and hiking boots. Back in the kitchen she glanced at the outdoor thermometer attached next to the window over the sink. It was still in the fifties, so she decided to skip a jacket. Her sweatshirt and the exertion of hiking should keep her warm.

As she stepped out the door, an ancient

pickup rattled to a stop at the bottom of the front steps. Painted on the side of the truck was CLARK AND SONS PLUMBING.

An old man hopped out of the cab, grabbed a toolbox from the back, and moseyed up to Skye. "Where's the kitchen?"

"Excuse me?" Was this Beau's plumber? Hadn't he heard the contractor was dead?

"I'm here to fix your faucet."

"Oh, how much will that cost?" Skye did some quick calculations. It would be great to have running water in the kitchen again, but wouldn't it be more economical to wait for the new contractor to take care of it?

"Nothing. I owe the chief a favor. He called this morning and collected on it."

So Wally had sent her a plumber. She'd had guys send her flowers, bring her candy, and even give her an occasional piece of jewelry, but this felt different. She felt cherished. Should she accept?

As she was thinking, the man added, "The chief said to tell you that I'm a gift with no strings attached."

"Well, in that case, okay. But only fix the faucet. I know there are a lot of other plumbing problems, but don't do anything about them."

He took off his cap and scratched his head. "The chief said you'd say that, and that was fine."

"I'm on my way out for a couple of hours. Do I need to stick around?" Skye figured anyone working for the police chief probably wouldn't steal anything.

"Nope. It'll be fixed when you get back."

After showing the plumber to the kitchen, Skye grabbed a box of dry cat food, a long stick with a nail on the end, and a black plastic garbage bag, and started out walking south on the inside of the ditch along the road that ran in front of her house. Every few steps she shook the box or called, "Here, kitty, kitty."

Skye had done this at various times every day since Bingo went missing, choosing a different direction for each search. So far, no luck.

As she walked, she used the long stick to poke into the underbrush. She found lots of beer cans, snack bags, and candy wrappers, which she deposited in the trash bag, but nothing to indicate Bingo had ever passed that way.

The fields along the road hadn't been harvested yet, the yellow stalks of corn were heavy with ripe ears. Skye smiled, remembering how her father would laugh himself silly when he spotted weekenders from Chicago stopping along the road and picking the corn from his fields.

One day she had asked why he didn't stop them from stealing, and Jed had said, "They'll get their just deserts when they try to eat what they've stolen. They don't realize that field corn is silage, grown to feed livestock, not humans. Imagine the looks on their faces when they bite into the steaming ear, full of butter and salt. Instead of the wonderful taste of sweet corn, they get a mouthful of crap."

Skye shook her head. Other farmers in the area ran the city thieves off with shotguns, but her dad considered them an afternoon's entertainment.

She had been walking for nearly an hour, and her feet were starting to hurt, so she looked around for somewhere to rest before turning back toward home. She crossed the blacktop, planning to search the other side as she returned.

The ditch on this side was much deeper, and the water it held from recent rains raced along at a fast clip. Skye looked for a place to cross and found an easement that had been built for tractors to use to get into the fields.

A few feet past the entrance, Skye could see a line of trees separating one farmer's field from the adjoining one. A couple of the evergreens had been knocked down, and Skye thought she could sit on one of the fallen trunks and rest.

She picked her way through the knee-high grass, trying to avoid the muddiest spots, but they were hard to see through all the weeds. She was nearly to the other side when her foot came down on something hard. Poking it with her stick, she tried to figure out what it was.

Finally, she squatted and pushed away the weeds. It was a book so saturated with dirt and rain its cover was completely obscured. The pages were swollen and stuck together, too, but she picked it up and rubbed the muck off on her denim-clad thigh.

After several attempts to clean the front enough to see the title, Skye could barely make out the word "Artists" and what she thought was a date — "1930." She pried open the cover and saw that it was from the Scumble River library. Why would anyone throw a library book along the side of a road?

Shrugging, she stuck the book in the garbage bag. At least if she couldn't find Bingo, she could clean up her little part of the world by putting litter in its place.

CHAPTER 10
FBI's TEN MOST
WANTED FUGITIVES

It was nearly six when Skye got back to the house. The light on her answering machine was blinking enticingly, but she fought temptation and went directly upstairs. She didn't want to be half dressed when Wally showed up for their date. Knowing him, he'd come early, and being in a state of dishabille when he arrived would not send the right message concerning her wish to slow down their relationship.

Skye hurriedly showered. Her thick, wavy hair — feared by shorted-out flatirons everywhere — severely limited her choice of styles. She could scrape it back into a French braid, let it dry naturally into uncontrollable curls, or tame it with electric curlers and a significant amount of mousse and hair spray. For tonight she chose the latter.

Makeup was less of a problem. A little light bronzing powder to brighten her pale complexion, some amber shadow and dark brown liner to bring out the sparkle in her green eyes, and a few strokes of mascara to emphasize her long lashes, and she was finished.

Choosing the right outfit was the last hurdle. It would help if she knew the type of restaurant Wally had in mind. Why did men invariably forget to mention those important facts when asking for a date?

Skye walked up and down the length of the worn Persian carpet between her bed and the closet, clad only in her bra and panties. What to wear, what to wear? Something cold brushed her shoulder. Startled, she whirled around. A shiver ran up her spine. She was alone in the middle of the room. What had touched her?

Her heart was still doing the conga, but she drew a shaky breath and reassured herself. It must have been a draft. But where had it come from? Was there a tear in the plastic that covered the window holes? She went over to see. No. The sheeting appeared to be intact.

Maybe the French doors that led out to the second-story balcony were ajar? She moved over and grasped their handles. While she was pulling on them to make sure they were shut tight, she heard the jangle of wire hangers. She spun around and ran back toward the closet.

On the floor lay the new outfit she'd bought at Nordstrom's last weekend. At first Skye smiled — it was the perfect thing to wear tonight. But then she frowned — how did it get from the rod to the floor? Could the breeze she had felt earlier have swept the clothes off their hangers?

That must have been it. There was no other logical explanation. Skye's mind skittered around the idea that Mrs. Griggs's spirit might be trying to help with her wardrobe selection, but she shoved that thought away. She wasn't going down that path.

Besides, time was slipping away. Her priority was getting dressed, not examining the possibility of a poltergeist. Skye shimmied into the copper-colored A-line skirt, smoothing the soft corduroy over her hips. Next she slipped a cream cashmere turtleneck over her head, and then shrugged into the copper-on-copper, floral brocade box jacket. Twisting in front of the cheval mirror, Skye decided the only jewelry she needed were her gold love knot earrings.

Skye was pulling on brown suede boots when the doorbell rang. Glancing at her clock radio, she saw it was ten to seven. She liked that Wally wasn't precisely on time. A little early or a bit late was fine, as long as it wasn't exactly on the dot as Simon had always been.

The bell rang again as she ran down the stairs, and Skye realized another item to add to her endless list of home improvement projects was an intercom. It was a long way from her bedroom to the front door.

Using the peephole, Skye confirmed it really was Wally ringing the bell, then let him in.

He strode into the foyer, stopped and stared at her, then growled low in his throat. "Mmm. You look like a cinnamon roll, good enough to eat, or at least lick all over."

Skye's pulse leapt in response, but she managed to keep her voice even when she said, "Thank you. You look pretty yummy yourself." He looked roguishly handsome in black twill slacks and a black-and-white herringbone sports jacket that matched the black and silver of his hair.

The wind had added a warm glow to his olive complexion, and he moved toward her with an athletic grace, sweeping her into his arms. "I could call and postpone our dinner reservation. We could have dessert first."

"Remember our agreement." She gave him a quick kiss on his nose, then squirmed loose. "No dessert."

"But I'm starving."

Skye crossed her arms and shook her head.

"Then I suppose we'd better go to dinner."

Skye grabbed her purse and stepped out the door. "Where are we going?"

"The Country Mansion in Dwight."

Before she could comment on his choice, she glimpsed the taillights of a white car pulling out of her driveway.

Turning to Wally, who was tugging on the knob to make sure the lock caught, she pointed. "Did you see that car?"

"What car?"

"I thought I saw a car pulling out of my driveway."

"Maybe someone was turning around." Wally took her elbow as they walked down the porch steps.

"Yeah. That must be it." Skye allowed herself to be distracted by the sight of the bluish silver Thunderbird convertible parked out front.

She realized she couldn't remember seeing Wally in any vehicle except a police cruiser. His choice of private car was a revelation. She would have pictured him in a pickup or a Jeep, or even a Cadillac, but the Thunderbird was such a carefree, fun choice, it surprised her and suggested that maybe she didn't know him as well as she had thought.

As Wally held the door open, Skye slid into the passenger seat. "Cool car. I love the color. What's it called?"

He mumbled, "Sky blue."

She grinned. "Now I *really* like it." She didn't flatter herself that Wally had chosen the color based on her name alone, but she found it sweet that it might have influenced him. "It's a shame it's too cold to put the top down."

"Yes, it's great zooming down some of these deserted country roads with the top down and the radio blasting on a warm sunny day."

"I don't remember seeing you driving it before."

"I've only had it since April." His expression was a little sheepish when he added, "It was a belated fortieth birthday present from my dad. The card said it would help with my midlife crisis."

Skye was speechless as Wally walked around the hood and climbed behind the wheel. His parents were another area of Wally's life she knew nothing about. He never mentioned them. She was aware he hadn't been born in Scumble River, having moved there eighteen years ago when he was hired as a rookie police officer, but she had no more than a vague idea of what his first twenty-two years of life had been like. How could she have even considered sleeping with a man she knew so little about?

"What?" Skye asked, Wally's question bringing her out of her thoughts.

"I asked if you'd been to the Mansion recently."

"No, not for ages." Skye settled into the soft leather seats.

Wally grinned. "Good. I was afraid it might be a favorite haunt of yours and Reid's."

"Nope." Skye squirmed a little, uncomfortable talking about her ex. "Simon didn't like the Mansion. He preferred more modern places in the city. He liked to try new things." Skye gave a sardonic laugh. "Especially girlfriends, as I found out."

"His loss, my gain." Wally trailed his fingers down her cheek, then shifted the car into REVERSE and turned it toward the road.

Skye buckled her seat belt as he zoomed out onto Brook Lane. She could feel her tension dissolving as they drove. She was silent until Wally merged onto

I-55; then she said, "Thank you for the plumber."

"Did he get your faucet fixed?"

"Yes. It was really sweet of you to send him to me."

Wally gave her a crooked smile. "I figure any guy can send flowers, but how many have a plumber on call?"

"I'm guessing that would be zero." Skye relaxed, then straightened. "Did you get my message about someone being in my house while I was at the police station this morning?"

"Yes." Wally smoothly shifted gears. "I passed the info on to the sheriff. Have you arranged to have the locks changed yet?"

"Sort of." Skye described her encounter with Dulci Smallwood and concluded with, "Have you heard of her? Is she on the ten most wanted list or anything?"

"No, and it's an unusual enough name that it would stick in my mind."

"I wonder what she did." Skye turned slightly and gazed at Wally's handsome profile.

"Well, even though Loretta and I are usually on opposite sides of the interrogation table, I like her, and I'm sure she'd never do anything to hurt you. Whatever Dulci's legal problems are, they probably don't have anything to do with her contracting business."

"That's my guess, too." Skye was silent for a while. She appreciated the fact that Wally didn't immediately tell her she shouldn't hire Dulci. She also found his open-mindedness regarding both Loretta and Dulci refreshing. Simon would probably have told her to hire someone else, saying that while there might not be anything against Dulci, why take the chance when there were safer routes to follow. That was the difference between the two men. Simon meant safety and stability, and Wally offered a chance to stretch her wings and try new things.

Wally plucked a CD from the holder attached to his sun visor and slid it into the car's player. Immediately Gary Lewis started to sing "Save Your Heart For Me." Wally took Skye's hand. "I hope you like oldies."

"Oldies, country, some jazz, a little classical, pretty much anything but acid rock and rap."

"My favorites are the forties through the seventies. They lost me at disco."

Skye bit her lip, but a small bubble of laughter escaped anyway.

"What?" Wally asked in a mock angry tone.

"I'm imagining you in a white suit dancing under one of those big mirrored balls to 'Saturday Night Fever.' "

"Never happened." Wally parked the T-bird in the Mansion's parking lot and got out to open Skye's door.

"Never?" she teased.

"Maybe once." He laughed. "But there were no pictures taken."

"That's what they all say." She took his arm and they walked across the gravel to the long sweep of concrete stairs.

When Wally pushed open the double glass doors, the white lace curtains on the inside rippled in the breeze. Skye stepped over the threshold and scanned the enclosed porch. People waiting to be shown to their tables sat on white wicker sofas and chairs.

Wally guided her through another set of doors, then went to speak to the hostess. While he checked on their reservation, Skye examined her surroundings. To her left was a beautiful wooden staircase. Against its railing was a half oval antique china cabinet and an old oak icebox.

Skye studied the stemmed green crystal glasses on the glass-enclosed shelves that hung on the opposite wall. She had noticed similar ones in the china cabinet at Mrs. Griggs's. She should ask someone here if they were valuable.

Before she could find anyone to question, Wally took her arm and said, "Our table's ready."

An enticing aroma of cinnamon and freshly baked bread surrounded them as they passed the bakery and walked down a narrow hall. The Mansion was famous for its pastries.

"This way, please." The hostess led them into a large room filled with diners. She indicated a corner table partially shielded by a folding screen on one side and a large floral arrangement on the other, and asked, "Is this what you wanted, Chief Boyd?"

"Perfect."

Wally helped Skye into her chair, then sat next to her with his back to the wall, moving the silverware and napkin to accommodate his seating choice. Skye tried to hide her giggle by putting the menu in front of her face, but Wally asked, "Now what's so funny?"

"Why did you pick that chair?"

"It was the one next to you."

"So was the one on my other side, and the place setting was over there."

"Then I don't know." Red climbed up

Wally's tan neck and cheeks. "What's the big deal?"

"It's just that I do that, too," Skye hastened to explain. "I like to sit with my back to the wall. My Grandma Leofanti used to say it was an Italian thing. It's actually pretty funny at family gatherings with everyone fighting for the wall seats."

"It's also a cop thing. You should see the maneuvering at the annual law enforcement luncheon. It looks like we're playing musical chairs."

Skye smiled and slipped her hand into Wally's. She liked the way he could laugh at himself and take a bit of teasing.

The waitress approached carrying a silver wine bucket on a floor stand and said, "Hello, my name is Rhea Ann and I'll be taking care of you tonight. When would you like the champagne you ordered, Chief?"

Wally looked at Skye. "Would you like it now, or would you prefer it later, with dessert?" There was a devilish glint in his eye.

"Let's have it now. Dessert is so far away," Skye answered with an equally mischievous grin.

Wally nodded to the waitress, who began the ritual of uncorking.

When the server left with their appetizer orders, Wally raised his glass. "To the girl

I've been waiting for all my life."

Skye started to reply in kind, but put on the mental brakes. If this relationship was going to slow down, she would have to be the one to set the tone. Instead she said, "To our first date."

There was a brief, awkward silence. Skye had a lot to ask and tell Wally, but all of it pertained to the murder and she didn't know how he'd react to that topic. Simon hated it when she talked "business" at the table, and she didn't want to annoy Wally if he felt the same way.

Finally she asked, "How was your day?"

At the same time Wally said, "I hear you were out at the Rec Club this morning."

They both started to answer at once, but Wally insisted Skye go first.

"That's right. I wanted to see the spot where Beau's truck was found. There wasn't any police tape or anything. Wasn't I supposed to be there?"

"The county techs were finished with it, so being there was fine." Wally buttered a roll. "But I wondered why you didn't tell me you were going."

"I didn't think it was important enough to mention." As Skye sipped her champagne, a question popped into her head. "Who squealed on me?"

"The caretaker. We asked him to keep a list of any odd people he noticed."

"Odd?" Skye choked on a bubble and put down the glass. "He thought I was odd?"

"Odd that you'd be at the lake with no boat or fishing gear."

Their waitress served their appetizers, took the order for their entrée, and refilled their champagne glasses before leaving.

Skye plucked a homemade toast point from those arranged around a small oval casserole dish, scooped a bit of the artichoke and crab dip onto it, and took a careful bite. All she needed was to have the appetizer spill down the front of her cream turtleneck and have to wear a food-spattered garment for the rest of the evening.

Wally followed suit with the dip, then asked, "Did you find anything out there we missed?"

Skye swallowed. "No, but a couple of questions did occur to me."

"Oh?" Wally popped the crab-topped triangle of toast in his mouth.

"Like, how did the person driving the truck get into the club?"

"Beau was a member. The perp probably used Beau's key to get in." Wally swallowed and added, "Since his key ring is missing, we don't know for sure."

"What's the theory as to why the killer chose that lake rather than a deeper, more remote one?"

"Impulse, poor judgment, didn't know the territory." Wally shrugged. "We have no idea. Pick one."

"Any sign of how the killer got home after ditching the truck?"

"Not so far. The techs are examining footsteps and tire tracks as we speak."

Skye sagged back. "So, no progress at all. At this rate Sheriff Peterson will be sending someone out to measure me for my prison jumpsuit."

Before Wally could answer, their salads were served. Wally ate a forkful, then said, "Don't worry. I had some good interviews today with his friends and associates, and I'll keep at it tomorrow."

"How about the two guys who worked for Beau? Where were they? They should have been working on my house, but it looked as if they hadn't been there all day."

"Quirk talked to them this afternoon. Both said Hamilton called that morning and told them not to show up for work, so they hired on with a different contractor for the day. They were with that crew over in Laurel from nine a.m. to five p.m., so they both have an alibi."

"Darn." Skye took a sip of water.

"Something will turn up." Wally patted her hand. "I talked to Hamilton's sister again."

"Did she have anything useful to say?"

"She claimed everyone loved her brother, but Alana's boyfriend gave me a few names of Beau's ex-girlfriends while Alana was out of the room."

"Who did he say Beau had dated?"

"Yolanda Doozier, Raette Craughwell, and Nikki Price. I'm guessing they all have been around. Do you know any of them?"

"I went to school with Yolanda, and Nikki is my mom's exercise instructor, and if you mean 'been around' as in 'previously enjoyed companion,' then yes, that would fit them both. But the other name doesn't seem familiar."

"Rae —" Wally started to say as a buxom redhead scuttled around the floral arrangement secluding their table from the rest of the restaurant.

She slid to a stop, and screeched, "I knew it! I just knew it! One second." She dug in her cavernous purse, pulled out a disposable camera, and ordered them to smile. Before Skye or Wally could react, she aimed and pressed the button. "You two didn't think you could get away with it forever, did you? There's no wiggling out of it. I have proof."

CHAPTER 11
ELEVENTH HOUR

"Proof of what?" Skye asked the woman, then looked questioningly at Wally. Was their intruder a wacko? She seemed familiar, but Skye couldn't quite place her. She met hundreds of parents each school year, but usually only for one conference. While they remembered her as the person diagnosing their child, she couldn't always match names and faces outside of school.

Wally gave a tiny shrug and a small shake of his head, indicating he didn't know who the woman was either. He also moved closer to Skye, and she could see he was tensed to leap into action if the woman's behavior changed from nutty to threatening.

"I told my husband it was you two, but he wouldn't believe me." The redhead looked expectantly at Skye.

Skye thought it best to go along with the woman, in case she really was a lunatic, so she said, "It's us all right."

"Everyone else thought you were engaged to that nice funeral home director. I mean, after your awful experience with that horrible high school English teacher, they were pretty sure that's what had happened, but I noticed lately we weren't seeing you with him as much." The redhead put her hand to her chest. "Don't tell me the funeral home guy was sleeping with young girls, too?"

Skye winced at hearing her past love life summed up so starkly, but the woman was oblivious and kept talking. "So, when did you and the chief get together? I started noticing the looks and the touches during the Route 66 Yard Sale."

The redhead's high-pitched, affected drawl and breathless chatter were beginning to ring a bell in Skye's memory — not the pleasant tinkling silver variety, but the annoying Salvation Army Santa kind, the ones they ring continually from the day after Thanksgiving until Christmas Eve.

Skye scrunched up her face and ventured a guess. "Mrs. Van Horn?"

"Why yes, dear, but call me Priscilla. Don't tell me you didn't remember me after I helped you figure out who killed poor Lorelei Ingels."

"Of course I remember you." Skye thought quickly. "It's just that you've lost weight."

"You think so?" Priscilla preened.

Skye nodded and asked, "How is Zoë doing?" Skye had met Priscilla Van Horn and her daughter a year and a half ago, when Zoë's best friend, Lorelei Ingels, was found dead on the stage of Scumble River High School.

"She's downtown at Columbia in their theater program." Priscilla once again dug through her huge purse, this time producing a bundle of pictures, which she shoved at Skye. "Now that Zoë's out of Lorelei's shadow, she's getting lead roles." Zoë had played second fiddle to her friend for years, and Lorelei's death had given Zoë her big chance. "She's barely a sophomore and already the head of the acting department has taken a personal interest in her. He's giving her private tutoring."

Skye started to say something about an older man and a vulnerable girl, but thought twice. The Zoë she remembered could take care of herself.

Priscilla Van Horn was visibly waiting for Skye's admiration, so Skye said, "That's terrific. What a wonderful opportunity." Skye made a show of looking through the photos and oohing and ahing before silently passing them to Wally. Then she asked carefully, not knowing what to expect, "Uh, Mrs. Van

Horn, I mean, Priscilla, you still haven't told us why you took our picture or what you have proof of."

"Oh, the picture is for my bunco club." For the first time since she had appeared, Priscilla looked a little uncomfortable. "All the members are women with children at your schools, and we sort of took an interest in you after you solved the Ingels case."

"An interest in me, why?"

"Well, mostly in who you're dating." Priscilla smiled ingratiatingly. "You know Scumble River is pretty dull and we sort of thought it would be fun to see if we could predict who you would date, who you would end up marrying, and when those things would happen. Then someone thought it would make it even more interesting if we placed bets on it."

Wally snorted, and Skye shot him a dirty look before turning back to the redhead. "You mean your bunco club is running a betting pool on my love life?"

"I wouldn't put it that way exactly."

"Then how would you put it?" Skye's voice was rising and she was fighting to hold on to her temper.

Priscilla waved her hand as if she were chasing away a fly. "Don't worry about it, dear." She glanced coyly at Wally. "It looks like it will all be over soon." She pulled out a vacant chair, sat down, and lowered her voice. "While I have you two alone, did I hear Beau Hamilton was murdered and you found him, Skye?"

Wally cut in smoothly before Skye could respond. "Yes, Mrs. Van Horn, and I heard you were one of Beau's less-than-satisfied customers."

Priscilla froze, then abruptly stood up, her chair teetering. "I don't know who told you that. He remodeled my master bathroom and it was fine."

Wally had been holding the snapshots of Zoë throughout Priscilla's explanation of her club's interest in Skye, but now he handed them back to Priscilla without having looked at them and said, "I'd like to talk to you about your relationship with Beau tomorrow. I'll stop by your house at one."

"*Relationship!*" Priscilla squawked. "I didn't have a *relationship* with Beau Hamilton." She backed away from the table. "Anyway, I'm leaving to visit my mother in Texas tomorrow morning."

"What time?"

"Nine."

"Fine. I'll be there at eight."

Priscilla took another step backward,

protesting, "But I'll be busy packing."

"We can talk while you pack. It shouldn't take long." Wally's face was expressionless.

Skye could see the wheels turning in Priscilla's head, and it was plain the gerbils running on them weren't gaining any ground. Finally she let out a frustrated cry, stomped her foot, and whirled around. As she tried to flee, her high heel caught in the basket of flowers on the floor behind her. She tripped, falling to the ground in a shower of chrysanthemums, ferns, and cat-tails. A spider mum landed on top of her upswept hair.

Before either Skye or Wally could move, Priscilla shot up and rushed out of the restaurant. The mum's spiky petals covered her eyes like a veil, and a yellow ribbon from the arrangement wrapped around her ankle and trailed after her like the train on a wedding gown.

Skye was the first to giggle, followed closely by Wally's snickering. They looked at each other, and Wally started humming "Here Comes the Bride." Immediately, they were both laughing uncontrollably as they stared at the fleeing woman scattering flower petals and florist ribbon in her wake.

Finally, Skye stopped laughing and returned her gaze to Wally. "That should be quite a conversation you have with her to-morrow."

"What do you want to bet she won't be there if I wait until tomorrow morning?" Wally reached into his pocket for his cell. He spoke quietly into the phone so he wouldn't disturb the other diners. "Quirk, I want you to watch the Van Horn house tonight. She should be pulling into the driveway in about twenty minutes."

He listened, then replied, "I don't know the address. Look it up. Priscilla Van Horn. If she tries to leave the city limits after getting home, bring her into the station and hold her for questioning."

Wally clicked off his cell and smiled at Skye. "I sure hope I don't have to arrest her, since she was the only one betting on me to win your heart."

Skye giggled. She never knew Wally had such a quirky sense of humor. She could feel the tension in her neck and shoulders easing.

The waitress was hovering, waiting to serve their main course, and Wally nodded at her. She hurried over and placed Skye's duck à l'orange in front of her.

As she centered Wally's filet mignon between his silverware, she said, "The owner sends his apologies for that woman

160

bothering you, Chief Boyd. Next time we'll try to arrange for more privacy."

"She certainly isn't any fault of the restaurant's, but thank you."

After the server withdrew, Skye said, "They seem to know you well. Do you come here often?"

"Not really, maybe half a dozen times a year, but I wanted everything to be perfect tonight, so this afternoon I came over and arranged things in person."

"Impressive." Skye tilted her head. "You keep surprising me."

"Then my plan is working." Wally sliced off a bite of steak and raised it to his mouth. "Any luck finding Bingo?"

Skye felt her chest tighten. She fought not to sound teary when she spoke. "No, I was out looking for him again today and there wasn't any sign of him."

"He really seems to have disappeared. Usually if we get a lost pet report, either the animal is found sitting on the owner's doorstep, someone nearby sees a flyer and recognizes the cat or dog that's been hanging around their backyard, or sadly, we find them run over."

"I need to know what happened to him."

"Don't give up yet," Wally encouraged. "He may still turn up okay."

Skye nodded and tucked her worry for Bingo away. She certainly wasn't about to stop looking for him this quickly.

They finished their entrées and were looking at dessert menus when something popped into Skye's head. "Oh, I did find one odd thing while I was out looking for Bingo."

"What?"

"A library book that had been thrown away."

"Some kid must have lost it on the way home from school or something." Wally's attention was focused on his choice. He laid the menu down and said, "Key lime pie for me. What are you having?"

"I'm stuffed. I'll just have a decaf cappuccino, if they have that."

After they ordered and were served, Skye said, "You must have an amazing metabolism to eat all that and still be in such great shape."

Wally quirked an eyebrow and grinned. "You think I'm in great shape?"

The color rose in her cheeks. When would she learn to keep her mouth shut?

"I like your shape, too." Wally appeared to notice her embarrassment and his grin widened.

"But I'm not, I mean I don't . . ." Her

face felt like it was on fire. "I don't look like a Victoria's Secret ad," she finally managed to say.

"No, you don't." Wally scooted his chair closer and put his arm around Skye. He lowered his voice. "You were cute when you were sixteen, and back then you had a body straight out of the swimsuit edition of *Sports Illustrated,* but when you came back here three summers ago, you took my breath away."

"Really?"

"You're soft and curvy and you feel like heaven in my arms."

"Wow." Skye was shocked and somewhat skeptical. "But the magazine pictures *look* better, right?"

"To some men. To me they look like boys who have had boob jobs."

Skye hooted. "You are too much, Chief."

"And you are exactly enough, sugar." Wally's kiss was sweet, with just a hint of passion.

They lingered over their coffees, then moved to the bar and talked for another half hour. Wally had a glass of port and Skye had a grasshopper. As they walked to the car and drove home, she wondered if the glow she felt was from the alcohol or Wally.

When he parked in front of her house,

Skye turned and said, "It's been a fabulous evening."

"That sounds like goodbye."

"It is, for now."

Wally was silent for a moment, then asked, "But you'll go out with me again?"

"Definitely."

Wally got out of the car and walked around the hood. He opened the passenger door and helped Skye out. As they climbed the steps to the porch, he paused by the front door. "I won't always give in this easily."

"I know. And I won't always want to say goodbye this early. But we need to take this slow and be sure. We've both made some mistakes in the past."

Wally cupped her chin in his hand and kissed her until they both were breathless. "This doesn't feel like one of those mistakes."

"You're right. It doesn't." She unlocked the door and stepped inside. "But the best reason to do the right thing today is tomorrow."

"In that case, I'll call you tomorrow, after I question Priscilla Van Horn."

"I won't be home until the afternoon. I'll be at church in the morning, then I want to talk to my brother."

"Something up with Vince?"

"Probably not. But Mom's in a tizzy and I hope I can smooth things over."

"Okay." Wally went back down the steps. "Good night."

Skye watched until he started to back the car away, and then she reluctantly closed the door. She looked at her watch. It was a few minutes before eleven, but it felt as if she had only been gone a couple of seconds. Being with Wally made her feel like time stood still.

She went into the parlor, intent on listening to the phone messages she had ignored earlier that day, but before she could even push the PLAY button, the doorbell rang. Half smiling, but determined not to let Wally in even though she wanted to, Skye flung open the door.

The figure on her porch wore a black skirt ripped from the hem nearly to the waistband, a red blouse half untucked, and black slides with one of the heels broken. She swayed, almost collapsing, and cried out, "Help me."

CHAPTER 12
TWELVE O'CLOCK
HIGH

"Oh, my God." Skye put her arm around the woman and drew her inside.

By far, Alana Lowe was not the first unexpected visitor to show up at Skye's front door; in fact, Alana wasn't even the most surprising — Simon's mother, who at the time was supposed to have been dead for twenty years, got that trophy — but Alana did win the prize for arriving in the most shocking condition.

"What happened to you?" Skye led her to the parlor and seated her on the sofa.

Alana didn't answer and Skye was afraid the woman was in shock. Beyond a few superficial scratches, there didn't seem to be anything physically wrong with her — no bleeding, nothing broken, and she didn't appear to be in pain — but mentally Alana had withdrawn.

Skye kneeled beside the settee and tried to make eye contact. "Alana, it's me, Skye.

You're safe now. Tell me what happened to you."

Alana continued to stare past Skye's shoulder. Every once in a while she jumped as if she had been slapped, but she never uttered a word.

Skye wasn't sure what to do. She knew that Alana had always been emotionally fragile, but something had evidently pushed her over the edge.

She bit her lip. Who to call: the sheriff or Wally? Conceivably, since this was Beau's sister, there was a good chance that whatever had happened to her was connected to her brother's murder. Wally was investigating Beau's murder just as much as the sheriff was. She would call Wally. Should she call the ambulance, too?

Rising to her feet, she walked over to the end table, picked up the receiver, and dialed the police department. Too bad she didn't know Wally's cell phone number. She needed to remember to get that from him. It would save a lot of time if she didn't have to go through the dispatcher.

After six rings, someone finally picked up and Skye said, "Hi, this is Skye Denison. Is Chief Boyd there?" She guessed he would probably check in at the station after dropping her off and before going home. "He is?

Great. Could I speak to him please?"

Skye watched Alana closely as she waited. So far the woman hadn't moved, not even to look around.

When Wally answered, Skye told him what had happened and asked, "Do you think we need an ambulance? I'm afraid she may have been raped."

"I'll be there in less than five minutes. We can decide then."

They hung up and Skye tried once again to get Alana to talk. She sat beside the woman and took her hand. "Okay, the police are on their way. Everything will fine."

When Skye said "police," Alana jerked her hand from Skye's, drew up her legs, and wrapped her arms around them, moaning, "No. No. No."

Skye wrinkled her brow. What in the heck had happened? "Alana, did the police do this to you?" Skye knew it couldn't have been Wally, and Officer Quirk was by the book, so who did that leave?

Buck Peterson! That man was as far from regulation as a corked baseball bat. Skye cupped Alana's chin and turned the other woman's face so they were eye to eye. "Did Sheriff Peterson hurt you?"

Alana let out a single scream and stood up. After a few seconds she blinked, focused on Skye who had followed her off the couch, and begged, "Please help me." Then she sank back down and sobbed.

Skye patted Alana's back as the woman cried, knowing that it was the only thing she could do for her at the present. But her mind raced, imagining what Peterson had done to this fragile woman.

When the doorbell rang, Skye handed Alana a box of Kleenex and rushed to answer it.

Wally strode in, gave Skye a quick hug, and asked, "Has she said anything?"

Skye described what had happened since her call to him, then pulled him as far away from the parlor entrance as the foyer allowed and lowered her voice. "Do you know Alana at all?"

"No, I've seen her around town, but the first time I really talked to her was about her brother."

"That's what I figured." Skye struggled to explain the art teacher to Wally. "I met Alana when I first started working at the high school. The more I got to know her, the more I didn't know her, if you get what I mean."

"Sort of. From our conversation this morning I gathered she's an odd duck."

"That's one way to put it. In the past three

years of working with her, I've found her to be a bizarre combination of sophistication and vulnerability. She dresses like a New York socialite, but is almost as naïve as my mother. She motivates her students to produce amazing works of art, but goes to pieces if one of the kids talks back to her."

Wally ran his fingers through his hair. "Not your usual Scumble River teacher?"

"Exactly. She asks for my help a lot at school, with everything from dealing with difficult students to looking at drawings she's afraid are the work of psychopaths."

"Not the most stable teacup on the shelf?"

"Right." Skye nodded, then continued to explain, "What I'm trying to say is that it would be easy for someone to tip her over the edge, but you can believe what she tells you. She doesn't have any problem distinguishing reality from fantasy."

"Okay. I get it." Wally started to go into the parlor, then turned back. "You do know that if Peterson did something to her, I won't look the other way out of misguided loyalty to a brother officer, don't you?"

"I know, but I had to make sure."

Alana had made a remarkable recovery in the few minutes she had been alone. She had tucked in her blouse, smoothed her long, black hair back into a chignon, and was sitting primly on a Queen Anne chair holding her torn skirt closed when Skye and Wally entered the parlor.

Wally immediately pulled another chair up to her and said, "Ms. Lowe, I understand you need some help. What can we do for you?"

Alana shot Skye a fearful glance and seemed reassured by her nod. "It all started this afternoon. I was doing my nails. My boyfriend, Neville, had to go into the city for a while, and you had told me there wasn't anything I could do about poor Beau's services yet."

Wally looked at Skye, who shrugged. She had forgotten to mention that with Alana there was no short version.

"Anyway, I had just put on the top coat of polish when I heard knocking on the door. I was a little slow to answer because I didn't want to ruin my manicure, and when I did, it was Sheriff Peterson and one of his deputies. They slammed open the door and made me come with them right away. I couldn't call anyone or leave a note or anything."

Skye patted her hand. "They did the same thing to me last month." She said to Wally, "It sounds like they're getting out of control over there."

Alana nodded, then continued, "Sheriff

Peterson made me wait in the car with him while his deputy searched my house. He had a warrant and said I couldn't stop him."

It was Wally's turn to nod before asking, "What happened next?"

"They took me to the sheriff's office in Laurel, and the sheriff made me go into a room with him. At first I thought we were alone, but there was a woman who sat in the corner and took notes."

Skye encouraged her. "Go ahead, Alana. You'll feel better once you get it all out."

"He said a lot of awful things, but finally he said that Beau had been a drug lord, and that one of his dealers had been arrested and confessed to shooting him, and that they thought I was involved in the drug business, too."

Skye blinked, but managed to suppress a gasp. She asked Wally, "Did you know anything about this?"

"No," Wally gritted between closed teeth. "That son of a bitch Peterson did this all behind my back."

"What happened after that?" Skye asked Alana, seeing that Wally was clearly too angry to speak.

"He kept badgering me to admit Beau and I were part of some huge Chicago drug gang, but we weren't and I wasn't about to say we were." Alana straightened in her chair. "People kept coming in and out, and then the sheriff would leave me by myself for what seemed like hours at a time."

"What a jerk," Skye muttered.

"He kept giving me coffee, and then he wouldn't let me go to the bathroom. He thought he could break me down, but I've been a teacher for nearly fifteen years and I often don't get a potty break for the whole school day. He didn't know who he was dealing with."

"Good for you." Skye squeezed Alana's hand.

"Finally, a deputy came in and whispered something to the sheriff. Peterson turned red and threw a chair against the wall and left the room. But this time, only a few minutes went by and the police matron who had been taking notes came back and told me I could go."

"Do you know why they let you leave?" Wally asked.

"I heard them saying they couldn't find drugs or any evidence of a drug operation at my house."

"How long did they have you there?" Skye asked.

"A long time. It wasn't even noon when they picked me up, and it was past seven thirty when I walked in my front door."

"So, did this happen when they drove you back?" Skye indicated Alana's state of disarray.

"No. Once I got home, I took a shower and ate something, but I couldn't rest. Neville was still gone and I had to talk to someone so I drove out here."

"Are you and Skye good friends?" Wally frowned, and it was evident to Skye he thought Skye had kept something important from him.

"We're school friends," Alana explained. "We're not real-life friends, like Skye and Trixie are, but Skye's always been nice to me, and helped me when I had problems with the students or administration, and I couldn't think of anyone else to talk to." She paused, then gave Skye a little smile. "Besides, you've figured out all those other murders, so I wanted to ask you to look into my brother's. He was not a drug dealer."

Skye made a noncommittal noise.

Alana continued, "You weren't home, but I decided to wait a while. I was sitting on your swing and I must have nodded off, because suddenly someone pulled some kind of bag over my head, tied up my hands, and picked me up."

"Oh, my God!" Skye's heart skipped a

beat. "You poor thing."

"Whoever it was carried me around the house and into the woods out back. I have a good sense of direction so I was able to tell where he was taking me. He tied me to a tree and left me there. I eventually managed to get free and find my way back to your front door."

Wally was already reaching for the phone. He punched in the number and ordered, "Get me Quirk." A minute or two went by as he paced impatiently. Finally he said, "Quirk, get hold of someone at the sheriff's office and find out what the hell is going on." After explaining about Alana's attack and the drug dealer being arrested for Beau's murder, he continued, "Before you do that, though, contact all off-duty officers and have them come over to the old Griggs house on Brook Lane. Tell them to search every inch of the property." He barked a few more orders, then hung up and turned to Alana. "Do you want to go to the hospital?"

"No. I'm okay. Whoever grabbed me didn't hurt me. Could I call my boyfriend to come over, though?"

"Certainly. But I do have a few more questions, if you're up to it."

"Sure. Is it okay if I use the restroom

first?" Alana looked from Wally to Skye.

"Definitely. It's right this way. There's some safety pins in the medicine cabinet if you want to fasten your skirt." Skye guided Alana out of the parlor and down the hallway. "Would you like something to drink? Coffee, tea, soda, maybe some wine?"

"I'd love some wine. Thank you."

After Alana called her boyfriend, and Wally's men had arrived and been instructed where to search, Skye, Alana, and Wally gathered back in the parlor and Wally said, "I made a quick check of the house just now and found a couple of interesting things." He paused to take a gulp of the coffee Skye had brought him. "There are marks on your new front lock, indicating someone tried to jimmy it, and the plastic covering one of the window holes in the back has been slit."

"Shit!" Skye banged her cup into its saucer, wincing when it clanked. "Those windows being out make it almost impossible to secure the house."

"Yeah. I should have thought of that after you told me about this afternoon's break-in." Wally scowled. "I'll get someone out here first thing in the morning to board up the openings."

"No! The plumber was enough," Skye protested. She couldn't let Wally start to take care of her. They needed to build their relationship on an equal footing.

Wally shrugged noncommittally, then turned to Alana. "When you first arrived here this evening, were there any vehicles in the driveway?"

"No."

Skye closed her eyes, trying to drag an elusive piece of information from her subconscious. She knew there was something she wanted to ask Alana, but couldn't get it into words.

Before anything came to her, the doorbell rang and she ran to answer it. She opened the door to a dapper-looking man about fifty years old. He reminded her of a 1950s movie star.

He held out his hand. "My name is Neville Jeffreys, I'm Alana's friend."

They had met briefly at school a couple of weeks ago, but Skye figured the man was too shaken up over his girlfriend's assault to remember. "Skye Denison." She shook his hand and stepped aside so he could enter. He was only a bit taller than she, with a slim build and a dancer's grace. He had ebony hair worn slicked back, and dark, nearly black eyes. "We're in the parlor. It's this way." She pointed to her left, then followed him down the hall.

When they entered the room, Neville immediately went to Alana and took her into his arms. "Sweetheart, I'm so sorry I wasn't here to help you."

"It was so awful. He could have killed me." She broke down again, sobbing, and Neville patted her back and smoothed her hair.

Skye and Wally stepped into the hall to give the couple some privacy. "This all ties into Beau's death somehow, doesn't it?" she asked.

"That would be my guess."

"Did Quirk get any info on the guy they arrested?"

Wally nodded. "His name is Terry Edwards. He's from Clay Center. He's strictly small-time. He occasionally sells a little coke and meth to his buddies, but only enough to support his habit. He's not a big-time dealer by any means."

"You know him?"

"Everybody knows Terry. He's an old hippie who likes to stay high and keep to himself."

Skye sighed. "He didn't kill Beau, did he?"

"Probably not."

Skye sagged against the wall. For a fleeting second, it had been so nice to think that Beau's murderer was behind bars and she was no longer a suspect. "So Sheriff Peterson is on the wrong track?"

"Probably." Wally exhaled noisily. "And unfortunately, even if you're on the right track, you'll get run over if you just sit there. But Peterson doesn't care. To him, the case is solved, and he can put a win in his column."

"But at least if the sheriff *thinks* he has the killer, he no longer has any reason to suspect me. And won't get in your way while you investigate."

"My little Pollyanna," Wally murmured as he leaned in to kiss Skye.

"What? You think I'm too optimistic?" She turned her head so his lips landed on her cheek. "How can Peterson still suspect me if he claims to have a confession from Terry Edwards? That doesn't make any sense."

"Let's just say that Peterson won't take it well if he finds out I'm still investigating. Which means he'll try and retaliate. What do you think the best way to get at me would be?"

"Me?" Skye asked. "But how?"

"How about hassling you, like he did Alana, about being involved in Beau's alleged drug ring?"

"Crap."

"I could not investigate, and publicly

agree that the sheriff is correct in his arrest."

Skye felt a tug of temptation. "There's no way I can let an innocent man go to prison simply to make things better for me, is there?"

"No." Wally hugged her. "The Skye I know and love would last about an hour and a half before she had to make things right."

"Wrong." Skye poked him in the chest with her index finger. "I could last two hours, at the very least."

The grandfather clock in the foyer began to chime as they returned to the parlor. Skye had already counted the twelfth bong when it dawned on her that a moment ago Wally had said he loved her. Had his declaration been a figure of speech, or did he really mean it?

CHAPTER 13
LUCKY THIRTEEN

Neville and Alana were sitting side by side on the sofa when Skye and Wally entered the parlor. Neville whispered something in Alana's ear that made her pale cheeks turn pink, but as soon as he spied Wally, he said, "Unquestionably there's a madman out there. What are you going to do to protect Alana?"

Wally took his time answering. He waited for Skye to sit down, then leaned forward, hands gripping the back of her Queen Anne chair. "I've got my men searching the area right now. We're hopeful that they'll find something for us to go on."

"That's not good enough. She needs twenty-four-hour protection."

"Mr. Jeffreys, we're a small police department. I haven't got that kind of manpower." Wally straightened. "My officers are fully aware of what's happened and will regularly patrol Ms. Lowe's street, but she has to take reasonable precautions, too. No more running around the countryside on her own."

"If that's the best you can do, I'd better hire a private bodyguard to ensure her safety." Neville squeezed Alana's shoulder. "What else can we do?"

Alana spoke hesitantly. "Chief Boyd, how about the sheriff? Should I get an attorney?"

Skye knew it would be difficult for Wally to be candid, so she answered for him. "If I were you, I'd line up a lawyer now, get someone on retainer, and if Sheriff Peterson comes to question you again, refuse to say anything until your attorney is present. Do you know any?"

Neville broke in. "I know several lawyers in the city. I'll make sure Alana has one at her disposal."

"Good. Peterson may put you in a cell to wait for your lawyer, trying to get you to talk before he or she arrives. Don't give in. Tough it out."

Alana nodded her understanding, but said, "I'm not too good at being strong."

"Don't worry, sweetheart, I'll make sure everything is okay." Neville stood up, drew Alana to her feet, and asked, "Since it's obvious there's nothing you can do to help us, can we go now?"

Wally's expression darkened with Neville's

insult, but he answered civilly, "Yes. I'll be in touch to let you know what we find."

Skye stood, and they walked the couple to the door.

As they turned to go, Alana said to Skye and Wally, "Beau had a lot of faults, I know that even if I pretended not to, but he would never be involved in using or selling drugs."

"Sometimes we don't know our siblings as well as we think we do." Wally stood holding the door. "Can you really make that statement?"

"Yes." Alana took a deep breath. "It's not information that I usually share with people, but our mother was shot by a drug addict. I was fifteen and in school when it happened, but Beau was only five and home for the afternoon from kindergarten."

Neville put his arm around her and whispered, "You don't have to do this."

Alana swallowed a sob and continued. "My mother was an artist and we lived in a loft apartment in what they called a transition neighborhood of New York City. The addict shot her for seven dollars, a carton of cigarettes, and a bottle of wine."

Skye murmured, "How awful."

"When I came home from school that day, I found my mother dead and Beau hiding in the cupboard under the sink. He didn't speak to anyone but me until he was nearly thirteen." Alana shut her eyes and took a deep breath. When she opened them again, her voice was steady. "One thing I know for sure. If he didn't get involved with drugs while we were in the foster care system, he never would."

Skye nodded. She had seen what the foster care system was like when she worked in New Orleans. It wasn't that the people working for the organization didn't try. It was that the task was too huge for the funding provided.

It had been the same in Illinois. The citizens didn't want to admit they'd rather have throwaway children than pay higher taxes, while babies continued to be born to mothers who either didn't want them or had no idea how to care for them.

Every time she had to deal with the Department of Children and Family Services, it left a bitter taste in her mouth because there was so little either she or they could do. Skye pushed those thoughts away and concentrated on the matter at hand by asking, "How about your father? Wasn't he able to take care of you and Beau?"

"We had different fathers. Mine died in a Vietnam protest march, and no one knew how to contact my brother's." Alana wiped a tear from her cheek, then took Skye's hands. "Please help me find out who really killed Beau."

Skye promised, knowing as the words came out of her mouth that Wally wouldn't be happy with her pledge. "Alana, I believe that Beau wouldn't sell drugs, and I won't let Sheriff Peterson sweep his death under the rug and forget it. I'll find out what really happened."

"Thank you."

Closing the door after Alana and Neville left, Skye braced herself for Wally's anger, but he surprised her by saying, "Promises like that are tough to keep. I found that out the hard way when I was a rookie."

Skye opened her mouth to retort, but Wally was right. They were tough to keep, but not impossible. Instead she said, "You told me you thought the sheriff had the wrong man, and that you would keep investigating, didn't you?"

"Yes, and I am. But investigating is one thing, getting results is another."

"Do you think Alana's in danger?"

"No, I think she was in the wrong place at the wrong time." Wally leaned against the wall and folded his arms. "It seems fairly patent to me that whoever abducted her did it because she had him trapped in the house."

"That's what I figured, too."

"Which means you're the one in danger since all that's between you and the outside world is a thin layer of plastic where your windows should be."

Skye nodded. "I know." She paused. "Unless he found whatever he was searching for. What do you think that was?"

"Evidence from Beau's murder would be my best guess." Wally straightened. "Maybe he stashed the murder weapon somewhere in here."

Skye snorted. "Good luck to anyone trying to find it. There's so much junk packed in this house it would be like looking for a grain of salt in a shaker."

"You shouldn't stay here alone."

"Well, I'm not moving back to my parents'."

Wally grinned. "You could come live with me."

"Right." Skye rolled her eyes. "That would go over oh-so-well with the folks in town, not to mention my mother, who would kill you."

"I think I could take on a five-foot-two, hundred-and-thirty-pound middle-aged woman."

"How much do you want to bet?" Skye took his hand and tugged him toward the door. "Anyway, I'll be fine. It seems pretty clear that whoever is looking for something only comes around when I'm not here. And even though Alana surprised him, he didn't hurt her, only got her out of his way."

"He sure hurt Beau." Wally reluctantly went out the door. "I left my cell phone number on the side table in the parlor. Call me tomorrow morning before you go to church."

"Yes, sir!"

He kissed her, and as he walked away, raised his voice to say, "Anyway, you'd better sleep with your shotgun beside your bed tonight."

"I always do." When she had moved back to town, Skye's father had given her a shotgun for protection. At first she didn't want to take it, but she soon realized that being able to defend herself was necessary if she was going to live alone, far from neighbors and streetlights. Good thing she was an excellent shot, having hunted with her father and brother all through her adolescence.

Alana's car! Where was Alana's car? Skye's hurried steps came to an abrupt stop as she rushed across the gravel driveway toward the garage the next morning. Hadn't Alana said she had driven to Skye's house last night? And Neville had come and taken her home, so where was the extra car?

Skye pivoted, scanning the surrounding area. Nothing. Had Wally realized that the vehicle was missing? How about Alana? Surely she would have noticed — though maybe not. She was extremely upset. She probably wouldn't become aware of the car's absence until she went to drive it.

Looking at her watch, Skye realized that she'd be late to church if she took time to return to the house and call Wally again to tell him about the missing vehicle. They had already touched base once that morning, but neither had anything new to report. Skye paused briefly, half turning to go back inside, but God won, and she continued on to the garage.

She slid behind the wheel of the Bel Air and promised herself she'd get in touch with Wally as soon as Mass was over and she could reach a telephone.

Reminding herself to call Wally made her remember her mother's six a.m. wake-up call. May had phoned that morning wanting to know why Skye hadn't returned May's calls from the day before. Skye had been forced to fill her mother in on what had happened to Alana, and admit that after everyone left she had fallen into bed exhausted and never listened to the messages on her answering machine.

May's anxious voice demanding that Skye move back home echoed in Skye's head as she drove. It had taken her nearly half an hour to convince her mother that she was safe staying at the Griggs house.

The parking lot behind the church was packed when Skye arrived. She rarely attended the eleven thirty service, preferring the nine o'clock, and hadn't realized the later Mass was so popular. She finally gave up and eased her car into a spot on the street, hoping her bumper wasn't too close to the nearby fire hydrant.

As she entered the building, she scanned the congregation for her brother. Her mother had taken a moment from worrying about Skye's safety to ask if she had talked to Vince about his mysterious behavior. May had been extremely displeased to learn that Skye hadn't done so yet, and fully expressed her unhappiness. Skye was determined to draw a line through that chore on her to-do list and get her mother off her back as soon as church was over.

Skye spotted Vince in a pew toward the

back, near a stained-glass window portraying the Crucifixion. She genuflected, then excused herself as she crawled across the couple occupying the aisle seats.

The woman sitting to Vince's left frowned as Skye took the spot to his right and kissed him on the cheek. Skye was used to being the object of other women's resentment when she was with her brother. He was extremely handsome, tall with finely carved features, and radiated charm.

Today he wore brown corduroy slacks with a golden yellow sweater that matched his hair. Like his mother and sister, he had the Leofanti eyes — a bright emerald green.

Vince greeted her with a smile that quickly turned suspicious. He leaned down and whispered in her ear, "What are you doing here?"

"Attending Mass," Skye answered. This wasn't the time or place to explain.

"Why didn't you go to the nine o'clock?"

"Come with me afterward for a cup of coffee and I'll explain."

He nodded agreeably, not one to fret for long, and they both stood as the processional started to play.

Skye tried to focus on the service, but her thoughts kept turning to what had happened in the last few days. *First Bingo disap-*

pears, then Loretta turns up. Beau is murdered and another contractor appears out of nowhere. Vince pulls a disappearing act. Beau's sister is threatened by the local sheriff, and attacked by some unknown assailant who it would seem wants something from my house, which is virtually open to the public due to Beau's incompetence. And to top it all off, Wally had started to pursue Skye at full force.

She sighed, and tried to concentrate. Father Burns had begun his sermon, and he almost always had something relevant to say. Today he was talking about trust, and all the examples in the Bible of man trusting God and things turning out okay. He concluded by saying, "You must not only trust in God, but in what God has put inside you. In trusting yourself, you demonstrate your trust in God."

Skye pondered those words for the rest of the service. Interesting that trust had been on her mind so much lately, and that Father Burns should choose that message to impart to the congregation.

As they stood up for the recessional, Father Burns said, "Remember, blessed are those who can laugh at themselves, for they shall never cease to be amused."

Skye smiled. The priest's gentle wit was a shock to first-timers, but his long-standing parishioners looked forward to what he would come up with each Sunday.

She and Vince shuffled in step with the crowd down the aisle toward the exit, pausing to bless themselves from the holy water font. In front of them, shaking hands with Father Burns, was Bunny.

Skye moved behind Vince, hoping Simon's mother wouldn't see her. Although she was beginning to realize she needed to talk to Simon one more time, she still didn't want to discuss their love life with his mother.

Even huddled behind Vince, Skye couldn't help hearing what Bunny was saying to the priest as the older woman gripped his hand with both of hers. "Father, I was watching a movie sequel on TV yesterday and it got me thinking."

"Yes, my dear." The priest's voice was kind and his expression endlessly patient.

"Don't you think that the story of Jonah in the Bible was the original *Jaws?*"

Skye peeked over Vince's shoulder in time to see a flicker of amusement in Father Burns's eyes, but he answered with a straight face. "You might be right. Perhaps if you study the Bible, you'll find even more movie inspirations."

The redhead nodded seriously, then brightened. "I bet I could find something to write about in there that would make me a million dollars."

The priest deftly moved Bunny along, saying, "Don't forget the church's cut if you do."

Skye hung back, letting Vince talk to Father Burns alone until she was sure Bunny had exited.

Then she greeted the priest, who patted her hand and said, "Skye, I was so sorry to hear about your terrible experience finding poor Beau Hamilton."

"Thank you, Father."

"If you want to talk, I'm here." The priest was tall and thin with the face of an ascetic. "You know, sometimes even those who counsel others need counseling."

"I'll keep that in mind," Skye answered, then asked, "Did you know Beau?"

"Yes, he was a parishioner."

"Really?" Skye was taken aback.

"You seem surprised. Why?"

"I never noticed him at Mass or any other church function."

"And?" Father Burns's faded blue eyes quizzed her.

"And he didn't act very . . . very . . ." She trailed off, not knowing how to complete her thought.

"Beau had a difficult life, and often made poor choices because of that, but he kept trying to be better, which is all God asks of us."

"Sorry, Father." Skye's face flamed and she wished she could twitch her nose and disappear. "Someday I'll learn not to judge other people so harshly."

The priest nodded, and as he turned to the next member of his flock, he said to Skye, "That's a good lesson to learn about judging yourself, too."

Skye thought about Father Burns's comment as she and Vince made their way down the outside steps.

At the bottom, Vince asked, "McDonald's or the Feed Bag?" There weren't many places in town open on Sunday.

She weighed the choices in view of wanting privacy, and finally said, "Let's go to McDonald's. We're less likely to run into as many people we know there."

"Okay."

"I'll meet you there." Skye started off to the right. "The lot was full so my car's parked on the street."

He nodded and headed in the opposite direction.

When Skye got to the Bel Air, she noticed

a white rectangle under her windshield wiper. Shoot. She must have been too close to that hydrant after all. She ripped the slip of paper free and turned it over, then smiled. It was a warning ticket signed by Wally. He had fined her thirteen kisses for stealing his heart.

Then Skye's smile faded. Things were going too fast with Wally. She had never been one to rush into a relationship. She liked to take her time and assess the situation.

On the other hand, her record with men was abysmal, and perhaps it was time to change her ways. One of Father Burns's previous sermons came back to her.

He had quoted Barbara J. Winter. "When you come to the edge of the light and are about to step into the darkness, faith is knowing that one of two things will occur. Either there will be something to stand on or you will be taught to fly."

Maybe Wally was God's test of faith for her.

Chapter 14
Fourteen Seconds

When Skye arrived at McDonald's, Vince had staked out a booth in the back corner and had two cups waiting on the table.

Skye slid into the seat opposite him and pried open the plastic lid. Steam rose, along with the soothing scent of tea. "Thanks. I've been drinking so much coffee lately, I thought I might have to resign from the Earl Grey Society."

"You're welcome." Vince poured the contents of two sugar packets and two tubs of nondairy creamer into his cup, stirred, then said, "So, what's up?"

"Mom's dander."

"Oh. My sin of lateness, right?"

"That and refusing to say why."

Vince sipped from his cup, then added another packet of sugar. "They caught me off guard. I should have had an excuse ready."

"Exactly. With Mom you never have the

right to remain silent — anything you don't explain will be misinterpreted, then used against you."

"It's too late now for a simple explanation, like 'I slept in,' isn't it?"

"Way too late. You broke the fourteen-second rule. You know that if you don't have an answer for Mom in under fourteen seconds, she thinks you're keeping something from her." Skye shook her head. "Why were you so behind schedule opening up the salon? That's not like you. Even when your band plays until two in the morning you're always at work on time."

"It's private."

"So I gathered. But you can tell me. I promise not to tell Mom."

"It's better if you don't know right now." Vince made circles on the tabletop with the liquid that had spilled from his cup.

Skye gave him a calculating glance. The last time he wouldn't tell her something, he'd been dealing with a stalker, and one of his band members had ended up dead.

"Help me come up with something to tell Mom," he said now, "and you'll be the first to know the real story when I'm ready to talk about it."

Skye knew that trying to force someone to come clean was useless, so she nodded.

"Okay, here's what I'll report to Mom. You went out Friday night with your friends, got drunk, and ended up spending the night on one of your pal's couches."

"Why didn't I tell her that when she asked?"

"You were embarrassed in front of Aunt Kitty."

"That's good." Vince shook his head. "Don't take this the wrong way, but you're a darn good liar. Did they teach you that in graduate school?"

"Right. It was a two-part class. Fabrication 101 and Mendacity 204."

Vince snorted and coffee shot out of his nose. Skye handed him a napkin. No matter how good-looking they were, boys would be boys.

After cleaning himself up, he said, "Hey, I don't know why Mom is so worried about me. I don't go around finding dead bodies."

"No, you go around enjoying live ones."

"Very funny." Vince made a face. "What's the scoop on Hamilton's murder?"

"Did you know Beau?"

"Yeah, sort of. He hung around a lot at the bars the band plays at."

"Was he into drugs? Did he sell them?"

"No way." Vince's voice was firm. "Did someone say that he did?"

"Sheriff Peterson claims he was murdered because of a drug deal gone bad."

Vince whistled. "Well, that would be a neat solution, but I don't believe it."

"Why?"

"He didn't hang with that crowd at the bars, and I saw him walk away when drugs were being used."

Skye drummed her fingers on the table. "That's what his sister says, too."

"Now if you said he was killed because he fu— uh, had sex with the wrong girl, that I'd believe."

"You mean like a jealous boyfriend?"

"Or husband," Vince drawled. "Beau didn't care what their marital status was as long as they had big boobs and a tiny brain."

"Why did the women go along with that? Why would they risk their marriages for a fling? They had to know he was only using them."

"Well." Vince struggled to explain Beau. "He was hot and he was charming. And even if he was with that girl for only one night, for that night he concentrated only on her. He made her feel like she was the most beautiful, most important girl he'd ever been with." Vince grinned. "Girls eat up that kind of attention."

"Lovely. Why didn't you tell me this when

I decided to hire him to fix up my house?"

Vince shrugged. "What does his sex life have to do with renovating your house?"

"Weren't you worried he might try to get me into bed?"

"No. You're not his type at all."

"Thanks a lot." Skye swatted her brother's hand. "I am far from flat-chested," she teased.

"True." Vince reached up to play with his ponytail, but quickly jerked his hand back down to the table. "But don't forget the second qualification — your IQ is bigger than your bra size."

Skye barely heard Vince's last sentence; instead she stared at his head with her mouth hanging open. "Oh, my God! You cut your hair." At that instant she knew there were grounds to start worrying. He had worn a ponytail for close to twenty years and there was only one reason she could think of that he would ever cut it off. "Now I know there's a woman involved. Who is she?"

"I do not have a new girlfriend." Vince tried to look innocent. "Where did you get an idea like that?"

Skye pointed to his head. "You've worn your hair long since you got out of high school. The only reason you would ever cut it was if a woman talked you into it."

"I just got tired of long hair."

"Right." Skye let the sarcasm roll off her tongue. "Next, you'll be telling me you've decided to stop drumming and quit the band."

"Hey, getting rid of my ponytail doesn't mean a thing. It's no big deal." Vince's eyes gleamed with sincerity. "I don't know why you're making such a fuss about it."

"Sure." Skye didn't believe him for a second, but said, "Silly me."

"Good."

She let the matter drop, figuring one of the town's nosey parkers would tell her. Vince was crazy if he thought he could keep prime gossip material like his love life quiet from the good people of Scumble River.

"Well, I've got to get going." She slid out of the booth, stood, and kissed his cheek. "I'll phone Mom when I get home. Remember your story if she calls you to confirm." She waved as she walked out the door. "Talk to you later."

Pulling out of the McDonald's parking lot, she was torn — should she go home, report to May about her conversation with her brother, and then try to get in touch with Loretta for the tenth time? Or should she stop by Wally's and inform him of Alana's missing car, and Vince's certainty that Beau wasn't into drugs?

Even as the Bel Air veered toward Wally's house, the good angel inside her nagged her to call him from home. The annoying little cherub reminded her that if she wanted Wally to take things slowly in their budding relationship, showing up at his house was not setting a good example.

Feeling as deprived as if someone had snatched a chocolate truffle from her lips, Skye yanked the steering wheel in the opposite direction and drove home.

For once, no one was waiting on her porch, and the front door was still locked, but there was something different. Skye was halfway over the threshold when she backed up and looked around. She descended the porch steps and circled the house. Aha, that was it. Her windows had been boarded up. When she left for church the holes had been covered in black plastic; now plywood was nailed over all of them. It had to be Wally.

Skye ground her teeth. The nerve of that man. She had specifically told him not to do this. As she seethed, she stepped into the house and noticed a piece of paper that must have been slid under the door.

It read: "Your ma was worried, so me and the guys waited for you to leave this morning, then we boarded up your windows."

There was no signature, but Skye recognized her father's spiky handwriting.

She blew a piece of hair out of her eyes. So it hadn't been Wally. That was a relief. Although she'd bet her entire supply of Diet Coke that he'd been the one to rile May up. Still, at least he hadn't ignored her wishes and gone ahead and done it himself. And she had to admit, it was good to know her house was secure again.

Feeling a weight lifted off her shoulders, Skye ran upstairs to change out of her dress. She was determined to start sorting through the junk Mrs. Griggs had crammed into nearly every nook and cranny; just as soon as she finished her calls.

But the minute she entered her bedroom, Skye knew someone had been there, again. She immediately checked the French doors, but they were securely dead-bolted. After looking through her jewelry box and the desk drawer where she kept her emergency cash supply, she was certain that nothing had been stolen. Nevertheless, a perfume bottle was knocked over on the dressing table and the edge of a scarf was sticking out of a drawer.

Why was someone coming into her house and not taking anything? Unless they were taking Mrs. Griggs's belongings and Skye wasn't noticing.

Mmm. The note had said Jed had started as soon as Skye left, which meant . . . Damn! Her aggravation intensified when she realized the creep had gotten inside despite the windows being boarded up. There must be another way into the house. Skye searched her mind for an alternate entry point. Wait a minute. Could he be coming in through the part of the roof that was torn off?

Her head pounded and her rate of breathing increased as her frustration bubbled to the surface. Shit! Shit! Shit! She kicked over the vanity stool, then threw a perfume bottle against the wall. Neither action made her feel any better. What she really wanted to do was totally annihilate the swine who kept breaking into her home.

Scanning the room, her gaze locked on the glassy-eyed stare of Bullwinkle — the nickname she had given the moose head hanging on the wall above the bed. The stuffed trophy was butt ugly. Its mouth was unbelievably huge — Skye wondered if it had been taxidermically enhanced to gape open that wide. The left antler was broken and hung down like the stop sign at a railroad crossing, and the hide was so moth-eaten it looked as if it had been shaved by a nearsighted barber.

A predatory smile crept across Skye's face as she stomped over to the bed and crawled on top of it. The ancient wood creaked menacingly under her weight, but she ignored the threat and scuttled toward the headboard. She stood — swaying as if she were balanced on a giant marshmallow — reached for the moose head, and yanked with all her might. Nothing happened. It stayed firmly attached to the plaster, goofy grin intact.

Planting her feet more firmly, Skye grasped the head with both arms as if she were hugging it, and pulled. For a moment it looked as if the moose would win the tug-of-war, but then the nails holding it to the wall gave way with a loud screech and she flew backward.

Skye bounced along the mattress on her derrière like a ping-pong ball, finally landing at the opposite end of the bed, momentarily dazed. Less than a second later her eyelids flew open, but everything remained dark. Reaching up, she realized her head was stuck in Bullwinkle's mouth.

She lay there for a moment, catching her breath, then tried to extricate herself from the moose's jaw. Shit! The stupid thing wouldn't come off. Visions of what she looked like wearing a moose head made her shudder. Thoughts of having to be rescued by the Scumble River fire department, and the story that would spread around town immediately afterward, rushed through her mind, motivating her to try again and again to free herself.

On her third attempt, Skye found that if she inched the mouth over her ears one at a time, she could move it. Then with a mighty thrust she broke free. Struggling to her feet, she ran to the French doors, unlocked them, and flung them open. Sprinting back toward the bed, she grabbed the stuffed trophy, then staggered across the balcony and hurled the moose as far as she could.

Immediately she felt better. She might not be able to keep the mysterious intruder from her house, but she had conquered the hideous Bullwinkle.

Nevertheless, it was time to quit messing around and get the roof and everything else fixed so she could be secure in her own home. But how?

Dulci Smallwood! If the contractor could guarantee a new roof by the end of the week, Skye would hire her.

Skye would still talk to Loretta and find out what Dulci was charged with, but unless it was murdering a homeowner, she was calling Dulci today to tell her to get started.

Having made her decision, Skye quickly stripped off her soiled dress and ruined panty hose, and pulled on gray jogging pants and a black sweatshirt. She tugged on an old pair of tennis shoes and pulled her hair back with a barrette. It was time to get to work: first phone calls, then an inventory of the old place.

As she descended the stairs, the grandfather clock in the foyer finished chiming twice. She hoped that meant everyone she needed to talk to would be available.

Entering the parlor, she made a mental note to call the telephone company. She needed additional jacks in the kitchen and her bedroom. The phone's present location was both inconvenient and uncomfortable.

Perched on the stiff settee, Skye called and left a message asking Wally if he knew where Alana's car was, since it wasn't parked in Skye's driveway. She also left word about Vince's information regarding Beau's non-use of drugs.

Moving on to the next name on her list, she dialed May.

Her mother answered immediately. "What did Vince tell you?"

Hoping to keep the conversation short,

Skye decided to forgo her usual protestations about not being her brother's keeper and not wanting to be a stool pigeon, and reported succinctly, "He went out drinking with his buddies Friday night, got too drunk to drive, and spent the night on one of his friend's couches."

"Then why didn't he tell me that yesterday when I asked?"

"Aunt Kitty was there and he was embarrassed."

"Do you believe him?"

"I believe every word he said to me," Skye said with utter conviction, remembering she had been the one to come up with the story, not Vince.

"Okay." Without warning May shifted gears. "Now that that's settled, what's this I hear about you and Wally being out on a date last night?"

Skye opened her mouth to ask who had told May, but stopped before uttering a sound. It was probably more a question of who *hadn't* told her, after Wally's and Skye's encounter with Priscilla the Bunco Lady.

When Skye didn't answer May persisted. "I told you he's not the right one for you. You need to make up with Simon. He's single, rich, and Catholic — perfect."

"Mom, Simon is history. He cheated on

me. I can forgive a lot of things, but not that."

"Are you sure he cheated?" May questioned. "Has he admitted it?"

"I'm not discussing it, Mom."

"Remember what they say: Men are like wine. They start out as grapes. It's our job to stomp on them and keep them in the dark until they mature. Once that happens, they turn into something we would like to have dinner with." May paused, then continued, "Go ahead and stomp on Simon, but then forgive him. Once he gets this nonsense out of his system, he'll be a good husband."

Skye had felt better after disposing of the moose head, but her temper was still frayed, and May had just cut the last thread. "Unless you want me to sell this house, quit my job, and move somewhere far, far away, you'll let this go."

There was a long silence; then May said in a stiff, hurt voice, "I'm only trying to make sure you're happy. It's for your own good."

"I know, Mom." Skye took a long calming breath, then softened her tone, but not her message. "Give it a rest, okay? No more lobbying for Simon."

"Fine. I certainly don't want to be a bother. I hope you'll at least invite me to the wedding. That is, if I'm still around. I haven't been feeling well. In fact, I'm feeling dizzy right now. I'd better go lay down. Goodbye."

Skye sighed as she hung up. She refused to feel guilty. Her mother had been playing the "not feeling well" card for the past twenty years. If Skye was going to live in Scumble River, she had to establish boundaries with her parents. Unexpectedly she chuckled. Yeah. Like that would really happen.

CHAPTER 15
FIFTEEN MINUTES
OF FAME

Skye reached for the phone, wiggling to find a comfortable position on the hard sofa. Her muscles ached from hiking up and down the river's shore — she had only been back a few minutes from another unsuccessful search for Bingo. There was still no sign of the cat, and tears itched behind her eyes. She blinked them back and straightened her spine. She'd look again tomorrow. She wasn't giving up on her pet.

Clearing her throat, she punched in Loretta's home number. She had called the attorney so often in the past couple of days, she had memorized all of her phone numbers — house, office, and cell.

It rang three times and Skye was preparing her message for the machine when she heard, "Hello. Loretta Steiner speaking."

For a moment surprise robbed Skye of her ability to speak, and before she could gather her wits, Loretta said sharply, "Who's there?

I can hear you breathing. Don't make me trace this call."

"No. Wait," Skye blurted out, "It's me, Skye."

"Oh, hi. Sorry I haven't gotten back to you. I was going to call you today."

"It's about time. First you send me a mysterious contractor, then you disappear."

"Don't get snippy with me, girl," Loretta snapped. "I was doing you a favor, sending you Dulci. If you don't want her, don't hire her."

"Sorry, you're right. I had a fight with my mom, my cat is still missing, and someone keeps breaking into my house. I'm a little on edge."

"Me, too." Loretta exhaled loudly. "Look, let's start over."

"Okay. So where have you been? I must have called you ten times since yesterday afternoon. I was getting worried one of those criminals you defend had killed you."

"Sorry. Didn't I mention when I saw you on Friday that I was going away for the weekend?"

"No." Skye faltered. Had Loretta told her? "I don't think so, but Friday was such a bad day, maybe I forgot. Sorry." Skye paused, then said, "That reminds me, how did you hear about my contractor's murder? As far as I know it didn't make the Chicago papers or TV news."

There was a long pause, and Loretta finally said, "I think channel nine or maybe one of the cable stations mentioned it briefly. They said something about a contractor in Scumble River being found dead at the home of his employer Skye Denison. I only caught the end."

"Great. My fifteen minutes of fame, and I missed it," Skye mocked.

"You've had more fame than you need, girl. Don't tell me you've already forgotten being on TV when that antique dealer died during your yard sale."

"Oh, yeah," Skye agreed distractedly. If Scumble River had made the TV evening news, why hadn't anyone mentioned it? Surely someone at church would have said something. Skye had the feeling Loretta was lying to her, but why?

"So, you want to know about Dulci, right?" Loretta broke into Skye's thoughts.

"Yes. After my last experience, I don't want to get caught being stupid again."

"Okay, let's see. She's a great contractor. Fast, efficient, and not expensive. She employs women and minorities. I like her and she needs the work."

"Why?"

"Because she's honest and doesn't mince words." Loretta snickered. "Actually, she's a lot like you."

"Not why do you like her, why does she need the work? I mean, if she's so good, shouldn't she be booked up a year in advance?"

"It has nothing to do with the quality of the job she does."

"Then why?" Skye squirmed, still trying to get comfortable. "What aren't you telling me?"

Loretta was silent, then said carefully, "Due to lawyer-client privilege, there are things I can't share about Dulci, but none of that has anything to do with her ability as a contractor."

"Are the things you can't tell me going to bring the Mafia or the cops to my doorstep?"

"No."

"What is she charged with?"

"The best thing would be for you to ask her." Then Loretta said slowly, "No, I take that back. The best thing for you to do would be to hire her to fix up your house, and for you to stay out of her personal problems. Sometimes ignorance is bliss."

"If ignorance is bliss, why aren't more people happy?" Skye snapped back.

Loretta snickered and hung up.

As soon as Skye replaced the receiver in its cradle, the phone rang. She answered cautiously — there were several people she didn't want to talk to.

"Ms. D? This is Frannie. I need you to come to the alley right now." Frannie worked weekends as a waitress at the bowling alley's grill.

"What's wrong?" Skye felt her heart skip a beat at the teen's urgent tone. Frannie was usually calm and upbeat.

"Your mother came in here looking for Miss Bunny and she was mad. They're in the basement and I can hear things breaking."

"Wh— ?"

Frannie cut off Skye's questions. "Just come."

Skye frowned. Frannie didn't often ask for help. She must be seriously afraid.

By speeding, running a few stop signs, and not bothering to change out of her sweat suit or comb her hair, Skye made it to the bowling alley in record time. She parked the Bel Air in the crowded lot, jumped out, and ran into the building's entrance. As she neared the door to the basement, she heard shouts and the sound of breaking glass.

Skye skidded to a stop. What in the world

were Bunny and May doing?

Frannie rushed up to her. "You've got to stop them before they hurt each other."

"Don't worry. I'll take care of it." Skye's words were meant to comfort the teenager, but they did nothing to reassure herself.

The image of May and Bunny rolling around on the basement floor pulling each other's hair popped into Skye's mind as she tried the knob. The door wasn't locked. Starting down the steps, she wondered if there was a fire hose handy. How else would she separate the two enraged women?

She reached the bottom. There was no one in sight and it had become eerily silent. Skye crinkled her brow. Had they killed each other?

She hurried toward the back of the basement where walls had been erected to create two rooms. The door on the right was open and Skye could see that the room was empty, but the door on the left was closed.

Skye twisted the knob, and when it wouldn't budge she pounded on the cheap wood veneer, yelling, "Mom! Bunny! Let me in right now!"

Finally, the door was jerked open, a hand wrapped around Skye's arm, and she was yanked inside. Even after the hand freed her, the momentum kept her going until she skidded into the room's back wall. She whirled around just in time to see the door slam shut and Bunny and May position themselves against it. Skye stared at the pair standing shoulder to shoulder. Neither woman had a hair out of place, nor did anything in the room appear to be broken.

"What in blue blazes is going on?" Skye demanded. "You've terrified Frannie."

May and Bunny exchanged conspiratorial looks, but neither woman spoke.

"Answer me. Why are you two fighting?" Skye's glance was drawn to a large metal wastebasket that contained the remains of numerous broken beer bottles. She was beginning to get a bad feeling about this.

Suddenly there was a pounding on the door and a masculine voice demanded to be let in. Bunny flung the door open and Simon strode in. Before either he or Skye could move, Bunny and May scampered out of the room.

Simon and Skye froze, gazes locked, the mutual words, "What are you doing here?" dying on their lips.

The sound of a distant door slamming brought them out of their daze. Skye pushed Simon aside and ran for the exit.

He was on her heels and they both reached the door at the top of the stairs at the same time.

Skye tried the knob. It was locked. She yelled, "Let me out of here!"

May's voice answered, "You wouldn't talk to Simon, now you have no choice."

Simon stepped next to Skye on the top step and yelled, "Bunny, this isn't funny. Let us out, now."

"No," Bunny responded immediately. "You won't explain to Skye what happened. Now you'll either explain or stay in there forever."

"Mom," Skye threatened, "remember what I said earlier. If you don't let me out this instant, I'm moving away." She was bluffing, but hoped her mother wouldn't figure that out.

"This is your one chance for happiness. I'm willing to take the risk." May sounded resolute.

After several more minutes of screaming at their mothers and getting no response, Simon turned to Skye, "I sure wish I hadn't put that dead bolt on the outside of this door. I wanted to keep the customers from wandering down here. It seemed like a good idea at the time."

"So many things do," Skye murmured.

"I take it you got a frantic call from Frannie, too?"

Skye nodded.

"We've been had by a teenage dupe and two middle-aged con women."

"Yep."

Simon raised an eyebrow, then turned and sat on the step. "Not that I wanted it to happen this way, but I *have* been trying to talk to you."

"Really? You could have fooled me. It's not as if I'm hard to find."

"No. Merely hard to get alone."

"Ah, that *was* you I kept seeing pull out of my driveway." Skye frowned. "I thought so, but I only ever saw the taillights of your car, so I wasn't sure."

"Well, it was me, but every time I tried to come see you, Boyd was already there."

A voice from outside the door screeched, "I told you not to date Wally."

Skye blew out a puff of exasperation, edged past Simon, and walked down the stairs. Even locked in a basement, privacy was hard to come by in Scumble River.

Simon followed. "And you never answer your phone."

"Why didn't you leave a message?" Skye kept walking. There was no furniture in the main room, so she headed back to the

219

smaller room where their mothers had been. At least it had a few chairs and tables.

Simon tagged along. "There didn't seem to be anything I could say that was short enough to fit on an answering machine tape."

"Well, we're here now." Skye sat down in the metal folding chair next to the wastebasket. "Explain."

A stubborn expression settled on his face. "I went on a trip; I invited you to come along; you said no. I stayed with an old friend from college, which I told you I was doing. I have a clear conscience."

"A clear conscience is the sign of a bad memory." Skye folded her arms. "Such as forgetting to mention your 'friend' was a woman."

"Spike being female is irrelevant." Simon sat down across from her.

"Ignoring the facts doesn't change the facts," Skye scoffed. "If you have a logical reason why I shouldn't be angry that my boyfriend spent several nights with another woman, now is the time to tell me."

Simon's face had turned brick red. He took a deep breath, started to speak, stopped, then said, "Look, if you knew all the facts, you wouldn't be angry. But before I tell you, I need to believe you trust me."

"Why? Why can't you help me trust you by explaining?"

"It's a guy thing."

"Now I know you're hiding something. You never, ever say 'It's a guy thing.' " Skye shot out of her chair. "And you never say it, because 'It's a guy thing' really means that there is no rational thought pattern connected with it, and you have no chance at all of making it sound logical."

"That's not true." Simon ran his fingers through his hair. "I don't want to be one of those whiners who blame all their problems on their childhood, but every time Bunny left, I felt like it was my fault, so I need to know that no matter what I do, you won't leave me. I'd never do anything to hurt you, but you have to believe in me."

Skye could see the wounded little boy in his eyes, and the love she'd had for him in the past started to seep out of the box she had built around those feelings. She opened her mouth to say he didn't have to explain, but then she remembered Luc and Kent and the other men who had betrayed her, and said, "I understand what you're asking from me; I just don't think I can give you that unconditional trust you're looking for. I've been hurt too many times myself. Please, please, tell me why I shouldn't be upset when you spent the night with a woman."

For a moment, Skye saw something in Simon's expression. Would he finally tell her what had happened? At that moment she decided that if he told her the truth, no matter what that truth was, she would take him back and give their relationship another chance.

"The truth is —" Simon broke off what he had been about to say, his eyes narrowed; then he continued, saying the words tentatively as if testing the idea. "The truth is, you're doing this because I tried to take our relationship to the next level. You panicked when I suggested exchanging keys and leaving some of our clothes at each other's houses. Subconsciously, you've been looking for a reason to break up since I first asked you to do that."

Her mood veered sharply from forgiveness to anger. "How dare you try to blame me for what you did!" She gritted her teeth, reined in her temper, and tried once again to give him a chance to tell his side. "Instead of psychoanalyzing me, how about just coming clean?"

He chuckled nastily. "Come clean? How about before I come clean, you come clean and tell me why you've been spending so much time with Boyd." His words exploded in the air between them. "We've been together for more than a year. Then in less than a month, before you give us a chance to straighten things out, you're already seeing someone else."

Skye was silent, guilty feelings hampering her ability to defend herself. Finally she said halfheartedly, "That's different. I didn't sleep with Wally while I was still going with you."

"So, you admit it. You *have* slept with him." His curt voice lashed at her.

"No." His caustic tone made her flush in shame. Maybe she shouldn't have started to see Wally so soon. "I haven't slept with him. Can you say the same about you and Spike?"

Skye held her breath. This was it. If he told her the truth, she'd forgive him and they could try to mend their relationship.

Instead, he replied in reckless anger, "Now I see why you've been so 'upset' over the whole Spike issue. It's not because you really think I've betrayed you. It's because it gave you the perfect excuse to have an affair with Boyd." A sudden chill clung to his words. "You've been wanting to screw him as long as I've known you."

Simon's crude words shocked her. He

never talked like that, especially to her. At first the pain caused by his words immobilized her; then the hurt turned into white-hot fury. She reached down into the wastebasket, grabbed an empty beer bottle, shot to her feet, and flung it at him, screaming, "You're the one who was caught with his hand in the cookie jar. Stop trying to make this about me."

The bottle shattered against the wall next to him, and the sound seemed to snap something in both of them.

Skye's glare turned into a beseeching look and she whispered, "All I ever asked you to do was explain."

Simon slumped against the back of his chair. "If after all this time we haven't built up enough trust not to let suspicion destroy our relationship, then maybe we shouldn't be together."

Skye took a quick, sharp breath. Was that what she really wanted? She sank back down. "Maybe you're right." The words fell from her lips like the broken glass littering the floor between them. They left her mouth tasting of regret's bitter doubts.

Simon's head drooped, suggesting that had not been what he had hoped to hear. He said almost to himself, "I can't believe this is all it takes to break us up. We have so much in common and we never argue."

"Just because two people argue, it doesn't mean that they don't love each other; and just because they don't argue, it doesn't mean that they do," she replied in a low, tormented voice.

He closed his eyes, and when he opened them he said, "So, this is it?"

Pain flooded the small room. Waves of hurt and humiliation and loss roiled around them.

"Maybe." They seemed to have backed each other into a corner and Skye couldn't see any way out of it. She felt her throat closing up. "I just don't want to trust someone again, then end up feeling like a fool because I did."

"Human beings are nearly unique in the animal world in having the ability to learn from the experiences of others." Simon's expression was bleak. "Too bad we're also remarkable for our apparent disinclination to do so."

Fierce grief ripped through her. A part of her couldn't believe he was ending things this way. She bit her lip to control the sobs that threatened to break loose. No way was she letting him see her cry.

Silently, she got up and went into the other room. When he didn't follow, she stood facing the wall, staring at a safety poster illustrating the Heimlich maneuver, and ignoring both the tiny voice at the back of her mind that urged her to trust him and the tears running down her cheeks.

CHAPTER 16
SIXTEEN CANDLES

The next morning Skye parked the Bel Air in the high school lot, then sat staring at the hood of her car, thinking of yesterday's debacle. Simon had finally figured out a way to get their mothers to unlock the basement door, but it had taken nearly an hour for him to come up with the idea. The plan was simple — all he and Skye had to do was lie. They shouted to Bunny and May that they had made up, and after several reassurances their mothers let them out.

Both women took the news of their children's deception poorly. Bunny wept hysterically, and May gasped for breath, claiming she was about to faint. Simon and Skye had hardened their hearts and left them wailing and panting. Their mothers were blatantly out of control, and if May ever pulled another stunt like that, Skye really would have to consider moving away.

With a final shake of her head, Skye

pushed the memory away and got out of her car. She trudged across the cracked asphalt, up the shallow steps, and through the door. Mondays were always tough, but she dreaded this one even more than usual.

Although to Skye it seemed to have happened a long time in the past, rather than only three days ago, Beau's death and her involvement would be fresh news for the school employees. Word would have spread, and everyone would want to hear about it. The fact that Beau was the brother of one of the high school teachers would be the extra marshmallow on the already yummy cup of hot gossip.

That's why she was there so early. It wasn't even seven o'clock yet — school started for the kids at ten to eight, and the teachers didn't have to report until seven thirty-five — so Skye hoped to escape into her office before either the staff or the students started to arrive.

There had been only two cars in the parking lot when she pulled in. One belonged to the new PE teacher, the other to the school secretary, Opal Hill.

Skye checked the hallway. It was empty. So far, so good, but she still had to sign in at the counter in the office. This was the riskiest part. Opal would never question her, but the office was a major hub of activity in the mornings. Teachers checked their mailboxes, made copies on the Xerox machine, and chatted; students dropped off notes and bought lunch tickets; and parents lined up to ask questions.

As Skye neared the counter, she blew out a breath of relief; there was no one around. Even Opal wasn't at her desk. Skye quickly signed the attendance sheet, scooped the papers out of her mailbox, and turned to leave.

Before she had taken a complete step, a voice boomed, "Get your rear end into my office immediately!"

She was busted. And by the worst possible person. Skye slowly turned back and with dragging steps reported to the principal.

Homer Knapik had been the high school principal for as long as most people could remember, even back when Skye had been a student at Scumble River High. Lately, the last two or three years, Homer had taken to announcing his retirement in June, but so far he was always back come the end of August, much to the disappointment of his staff.

By this point the teachers were convinced that should Homer pass away, the school board would have him stuffed and mounted in the chair behind his desk. The sad part was, no one would be able to tell the difference, at least as far as the running of the school went.

Skye paused on the threshold to his office, hoping she could get away without actually going in. "Good morning, Homer. You wanted to see me?"

"How the hell do you manage to keep finding dead bodies?" Homer slapped down a file on his desktop.

He was short and round, reminding Skye of an extremely hairy Humpty Dumpty.

"Just lucky?" She cringed.

"Don't be a smart-ass with me. What are you, some kind of magnet for the dead?"

Skye gave up and fully entered the room. "No." This wouldn't be a quick chat. "At least I don't think so."

"Well, I want you to stop it."

"Okay."

"That's it?" The hair sprouting out of his ears bristled. "All you have to say is 'okay'?"

"Okay, sir?"

Homer's face turned a mottled red. "And I want you to stay out of the police investigation. No sleuthing."

"What if they ask for my help?"

"They won't. Buck Peterson had me on

the phone for over an hour Saturday morning, chewing out my butt. Believe me, you will not be invited to participate."

"Sheriff Peterson isn't the only one involved in this case."

"Everyone knows about the thing between you and Wally Boyd. This would not be a good time for the police chief to let you interfere with his work." Homer glared.

"I do not interfere." Skye refused to let someone who resembled a long-haired gerbil control her private life. "I help."

"Quit finding dead bodies. Quit finding murderers. End of discussion." Homer stood, abruptly, knocking over his chair. "Get out of my sight." Skye turned to escape, but he stopped her. "No, wait. I forgot. I want you to talk to Pru Cormorant."

Skye cringed. "Why?" The English teacher had been at Scumble River High for as long as Homer, and was a law unto herself.

"She sent this note home to one of the parents." Homer thrust a piece of paper in Skye's direction.

She read it out loud: " 'Since last year, your son has reached rock bottom and started to dig.' " She suppressed a giggle. "How did Mrs. Sage respond to this?"

"Badly." Homer sat back down, his two

oversized front teeth gnawing on his bottom lip. "And Cormorant refuses to apologize."

"And of course she's tenured, so you don't have much to hold over her head, right?"

His nose twitched in agreement. "Which means it's your job to convince her how psychologically harmful this kind of talk can be to the students in our care."

Skye stared at the principal as if he had started speaking Swahili. She had never thought she'd hear those words from his mouth.

Then he ruined it by adding, "Or whatever gibberish you think will work to keep her in line." He looked up from the file he had opened and asked pointedly, "Are you still here?"

After silently stepping across the threshold and closing the door behind her, she ran Homer's list of commands through her mind. Stop finding bodies, stop finding murderers, and stop Pru Cormorant from riling up parents. Nope. There was little chance that she could fulfill any of them.

Skye retreated to the relative safety of her office and sank into the chair behind the desk. She let her tote bag fall to the floor and closed her eyes. She was already tired, and the day hadn't even officially started yet.

Once again, her thoughts wandered back to yesterday. After getting home from her lock-in with Simon, she had spent the rest of Sunday trying to block the memory of what had happened between them from her mind.

Her call to Dulci, and the contractor's verbal agreement to start work on the roof the next day, had helped make Skye feel somewhat better, but then Wally had phoned and Simon's accusations had flooded her thoughts.

She struggled to keep focused while Wally told her they had found Alana's car abandoned at the Recreation Club, not far from where Beau's truck had been dumped. The interesting thing was that there had been wet patches in the trunk. Samples had been sent off for testing, but Wally said it smelled like river water.

He had also mentioned questioning Priscilla Van Horn, but she hadn't told him anything of interest. After agreeing to speak to Vince about Beau's apparent non-drug use, Wally had asked to come over. Skye had turned him down, her feelings too raw and insecure after her afternoon with Simon.

Instead, Skye had spent the remaining hours of the evening sorting through Mrs.

Griggs's treasures, managing to straighten one corner of a spare bedroom before falling into bed exhausted. She had uncovered mostly junk, but she did find a couple of items that might be worth something. They were locked safely in her trunk, where they would remain until her house had real windows and a roof.

A tentative knock on her office door brought Skye back to the present, and she called out, "Come in."

Justin and Frannie entered. They made an interesting couple. Frannie was outgoing and friendly, quite a contrast to Justin, who was reserved and suspicious. He was nearly six feet tall and rail thin, while she was five inches shorter and much curvier. They both had brown hair, but his was military-short and hers flowed to her waist.

Frannie hung back, smiling tentatively at Skye. "Hope you're not mad at me for yesterday, Ms. D."

"No, Frannie. I'm sure Bunny and May somehow forced you to help them."

"Well, they said it was the only way you'd ever find true happiness."

Skye grimaced. "Let's forget about it." She turned to Justin. "How was your weekend?"

"I mostly hung out with the kids from the *Scoop*." Justin thrust his chin out. "We were waiting for you to call us back about the prize."

Skye winced. With everything that had happened in the last sixty hours, she had forgotten to call them. Crap! Justin had major trust issues that had been exacerbated during the summer. He was just starting to come around again, but something as minor as an unreturned phone call could set back his progress.

"Oh, I am so sorry." Skye came around her desk and touched his upper arm, as close to a hug as she dared give in this day and age. "After what happened Friday night with poor Mr. Hamilton, I had to give a statement to the police the next day, and since my house is a total mess, I had to get busy finding a new contractor. And then Sunday, I was all tied up. Right, Frannie?" The girl nodded, and Skye finished up her justification. "So it's not that I don't care, it's that I was overwhelmed with what was happening."

When Justin didn't answer, Frannie gave him a hard look and said, "It's no big deal. Ms. D always comes through for us." She elbowed him in the side. "Doesn't she?"

His expression didn't change and he remained silent.

"Well, no matter how hectic things were,

it was very wrong to break my promise." Skye looked Justin in the eye. "And I'm truly sorry."

He shrugged and muttered, "Whatever."

Skye knew that was as much exoneration as she'd get from him, and changed the subject. "I truly am extremely proud of you and the others for winning the Blevins Award. We'll have to have a party."

"Yeah!" Frannie cheered. "You've got a big house now. Maybe we could have it there."

"If you all don't mind the mess from the renovation, we could have it this coming Saturday," Skye offered, wanting to let the teens know how pleased she was with their success. "I'll get sub sandwiches, chips, soda, and have my mom's friend Maggie make one of her famous cakes."

"Cool." Justin gave her one of his rare smiles.

Skye smiled back, then asked, "Have you thought about what you want to spend the five thousand dollars on?" She smiled to herself: Trust these two to find one of the few contests with a significant monetary prize.

Justin and Frannie glanced at each other, and he spoke. "We were thinking of buying computers for the school."

"That sounds like a great idea," Skye said. This was the beginning of her fourth year at the high school and they still had only one computer in the building available for student use, and it was not connected to the Internet. As far as she knew, Homer had a PC collecting dust in his office, and the secretary had one she used mostly as a word processor, but that was the extent of Scumble River High's technology.

"The whole newspaper staff agrees," Frannie contributed, bouncing in her chair.

Skye nodded. "We'll have to really consider how to do this, but off the top of my head, I think we should spend the majority of the money getting as much equipment as we can. However, we need to save a good chunk to hire someone to teach a computer class."

"The kids know how to use computers already, Ms. D." Justin protested. "Most have one at home."

"That may be true, but I don't think the teachers are as up-to-date." Skye held up her hand as Frannie started to interrupt her. "And even the students who have computers probably don't know everything they can do with them."

"But we want to spend the money for the kids, not the teachers," Frannie objected.

"Look at it this way. There is no way on God's green earth that the school board will approve this idea without trained staff to supervise."

"That's not fair," Justin griped. "It's our money."

"Have I ever claimed life is fair?" Skye asked. "If life were fair, would I be driving an aqua Bel Air? No. I'd have a cool black Miata."

Frannie giggled, and even Justin managed a small grin before saying, "Okay. But we need to find someone cheap to teach computers. Not anyone who expects big bucks."

As the homeroom bell rang, Skye ushered the teens to the door. "Don't worry, no *real* teacher ever expects to get paid big bucks."

After the kids left, Skye pulled a yellow pad from the top desk drawer and started a list of what she had to do. Number one was to find Bingo. Tied for second place was to figure out who Vince was dating, what personal secrets her new contractor was hiding, and if Alana Lowe knew anything she wasn't telling the police.

Skye wondered if the art teacher was at school today. If, as Alana claimed, Beau's death wasn't drug-related, then maybe she could point Skye in a different direction.

Skye chewed the end of her pen. What else

did she need to do? Mmm. Maybe she could talk to a few of Beau's recent clients. If Sheriff Peterson was convinced he had the killer in jail, surely he wouldn't object to Skye chatting with the dead man's customers.

Something else was niggling at her. Something she had meant to look at or ask or do. Something she had missed. What? She couldn't put her finger on it. Shoot. She hated when that happened. It would bug her all day, like an itchy tag inside the collar of a shirt.

Right now, the first period bell was ringing, and Skye had to get to work on her real job, the one they were paying her to perform. She put the legal pad in her tote bag and flipped open her calendar. What was on her schedule for today?

Her first appointment was at eight thirty, so she had some time to prepare. A mother had called to say she wanted to discuss enrolling her daughter in Scumble River High. Skye ran her finger over the student's name, Xenia Craughwell, then practiced saying it out loud. "Zeenia, Zenia, Zeena?"

She'd have to check with the mother to see how to say it correctly. If the girl was going to attend school here, Skye wanted to make sure they got the pronunciation right.

There were few things as unwelcoming as having the teacher screw up your name when she introduced you on your first day of class.

As Skye smoothed her hair and reapplied her lipstick, she wondered why Mrs. Craughwell had wanted a meeting before enrolling her daughter. Usually parents simply came by, signed the papers, and paid the fees on the same day their kids started classes.

Adding to Skye's unease, Mrs. Craughwell had refused to bring in her daughter's past school records, and specifically requested seeing either the psychologist or social worker. This behavior immediately set off warning bells in Skye's head, making her think the woman and her daughter had had prior experience with the special education system.

Normally, unless they arrived with an Individual Education Plan in hand or there were very unusual circumstances, the guidance counselor would take care of students who moved into the district. Xenia was already looking like an exception to the rule.

Skye finished freshening up, grabbed a yellow pad, pen, and her appointment book from the desk, and walked down the hall to Homer's office. So far, she'd been able to avoid the staff and their questions. Her luck held out as she entered the main office. Since it was between bells, the teachers were all in class and only Opal was present.

Skye paused, and asked the secretary, "Is Mrs. Craughwell here yet?"

"No, but I just reminded Homer she was coming." Opal continued her rapid-fire typing.

Since Skye had no desire to spend any time alone with Homer after his behavior that morning, she stalled. "Opal, do you get much use out of the computer, besides as a typewriter replacement, I mean?"

"No, uh, I'm not sure, I mean, yes," the secretary stammered.

Opal was a slight woman with a pouf of prematurely white hair. Today her eyes were pink-rimmed and her nose was twitching. She reminded Skye of the rabbit from *Alice in Wonderland,* except that Opal was never, ever late for anything, let alone an important date.

Skye decided to rephrase her question. "Do you think a computer class would help improve the computer's usefulness to you?"

"Homer says there's no money for that sort of thing, and I can't afford to pay for a class myself."

"And you shouldn't have to," Skye reassured her. "But if it were offered free at the school, you'd sign up?"

"If I could, yes. I take care of my mother, so it really depends on the time."

Skye nodded. "When is good for you?"

"Right after school. I could get the lady who sits with her to stay late."

Skye made a note of Opal's preference, and when she looked up, a woman in her early thirties had appeared. Small white teeth bit into a full bottom lip coated in frosted pink gloss, and long nails painted to match her lipstick gripped the edge of the counter.

She was tiny, probably not more than five feet tall, and she wore her platinum blond hair parted in the middle and straight down her back. Both her stature and hairstyle made her look about sixteen years old, if not for the wrinkles bracketing her mouth and eyes.

Skye took a not-so-wild guess and asked, "Mrs. Craughwell?"

"Yes." Heavily mascaraed lashes framed worried cornflower blue eyes. "I'm here to see the school psychologist and the principal."

Skye took a step forward and held out her hand. "I'm Skye Denison, the psychologist. We'll meet in the principal's office."

"I'm Raette Craughwell." The woman had taken the tips of Skye's fingers and was giving them a weak shake when the second period bell rang. She let go as if Skye's hand had turned into a cattle prod.

"Sorry." Skye made small talk as she led the woman down the short hallway to Homer's office. "The bells are a bit loud, aren't they?" As she chatted, she wondered. *Raette. Where have I heard that name before? It's fairly unusual, but I know someone said it to me not too long ago. Who was it?*

Suspending her rumination in favor of the task at hand, Skye gave a perfunctory knock on the principal's door and ushered the woman inside.

When Skye introduced Raette Craughwell to Homer, he glanced at her disinterestedly, then down again at the file he'd been reading, then quickly looked back at her. Popping up from his chair, he stumbled in his haste, but managed to approach the two women without falling.

Homer grasped Mrs. Craughwell's hand and said, "I'm Homer Knapik, the principal here. Have a seat. Get comfortable."

She sat in one of the visitor's chairs, clutching a little pink purse and a large manila envelope in her lap.

Homer took the chair next to her, looking

at her as if she were a dinner roll and he was a man on a low carb diet. Finally he licked his lips and said, "Now, tell me what I can do for you."

Skye, feeling totally ignored, but not altogether unhappy with that status, sat in a chair against the wall and observed. She made a bet with herself that at some point Homer would actually drool.

"I moved to Scumble River last June. I —"

"Then where has your daughter been since school started?" Homer interrupted. "We've been in session a month already."

"I was homeschooling her." Raette paused, then said, "I'm sure I didn't do as good a job as your teachers would have, but it seemed to be the best thing at the time."

He patted her hand. "Now don't underestimate yourself. Remember, amateurs built the ark and professionals built the *Titanic*."

Skye bit back a comment. Homer was well known for his negative views on homeschooling, but apparently if the mom was pretty enough he could overlook anything.

"Thank you. What a sweet thing to say." Mrs. Craughwell smiled before asking, "I was told this is a quiet community with safe schools. Is that true?"

Homer nodded vigorously, his hair flapping like the ears of a basset hound. "We are very vigilant against gangs, drugs, and violence."

Skye coughed. Yeah, so vigilant that they had completely missed the infiltration of methamphetamine last year. She hoped they had stopped the drug's use in the high school, but she wouldn't bet her parents' farm on it.

On the other hand, she was pretty sure they were free of gangs, with the exception of the usual cliques and groups.

Violence? So far, so good. They had had no major incidents in the school and only a few minor ones on the bus.

Homer patted Mrs. Craughwell's hand. "Your little girl will be safe with us."

"But will you be safe from her?"

"What?" Homer jerked back as if she had squirted him with pepper spray.

"Xenia has had some problems in her past schools," Mrs. Craughwell answered.

Skye raised an eyebrow, noting the woman had said "schools," not "school."

"I see." Homer floundered, moving his chair away from the mom. "Uh, what kind of trouble?"

"Well, she wouldn't go a lot of the time."

Homer's shoulders relaxed and Skye could read his mind. If the girl wasn't in school, she couldn't cause problems. Homer'd simply call the truancy officer and have him handle it.

"And . . . one of her schools claimed she had formed a gang." Mrs. Craughwell's high-pitched laugh was not convincing.

"What sort of gang?" Homer asked, his hairy brows meeting in the middle.

"It was silly really. She got this bunch of kids to go on strike."

"Strike?" Homer's eyebrows went from straight lines to exclamation points.

"You know, not do any homework."

"Is there more?"

"In her last school, she somehow convinced this group of girls that all of their fathers were evil and should be killed."

Homer popped from his seat like the next Kleenex in the box and backed toward his desk. He finally remembered Skye's presence and said to her, "This sounds like something in your job description."

Skye barely stopped herself from snorting. To Homer, anything he didn't want to deal with was in her job description. Instead she said, "Sure." She moved up and sat beside Mrs. Craughwell, then asked, "What happened?"

"They picked a day, bought rat poison, and were all set to do it when one girl came to her senses and told her mother about the plan."

"Did she call the police?" Skye was both appalled and curious. Xenia must have an enormous amount of charisma.

"Yes. The police put the girls under house arrest for six months. They could only go to school and home. No communication between them, and all the girls had to get counseling. If they broke those rules, they went to the juvenile facility."

"How long ago was this?"

"The six months ended four months ago. We moved here as soon as school was out. Everyone was so mad at Xenia and me, I thought it was best to try for a fresh start."

Skye paused to consider how to word her next question, then asked, "How did Xenia's father react to all this?" Skye waited, but the woman didn't answer. Finally after a full minute of silence, Skye tried again. "Did Xenia's father move here with you?"

"No." Mrs. Craughwell looked down at her purse. "I never married Xenia's father. I was sixteen when I had her, and he was only seventeen. He always refused to admit she was his child, and he left us when she was two years old."

"I see. And you've had no contact since then?"

Mrs. Craughwell shook her head.

"Does Xenia know his name?"

"I haven't told her."

Skye gestured at the envelope the woman was holding. "Are those Xenia's school records?"

Mrs. Craughwell nodded, then after a brief hesitation handed them to Skye, who opened the flap and quickly scanned the first few pages.

She said, "So, Xenia is turning sixteen in October? Then she's a sophomore?"

"Yes. Well, no. I mean she should be, but she didn't earn enough credits last year. That's why I've been trying to catch her up by homeschooling her. But she's really smart and she scores very high on the group achievement tests. Her previous school did some other kind of testing and they said she was fine, no learning problems. The papers are all in the envelope."

Skye was suspicious of Mrs. Craughwell's true motives for keeping her daughter home until now, but she was relieved to hear that Xenia had already had a case study. One less thing to hurry and get done. All she would have to do was read the report and see what had been recommended. "How did Xenia feel about moving here?"

Mrs. Craughwell smiled for the first time.

"She's excited. In fact, when I decided we had to move, Xenia was the one who found Scumble River and wanted to live here."

Skye felt another sizzle of shock. Why would a troubled teenager choose Scumble River?

CHAPTER 17
AT SEVENTEEN

Two hours later, Mrs. Craughwell finally left. Homer and Skye sat stunned, staring at each other. It was difficult to believe that a fifteen-year-old had wreaked the havoc Raette Craughwell had described.

Xenia had attended eight schools in her ten-year career as a student, and from what Skye could piece together from Mrs. Craughwell's rambling, most of the moves were made in order to avoid retention or expulsion.

Once Mrs. Craughwell got started talking, she had told Homer and Skye more about Xenia than they really wanted to know, and after her departure it took them several minutes to regroup. This girl would definitely be the toughest teenager either of them had ever dealt with. She was smart, resourceful, charismatic, and angry at the whole world. Most of the kids Skye had worked with possessed one or two of those traits, but having all four made Xenia dangerous.

Homer plucked at a tuft of hair growing from his ear and said, "What are we going to do with her?"

"I wish I knew." Skye felt as if she had just participated in the longest therapy session on record. It was clear that Mrs. Craughwell was at her wit's end, and it was equally clear that the solution didn't lie within the school's purview. "I'll read the case study report from her last school and see if they made any suggestions."

"We need a plan before she gets here tomorrow for classes. Did the mom say if she was riding the bus?"

"No." Skye shivered, imagining what could happen on a thirty-minute bus ride. "If she does, we'll need a plan for that, too."

"Shit." Homer closed his eyes and started to move his lips in and out. "I knew I should have retired last year."

Skye recognized a dismissal when she heard one. As the door closed between her and Homer's office, she heard him pick up the phone and say, "Opal, get me the superintendent right now. Tell him it's an emergency. Tell him Lizzy Borden Junior is starting school here tomorrow."

Trust Homer to put the most negative

spin possible on the situation — not that Skye felt all that positive herself. Still, as she headed down the hall, she was trying to come up with an idea to help Xenia fit in and start fresh. Normally Skye would try to pair the girl up with a classmate, but with Xenia's persuasive powers, that didn't seem fair to any other student. There had to be something that would channel Xenia's talents into more appropriate activities.

Skye's musings had brought her to the junction in the corridor. If she went left she'd return to her own office; if she went in the opposite direction, she'd walk past the art room. It was nearly eleven, the beginning of fifth period, which was Alana's plan time and the perfect moment to talk to her.

As Skye headed right, she rationalized that she was really checking to see if Alana was okay. She would not pump the woman for information on Beau's clients and/or girl-friends — although if the conversation went in that direction, and Skye got a lead in her investigation, she figured that was simply a twofer.

Alana's room was in the oldest part of the school, at the end of a row of lockers. Although the heating was iffy and there was no air conditioning, it did have a couple of coveted advantages over the newer class-rooms — a working door to the outside and windows.

When Skye approached, she smelled the customary odors of turpentine, clay, and permanent markers, but she also heard the unusual sound of raised voices. She accelerated her steps as the man's tone grew harsher.

Half afraid that Sheriff Peterson had returned to harass Alana, Skye dashed in. She stopped abruptly when she saw Neville and Alana standing by the outside door. Neville had his hands wrapped around Alana's upper arms and looked as if he were shaking her, but before Skye could be sure, his hold turned into an embrace.

Skye hesitated, not sure of what she had seen. She didn't want to interfere with a lovers' quarrel, but she also didn't want to let Alana down if she needed help. Compromising, Skye said, "Alana, are you okay?"

Neville answered, "Alana was feeling a little faint, and I was trying to get her outdoors for some fresh air."

Skye looked at Alana, not willing to let Neville answer for her. "Is that true, Alana?"

The art teacher nodded, her complexion pale and gray.

"I told you not to come to work today,"

he chided her, then turned to Skye and explained, "I was worried, so I came to see how she was doing. When I walked up, I saw her standing by her desk swaying, so I shouted for her to unlock the door. She managed to get it open, but as I stepped through she started to go down. I only managed to grab her before she hit the floor."

Skye relaxed. "Timing is everything." She had to stop seeing boogeymen everywhere. Neville was merely a caring boyfriend who got rattled when he saw his lover nearly pass out. "Evidently great minds think alike. I was checking to see how Alana was doing, too."

"I guess teaching today wasn't such a good idea." Alana smiled wanly from Neville's arms. "I felt okay this morning, but as the day went on I felt weaker and weaker. I sure wish they'd release Beau's body so I could plan his funeral."

"It shouldn't be too long now," Skye soothed.

Alana nodded, then asked, "Do you think Homer can get a sub for this afternoon?"

"I'm sure he can figure something out," Skye assured her. "I'll go tell him you had to leave. Is there anything else I can do?"

Alana pointed to her desk drawer. "Could you hand me my purse? Oh, and throw out my lunch. It's in the fridge in the teachers' lounge."

"Sure." Skye fetched the stylish black leather Prada satchel from the drawer and handed it to Alana. "How about if I stay with you while Neville brings the car around?"

"You don't need to. I'll be fine," Alana protested at the same time that Neville said, "Actually, since I wasn't going to be long, I parked right at the curb. We'll just nip out this door and you can lock up."

Skye nodded. "Okay. Then I'll take care of Homer and get rid of your lunch."

The couple waved as they left. After making sure the door was locked and nothing valuable was lying around, Skye retraced her steps to the office. Lucky for her, Homer was at lunch, so she was able to leave a message with Opal about Alana needing a sub.

Skye had been afraid if she told Homer in person, he would order her to teach art for the rest of the day, not caring that she was busy with her own work, or that her entire artistic ability consisted of tracing her hand to make a Thanksgiving Day turkey decoration.

Since she had avoided the wrath of Homer, Skye decided to take care of Alana's lunch disposal before she forgot.

The teachers' lounge was decorated in garage sale castoffs. Skye headed directly to the avocado-colored refrigerator huddled in the back, next to a counter with a sink full of used coffee mugs. She wrinkled her nose as she opened the door. The slight odor of spoiled milk and rotten lettuce lingered no matter how many times the fridge was cleaned.

Skye scanned the packed interior. Brown sacks, bright thermal carriers, and every type of takeout container crowded the shelves, but she unhesitatingly reached for a mini Gucci shopping bag. Examining it, she saw "Alana" in perfect calligraphy on the front.

Previously, Skye had never quite figured out how the art teacher could afford the designer labels she sported, but having now met Alana's wealthy boyfriend, Skye guessed they had all been gifts.

Resisting the temptation to peek inside to see what goodies Alana had brought for lunch, Skye lifted the cover of the big black trash can and upended the sack. She replaced the lid and moved a few steps away. As she paused to fold up the Gucci bag, intending to return it to the art teacher, the bell for first lunch rang.

Instantly the lounge was flooded with

teachers. Several crowded around an old library cart, which contained a huge brown microwave, circa 1980. The stained exterior did not dissuade them from battling to be first to use it.

Others went immediately to the three long metal tables that had been put together down the center of the room, intent on claiming one of the orange molded-plastic chairs that lined both sides. Each lunch hour was like playing a game of musical chairs; there were never quite enough seats for everyone, so the tardy were forced to sit on the sofa to eat.

The couch was covered in a prickly plaid fabric that could withstand a direct nuclear hit, and occupied the opposite wall, making conversation awkward. A sofa seat at lunch was like being stuck at the kiddie table during Christmas dinner.

Skye hesitated. Part of her said to get out of the lounge before the teachers started questioning her about the murder. Another part urged her to hang around and listen to see if the staff had any good gossip about Beau.

When the telephone located on a child-sized desk off in one corner rang, and one of the teachers who had occupied a sofa cushion was called away, Skye saw the opportunity as a divine sign and sat down.

First to notice Skye was Pru Cormorant, the English teacher Homer wanted Skye to "fix." Pru raised an overplucked brow and said, "Skye, we don't see you in here often. We're honored you chose to join us today."

Skye didn't usually eat in the teachers' lounge, primarily because in order to maintain her mental health she needed to be alone and regroup after a morning dealing with her high stress job. This was not a reason most of the staff would appreciate, so instead Skye smiled and voiced a more acceptable motive. "Thanks, Pru. It's so crowded here, I hate to take a seat from someone."

The English teacher narrowed her watery blue eyes. "That's very sweet of you. No wonder so many students on my speech team are switching to your little newspaper."

The kids were joining the newspaper staff because Skye and Trixie treated them fairly. The best story got the front page, not the story written by the teenager who kissed up to them the most. Pru was known for letting her favorites rule the speech team, and the teens were rebelling.

Skye bit her tongue to stop from blurting out a retort containing the words "teacher's pet." She had noticed that the other teachers weren't joining the conversation, and she knew this was because they didn't want to get on the wrong side of one of the school's queen-bee teachers.

Neither did Skye, so she held on to her smile and said, "You know teenagers, they like to try whatever is currently new."

Pru seemed unsatisfied with Skye's answer, but didn't pursue the matter. Instead, she said, "I hear you found another body. You must moonlight for the Grim Reaper." Pru tittered, and several of her cronies laughed along with her.

Skye took a deep breath. It would be so easy to make a smart-alecky comeback and lose this opportunity. Pru Cormorant was gossip central for the school, and Skye wanted to know what she had heard.

Giving a small shrug, Skye allowed a look of distress to cross her face, and then with a catch in her voice said, "I know. Isn't it awful? I'm sure glad the sheriff found the killer so fast. I simply couldn't imagine who would want to murder such a nice man."

Pru ran her fingers through her stringy dun-colored hair, tsking. "I'm surprised that you, a psychologist, were so easily taken in by such a con artist."

"Beau was a con artist? Really?" Skye laid the naïveté on thick.

"Everyone in town knew."

"You're kidding. Why didn't anyone tell me?"

"No one wanted to hurt dear Alana, of course." Pru's smile was superior. "And some people probably thought you hired him for the same reason so many other lonely women of a certain age did."

"What?" The word slipped out. Skye did not like where this was going and knew she shouldn't have allowed herself to be baited by the English teacher.

Pru licked her lips. "Well, he was extremely sexy and oh, so persuasive." She paused, but when Skye didn't respond, continued. "He was one of those real bad boys who are real good to women — at least in bed — but as a contractor he was hopeless. He hardly ever finished a job, and when he did, the work was so shoddy it had to be redone."

"I see." Skye refrained from hitting herself upside the head. How could she have not seen through him? Breathing deeply, she refocused. Recriminations at this point were useless. "But who did Beau cheat?"

Pru licked her lips again, this time as if about to sample a tasty morsel. "Let's see." Her pause was indisputably for effect.

"Did he work on the Bruefeld Estate?"

one of the male science teachers asked. "You know, the one they're turning into a spa."

"No. They brought in a Chicago company to do that work," Pru answered, sending a quelling look in the man's direction. "But Joy Kessler had a horrible time with Hamilton. She hired him to remodel the building for her new business and he never finished. She ended up having to pay someone else to complete the work."

"Oh, my." Skye added Joy to her list of suspects to interrogate.

"Then there's Jess Larson. You know, the new guy who bought the liquor store? He hired Beau to build that new banquet facility and bar, but after several months, he had to hire someone else, too."

"So a guy fell for his charms, too. It wasn't only lonely women." Skye processed that piece of information, then asked, "Why didn't any of these people file a complaint? I did check."

Pru tilted her Pepsi can and finished the last few drops before answering. "I hear that he had something on them all, and they didn't dare complain about his work."

"You mean he was blackmailing them?"

Pru flattened her soda can, crumbled her paper bag, and pushed back her chair. "I'm sure I couldn't say. Everyone knows I never gossip."

"Of course not," Skye agreed. "But if you know something for a fact, it isn't gossip."

"Well, when I suggested to Joy that she sue Beau, and tried to give her the number for my nephew, the lawyer, she said to forget it. It would be more trouble than it was worth." Pru disposed of her trash. "And later my nephew said that Jess had talked to him about filing a lawsuit, but called the next day and dropped it."

"How interesting." Pru's nephew must be as much of a big mouth as his aunt. So much for attorney-client privilege. Skye tried to think of anything else she could ask to keep up the flow of information, but nothing came to her in time.

Pru looked at the wall clock, then glanced pointedly at Skye still sitting on the sofa. "Now, unlike you, I have to get back to my classroom. The bell's about to ring and we mustn't leave the little darlings unattended."

Skye tensed to jump up, but then sat back. No matter what she did, there would always be some teachers who resented the freedom her job afforded compared to the constrictions of a classroom. Thinking of Homer's order to talk Pru out of writing scathing notes home about her students made Skye shake her head. She'd have a better chance of teaching Bingo to talk.

During the five minutes between the first lunch people filing out of the lounge and the second shift arriving, Skye sat absorbing what she had learned. Her glance swept the walls as she thought. Cork bulletin boards holding notices that had expired before the millennium changed were the only decoration, and they provided no inspiration.

She briefly considered sticking around to see what the next group of teachers would have to say, but decided she had used up her lunch period, and it wouldn't be fair to take another. She had too much real work to do to steal time away from it for personal business. As it was, she would have to take home a report to write to make up for the time she had spent with Alana.

Once she got back to her office, the afternoon sped by. Counseling sessions and classroom observations kept her busy until eighth period, when she finally got a chance to read Xenia's file. Skye had closed the thick folder and was mulling over ways to help the girl adjust to Scumble River High when the dismissal bell rang. A few seconds later, Trixie Frayne burst into Skye's office.

Skye hadn't seen Trixie since her friend's return from Lake Tahoe. It was good to see her looking as if she were a glowing seventeen again rather than an unhappy thirty-four. Trixie and her husband, Owen, had experienced a bad patch in their relationship during the past summer, and they were still trying to make things better between them.

Owen was a serious man who worked hard to get ahead, while Trixie was more fun-loving and believed that all work and no play made for rich heirs. Both had been trying to learn to meet somewhere in the middle.

Trixie plopped into the chair opposite Skye's desk and demanded, "What? I can't even leave town for the weekend without you getting into trouble."

"I am not in trouble." Skye pulled out the bottom drawer of her desk and put her feet up, getting comfortable. She knew this wouldn't be a short conversation. "A man was murdered. The sheriff found his killer. It's over."

"I wasn't talking about the murder, although from what I hear the sheriff couldn't find a library book if the Dewey decimal number was tattooed on his hand, so I doubt he has the real murderer."

"Oh, you mean my house." Skye wiggled in her chair. "No problem there either. I've already found a contractor to replace Beau."

"Not your house, you dork. Wally!" Trixie crossed her arms. "I hear you actually went on a real, honest-to-goodness date with him."

"Who told you?"

"Who didn't?" Trixie fluffed her short brown hair. "I even saw a picture."

"What?" Skye's feet hit the floor with a thump.

"It's on the Internet." Trixie smirked.

"You know how to surf the Net?"

"Not really. But since Owen bought the computer to keep the farm records, I've been teaching myself a little here and there. I'm a Freecell champ." Trixie examined her hot pink nails, rubbing at a smear of ink on her index finger. "Anyway, someone left me a phone message saying to check out the Bunco Babes Web site."

"Shit!"

"Don't worry. It's a good picture."

Skye moaned. She'd never have dreamed Priscilla would be computer literate. Skye had been under the impression that except for the teenagers, most Scumble Riverites either didn't have or didn't know how to use computers. Now Trixie was telling her that Priscilla Van Horn even had a Web site. Clearly, it was time to rethink her assumption. Maybe everyone in town was using computers except her.

"Do you want to come over and see it?"

"No. I know what we look like." Skye shook her head. "Is there any way you can get rid of the picture using your computer?"

"Not me. I'm a complete amateur. For that you'd need a hacker."

"Terrific. Where would I find one of those in Scumble River?" Skye chewed her lip. "I wonder if Wally knows it's there. And my mother."

"As I said when I got here, how did you get into so much trouble? I was only gone three days."

Skye filled Trixie in on all that had transpired — the murder, the house, Alana's kidnapping, the newspaper award, and, of course, Wally.

Trixie interrupted when she got to the police chief. "I thought you were going to hear Simon out before doing anything rash."

"Well, as it turns out, he and I talked yesterday." Skye explained May's and Bunny's part in bringing about the conversation.

"You're kidding." Trixie grinned. "I can't believe May would collaborate with Bunny for any reason. She must really want Simon as a son-in-law."

"I guess so. I'm currently not speaking to her, so I can't ask how the whole plan came together."

"I can just see you racing over to save the day." Trixie shook her head. "Were you afraid that May was playing Wallop-the-Trollop?"

"Huh?"

"You know, like that game they have in the bowling alley, Whac-a-Mole. Doesn't May call Bunny a trollop?"

"Among other things," Skye answered, not quite following Trixie's free association. "Anyway, I talked to Simon, and it didn't help at all."

"Oh?"

"He still insists he hasn't done anything wrong, and I should trust him enough so that he shouldn't have to explain."

"That's ridiculous. He goes on vacation alone, telling you he's staying with his old college buddy Spike. Spike turns out to be a woman, and you're not supposed to ask for an explanation? Please!"

"Exactly." Skye frowned.

"So it's really over?"

"He's leaving me no choice." Skye's frown deepened. "How can I be with a man I caught cheating on me? Surely if he had a good excuse, he'd have used it."

"True." Trixie nodded, then reached to pat Skye's hand. "But you know, it's like your Bel Air. Even if you traded it in for a brand-new Mercedes, you'd still have to deal with an occasional breakdown. And Wally won't be any less of a problem than Simon."

"Huh?" Trixie had lost Skye again.

"Because if it has tires or testicles, it's going to be trouble."

"So why do we bother with cars or men?"

"When they're running well, it's a fun ride."

Skye laughed. "And?"

"Great weekends in Lake Tahoe." Trixie smirked.

"Tell me everything."

"When we checked into the honeymoon suite, they gave us this brochure, 'Seventeen Ways to Use Your Private Hot Tub.' " When Trixie got to number three, "Add your favorite flavor of Jell-O," she stopped and winked. "You get the picture."

"Yes, I do." Skye leered. "So, what is your favorite flavor?"

Trixie ignored Skye's question and changed the subject. "Anything else happen while I was gone?"

"We have a new student transferring in tomorrow."

"Oh?"

When Skye finished giving her friend the rundown on Xenia Craughwell and her notorious behavior, Trixie asked, "Shouldn't a teenager like her be in some kind of private school?"

"Probably, but that would be the mother's choice since Xenia isn't special ed. The last school did a case study and didn't find her eligible for services. They said she wasn't emotionally disturbed, she was conduct disorder, and thus she didn't qualify."

"So what are you going to do with her?"

Skye smiled and leaned toward her friend. "Ah, that's where you come in."

Chapter 18
Eighteen-Wheeler

"No way!" Trixie squealed.

"Just for a little while," Skye wheedled. "We need to see what Xenia's really like."

"That fifty-pound file sitting on your desk didn't give you a clue?"

"She deserves a fresh start." Trixie rolled her eyes, but Skye continued, "Besides, there's some reason Xenia wanted to move to Scumble River. We need to know why."

"She thinks we're all country bumpkins she can twist around her finger?"

Skye took out a yellow pad. "That's a possibility." Jotting down Trixie's suggestion under "motivation," Skye added her own idea. "Or she wants to re-create herself."

"Or?"

"Or she's tracked her father down, and he lives here in town."

Trixie's eyes lit up. "What's her dad's name?"

"There wasn't a birth certificate in her

file. I need to ask her mother for it tomorrow."

"I still don't understand what making her my library assistant will accomplish."

"I'm hoping she'll bond with you, since you have such a good rapport with teens." Skye figured a little flattery wouldn't hurt her case. "She's really smart, and somehow she's kept learning, since her achievement tests show her way above grade level in all areas, so I suspect she likes to read." Skye doodled on her pad. "Also, since she'll be with you for her two study halls and before school, which are the most unstructured times of the day, you can see which kids she ends up hanging out with."

"Where will you put her the rest of the time?"

"In the top-level classes. I'm gambling she'll like the challenge, and those kids will be a good influence on her."

Trixie's expression was doubtful, but she said, "Okay, I'll take her on one condition."

"What?"

"You admit you don't think Sheriff Peterson has Beau Hamilton's murderer, and you tell me what you're up to in that case."

Skye weighed her options, then gave in. "You're right. I don't think it was a drug deal gone bad like the sheriff has decided.

271

I'm planning to talk to some of Beau's unsatisfied customers this afternoon, as I soon as I check on my new contractor."

"I'm coming with you."

"Not a good idea."

"Why?" Trixie demanded.

"Because I need to make my visits seem casual rather than an interrogation."

"How will you do that?"

Skye considered the people she needed to talk to. "Jess Larson should be easy enough. I'll stop at his store and buy something."

"Why can't I come with you?"

"Because it doesn't take two of us to pick up a bottle of wine."

Trixie frowned but didn't argue. "Who else are you going to talk to?"

"Joy Kessler. She recently opened that new exercise place for women, Joy's Jym, and offered me a free introductory session."

"I could go with you for that. I got a coupon in my mail for a free session, too."

Skye looked Trixie up and down, then raised an eyebrow. "And you would need to exercise why?" Trixie was a size four and never gained an ounce, no matter what she ate.

"Everyone needs to exercise. Size doesn't matter."

Skye thought it over. "Okay, the two of us

going to work out together shouldn't set off any alarm bells." Skye got up and started to gather her possessions. "Here's the plan. I'll stop and talk to Jess as soon as I leave here, then check on my contractor, change clothes and meet you at Joy's at five thirty."

"Roger. Five thirty at Joy's Jym."

Trixie and Skye left the building together. Trixie sped away first, gravel spraying out from under the wheels of her car. Skye's exit was more sedate; fishtailing a '57 Chevy was like peeling rubber with a tank.

She turned out of the parking lot and headed toward the Brown Bag Liquor Store. If she was lucky, she'd get there before the after-work crowd, and Jess would be available to talk. She didn't know him well — he was new to town, having purchased the business from his aunt when she retired last November — but he had seemed pretty open when she had needed to ask him some questions in February.

As she parked, Skye looked across the street at her Uncle Charlie's Up A Lazy River Motor Court. Its lot was empty. Not many people visited the area this late in September. The weather was too cold for swimming and boating, only doves and squirrels were in season to hunt, and the leaves hadn't reached their best colors yet.

Skye pushed open the door of the Brown Bag, her nose twitching at the yeasty smell of beer and stale cigarette smoke. The liquor store was empty except for Jess, who was sitting behind the cash register reading, but she could hear the sound of a television and male voices from the adjacent bar.

Jess looked up and waved as the bells over the door jingled. Skye waved back and headed toward the wine aisle. This was perfect. He was alone. She quickly made her selection, grabbing a bottle of Zinfandel, then slowed her steps as she approached the counter, trying to appear casual.

"Hi." Skye put the wine down. "Looks pretty deserted in here."

Jess stood and rang up her purchase. "It'll get busier in an hour or so when the guys start getting off work."

"Sounds like the bar is hopping, though."

"There always seems to be a steady stream of customers there, from when we open at ten to when we close at two." Jess held out his hand. "That'll be four ninety-three."

"I'll bet you're glad you had the bar built." Skye put a five in his palm. "With so many other taverns in town, you had to wonder if it would attract enough customers to be profitable."

"True, but I figured it would be a moneymaker." Jess handed her seven cents and put the wine in a bag. "This is the first watering hole they come to as they drive into town after getting off I-55."

"It's a good thing it was worth all the trouble you had getting it built." Skye leaned her right hip against the counter. "Didn't I hear you had to get a second contractor to finish it when your first one screwed up?"

Jess's smile widened. "So, you're investigating Beau Hamilton's murder." His brown eyes twinkled. "I thought Sheriff Peterson had that case solved."

Skye was caught short. Either Jess was a whole lot sharper than she had given him credit for, or her interviewing skills were deteriorating. Maybe both.

He walked out from behind the cash register and stood beside her. "I'll bet you want to know what happened between Beau and me, right?"

She nodded.

"Well." Jess rested his left hip against the counter and leaned toward her. "Beau came with wonderful recommendations and he talked a really good game, but within a week it was apparent to me that he was totally unreliable."

"Sounds like his pattern." Skye couldn't

quite figure Jess out. He was always friendly when she ran into him, even flirty, although she guessed he was at least five years younger than she, but there was something about him she was missing. "I was having the same problems with him."

"So I heard."

"What I don't understand is why there are no complaints filed against him. I certainly was ready to file one before he was killed."

Jess narrowed his eyes. "Did he know you were going to do that?"

Skye shrugged. "I certainly never made any secret of my dissatisfaction with his work, but I never specifically said I would file a report either."

"How did he respond when you told him you were unhappy with him?"

"He didn't seem at all concerned."

Jess held Skye's gaze for a long moment before nodding to himself, then saying, "I'm going to tell you something in confidence. I assume as a psychologist you know how to keep a secret."

"Yes, but if it has anything to do with the murder, I'll have to tell the police." Skye knew she risked having Jess clam up, but she felt she had to be up front with him.

"Okay. That's fair. The reason I didn't file

a report about Beau's shoddy work was that he found out something about me that I'd rather no one knew. In exchange for his silence I agreed to let him keep the money I had already paid him and not say anything negative about his work."

"Had you paid the full amount up front?"

"A third. He claimed he needed it for materials and to pay his crew." Jess hung his head. "How about you?"

"I gave him a third of the estimate, too, but I made him give me copies of receipts from his suppliers."

"You were smarter than I was. I had to pay for all the building materials again when I hired the new guy."

"I won't ask what he knew about you, but was it anything illegal?" Skye realized she was pushing it. Jess had no reason to tell her anything.

"No. Merely something personal that would ruin my fresh start here in town."

"Thanks for telling me." Skye held out her hand. "I wonder if he had something on everybody who didn't file a complaint against him."

Jess grasped her hand with both of his and squeezed. "I think that was his modus operandi. He nosed around while he was working, and if he found something, he used it to blackmail his clients."

"I think you're right." Skye squeezed back, then moved toward the door. "Thanks again. Bye."

Skye thought of what Jess had told her as she drove home. His theory made sense. She twisted her lips in a parody of a smile. Terrific. Her life was so dull, Beau couldn't even find anything to use against her for blackmail.

Her smile became genuine when she pulled into her driveway. Three women were hard at work on her roof, and Dulci and another woman were installing windows. Skye parked the car, hopped out, and walked over to where the contractor was working.

Skye waited for a break in the action, then said, "Wow. This is wonderful. How did you get the new windows so fast?"

"I found the ones Hamilton had bought." Dulci finished setting the frame into the space before continuing. "Loretta said you needed windows and a roof ASAP because someone keeps getting into your house."

Skye was overwhelmed with gratitude. Dulci was an answer to her prayers. First, she actually showed up to work when she promised to, but then she also tracked down the already-purchased windows, saving Skye a lot of money.

"Thank you. I forgot I said I'd look for the supplies Beau bought. How did you find them?"

Dulci concentrated on the level she was using on the window frame. "I figured he'd use somebody local so I called around. When I found out where he had purchased them, I asked where they'd been delivered. Turns out he had a building way the heck in the back of his sister's property that he used for storage. I went there this morning and picked them up."

"Alana was okay with that?"

"She wasn't there and the building wasn't locked." Dulci didn't look up.

"Funny, I don't remember anyone ever mentioning that building — even when the police were investigating Beau's murder."

"It doesn't look up to code, and I doubt he got a permit to build it — it's too close to the river. My guess is hardly anyone knows about it."

"I see." Skye let the implications sink in, then went back to the original subject. "How did you know they were my windows and not some other client's?"

Dulci answered expressionlessly, "They fit."

"Oh." Skye felt a little uncomfortable.

"Um, is it legal to just go take them like that?"

"Possession is nine-tenths of the law." Dulci looked at Skye out of the corner of her eye. "Besides, you paid for them. Did you want to wait for all the i's to be dotted and all the t's to be crossed, or do you want windows in your house?"

Skye briefly fought with her conscience. It lost. After all, as Dulci pointed out, she had paid for the windows, and since Dulci already had several installed, Skye certainly wasn't about to have her rip them out. "I want windows. Do you think you'll have them all installed by the end of the week like you estimated?"

Dulci eyed the house, counting under her breath, and finally said, "Sure, maybe earlier if our luck holds."

"That's wonderful." Impulsively, Skye hugged the contractor. "Thank you."

Dulci stiffened, then gave Skye's arms a quick squeeze before stepping back. "No problem."

Skye turned to thank the woman working with Dulci, but she had disappeared, so Skye turned back to the contractor. "I'm going to change clothes and run an errand. Is there anything you need before I leave?"

Dulci had already gone back to work, but

grunted "No" over her shoulder.

After throwing on a gray sweat suit, Skye scraped her hair into a ponytail and jumped back into her car. The drive to Joy's Jym was short, and she arrived in plenty of time for her rendezvous with Trixie.

As Skye sat waiting for her friend, she thought about the torture devices in store for her inside. She hated this kind of exercising, preferring a morning swim to sweating to the oldies.

One of her most terrifying childhood memories involved being dragged to what her mother had called an exercise salon. It happened at the end of her sixth-grade year. Skye had started to put on some weight, and May had decided to make her work out every day after school. The place was over in Brooklyn, and it was filled with middle-aged women who nagged at Skye to slim down, telling her she would never catch a boyfriend if she was chubby.

The women had scared her so much, Skye went on a strict diet, eating only a broiled chicken breast and half a cup of cottage cheese a day until she shed the extra pounds. Unfortunately, after she lost the weight, she found that she couldn't eat much more than that if she wanted to maintain her new slim figure.

When she discovered swimming a few years later, she found she could eat a few more calories, but from the age of twelve until her thirtieth birthday, she kept her weight down by dieting fiercely, weighing herself every morning, and fasting if she gained a pound or two.

The Christmas before she moved back to Scumble River, Skye had an epiphany — life was too short not to occasionally taste the chocolate, not to mention the home-made bread and pasta. She decided to exit from the diet roller coaster. It hadn't been an easy decision, and she had taken a lot of flak from people who had admonished her, "But you have such a pretty face. You can't let yourself go like that."

Skye had stood firm regarding her decision. She was tired of eating only eight hundred calories a day. She had reached her natural weight, her set point, and she was never going back to starving herself.

When her brother Vince had confronted her with the same lame argument the exercise ladies had used, that she would never find a man with her full figure, her answer was steadfast. "I know some people won't think I look good unless I become anorexic, but I'm finished obsessing about my weight. End of discussion."

It was now nearly four years since she had stopped her extreme dieting, and she still tried to eat healthfully and swim at least five days a week, but her life no longer revolved around how small a jeans size she could wear. And Vince had been wrong: Plenty of men had been interested in her. She had not always loved wisely, but she hadn't done that when she was thin either.

Trixie's "shave and a haircut" toot on the horn brought Skye back to the present. She reluctantly picked up her purse, slowly got out of the Bel Air, and trailed her friend into Joy's Jym.

Skye had been right in thinking five thirty would be a slow time. The place was empty. Skye and Trixie stood at the chest-high counter and looked around. There were six different machines spaced around the room. According to the sign, a patron should spend five minutes on each, for a total workout in half an hour.

If one ignored the exercise equipment, it was a pleasant room. Pale blue walls with feathery white clouds painted near the top and onto the ceiling. Lacy green plants were tucked into out-of-the-way corners, and fluffy periwinkle towels lay in convenient piles.

Skye had taken all of this in, and still no one had come to help them.

She was thinking of clearing her throat to attract some attention when Trixie yelled out, "Hey, anyone here?"

Joy came rushing from a back room, a container of yogurt in one hand and a plastic spoon in the other. She had the wholesome good looks of a Disney World Cinderella. She wore her dark blond hair pulled back into a ponytail, and her light makeup emphasized a pale gold complexion. She was dressed in a pink leotard and tights.

After ditching the yogurt container and spoon under the counter, she said, "Skye, Trixie, how nice to see you. Did you come to try out my place?"

Trixie smiled. "Yep, we thought it would be a fun girls' thing to do."

Skye held back a harrumph at the idea of exercise being fun, reminding herself why she was here and what she wanted to accomplish. Instead she said, "Hope you have time to show us the ropes. I'm a complete novice at this."

"Sure. You actually picked a great hour to come. I'm usually busy until around four thirty, then everyone has to get home to cook supper. Business picks back up around six, after everyone has eaten and done the dishes."

"Super." Trixie took off her sweat pants and jacket, revealing bright green tights and an orange leotard. "Where do I start?"

After Joy got Trixie going on the first machine, she turned to Skye. "Why don't you take your sweats off? You can begin over here." She pointed to a black hulk that looked a lot like a contraption from the Spanish Inquisition.

Skye shrugged out of her gray warm-up jacket, revealing a navy T-shirt, and said, "Um, I'm a little cold. I'll keep on my pants." Considering she had nothing but her pink Jockeys beneath them, this was really her only option. Who knew you needed special clothes to exercise?

Joy got Skye started, showing her where to put her arms and legs, and took a step as if to walk away.

Skye immediately botched what she was doing and called the owner back. "Could you stay with me? I'm really not good at this."

Joy gave her a beaming smile. "Sure. No problem. I won't let you get hurt. Don't worry."

As Skye went through the steps, she said, "This place is beautiful. Was it hard to get it looking this way?"

"Not once I got a decent contractor," Joy blurted out, then covered her mouth. "I mean, uh, thank you."

"Did you hear I was using Beau Hamilton to fix up the old house I inherited?"

"Yes."

"You used him at first, too, didn't you?"

Joy nodded.

"He sure was hot, wasn't he?" Skye winked. "Fun to watch that boy sweat."

Joy's lips curled in a small smile before returning to their neutral position.

"Too bad you can't judge a contractor by his muscles." Skye shook her head. "Did he do as bad a job for you as he did for me?"

"He was okay."

"Really? I heard he was so bad you had to hire someone else to finish the job."

Joy shrugged.

"So, why didn't you file a complaint?"

"It wasn't that bad."

"Joy, he's dead now. He can't hurt you," Skye reassured the skittish woman.

"Some things never die."

"Did he have a hold on you? Is that why you kept quiet?" By this time, Skye was panting like an eighteen-wheeler chugging uphill, and her words came out in gasps. Interrogation and exercise were not meant to go together.

"I can't talk about it." Joy looked up, tears in her navy blue eyes. "Please just let it alone, or you'll ruin my life."

Chapter 19
Cloud Nineteen

Skye stared as Joy ran into the back room. She tried to follow the distraught woman, but couldn't figure out how to get free of the exercise equipment. Trixie, on the other hand, gracefully vaulted from her machine and sprinted after Joy.

Skye ground her teeth as she heard their voices murmuring a few feet away. She couldn't make out the words from where she was trapped. By the time she managed to wiggle free, tearing the knee out of her sweatpants and breaking a nail, Joy and Trixie had reappeared.

Trixie was saying, "Don't worry. We won't tell a soul. I can't believe that fiend would hold something like that over you."

Skye opened her mouth, but Trixie shook her head slightly. Skye nodded.

Trixie put her sweat suit back on and said to Joy, "We'll come back another time to finish our free trial." Trixie motioned to

Skye to follow and then walked out the door.

As soon as they got outside, Skye grabbed Trixie. "What was that all about?"

"Let's go sit in your car." Trixie pulled Skye toward the Bel Air. "You know even the streets have ears around here."

Once they were settled, Skye turned toward her friend and commanded, "Tell."

"Beau was blackmailing Joy, that's why she never complained about his work. She let him keep the deposit, and hired someone else to finish the job."

Skye nodded. "That's exactly what Jess Larson said happened to him. Did Joy say what Beau was holding over her head? Jess wouldn't tell."

"It was about her little boy's condition."

"Alex? You mean the fact he has attention-deficit/hyperactivity disorder? That isn't exactly a big secret."

Trixie sighed. "It wasn't that he had ADHD, it was that Joy had begun to give him pills for it."

"I thought Joy and her husband were adamantly against medicating Alex. They certainly didn't inform the school he was taking anything. I thought my intervention plan was finally starting to work." Skye scratched her head. "But how could Beau blackmail her about that? It's not as if tons of other kids aren't in the same boat."

"The problem is her husband is *still* against medicating Alex. Joy is doing it without telling him." Trixie shook her head. "The poor woman just couldn't take her son's behavior anymore, and since she was with him a lot more than his father was, she decided to follow the doctor's advice, but keep it a secret."

"What an awful thing to blackmail some-one about." Skye shifted in her seat. "Beau really was a monster."

Trixie frowned. "I wonder if Beau found some dirt on all his clients."

"Everyone has secrets, and evidently Beau was good at finding the most sensitive ones."

"What did he have on you?"

"Nothing." Skye rolled her eyes. "Isn't that pathetic? My life is so dull, he couldn't find anything to blackmail me with."

"I'm sure you have some terrible thing in your past you want to hide," Trixie reassured Skye. "Maybe he just hadn't gotten around to threatening you yet."

"That must be it," Skye agreed, then quipped, "Or maybe he kidnapped Bingo and was going to hold him in exchange for my silence about his shoddy work."

"Still no luck in finding him, huh?"

"No. I can't think of anywhere else to look."

Trixie patted Skye's hand. "Want me to put up more posters?"

"Thanks." Skye's shoulders drooped. "But I think he's really gone. It's been six days and I've put up posters within a twenty-mile radius."

Trixie paused thoughtfully. "You know, maybe Beau *did* take him." She pursed her mouth. "If he did, where would he keep him?"

Skye had been kidding about the cat being stolen, but now she wondered. Beau knew she was getting fed up with him, and if he couldn't find anything to blackmail her with, maybe he *had* taken her pet.

Trixie continued as if Skye had answered her. "Where did Beau live?"

"He had a townhouse in the new development by the I-55 exit."

"Did the police search it?"

Skye shrugged. "I would assume so, but I don't know for sure. I'll have to ask Wally." Skye tapped her chin with her index finger, thinking. "But I bet he wouldn't keep Bingo there. Someone might see him."

"So, where?"

"I'll have to think about it."

"Okay." Trixie opened the car door. "I'll

see you tomorrow at school."

"Bye." Skye waited for Trixie to get out, waved, then backed up and took off for home.

The phone was ringing when Skye walked into the house, and she hurried to answer it before her machine picked it up.

Wally's sensuous baritone rewarded her efforts. "Hi there. Are you hungry?"

His question reminded her that she had skipped lunch, and her stomach growled in response. "Starving. Why?"

"I'm at the new Chinese place. How about I bring over takeout?"

Skye paused. A part of her was still smarting from her encounter with Simon. His accusation about dating Wally so soon after their breakup had hit a nerve. Maybe she should call a halt to things with Wally for a while.

Wally interrupted her deliberation. "Mmm. The smell of the hot and sour soup is making my mouth water."

Even if she disregarded the Simon issue, she had wanted to slow things down between her and Wally, discourage casual evenings together and only see him for regular dates.

Wally broke into her thoughts again. "Wow, they just gave me a taste of their egg rolls. They're amazing."

Skye admitted defeat. Wally had zeroed in on her weakness — Chinese food — and her craving won out. "Sounds wonderful." She could already taste the chicken-fried rice.

"Great. See you in twenty minutes."

Skye frowned at the receiver. He hadn't asked what she wanted. Should she call him back? No. She smiled. This would be a test. He claimed they already knew each other well. If that was true, he should know exactly what to order for her.

Her smile faded as she realized that she was dressed in torn sweats, her hair was a mess, and she reeked from her workout. Taking the stairs two at a time, she ran into the bathroom. Stripping, she leapt into the shower, then stood there panting. Phew. She was out of condition. Time to get back to swimming in the mornings.

A quick lather and rinse, and Skye jumped out of the shower. As she struggled to get the comb through her wet hair, she realized drying it was out of the question; there simply wasn't enough time. Instead she secured the sides with faux tortoiseshell combs and left the rest in damp curls down her back.

Next, what to wear? Nothing that looked

as if she had gotten dressed up just for him. She took a mental inventory of her closet, settling on forest green jeans and a cashmere sweater of the same color.

Skye slapped on moisturizer and applied mascara, then started to file her broken nail. As she finished evening out the ragged edges, the bell rang.

When she opened the door, Wally was leaning against the jamb holding two plastic shopping bags. He was still in uniform, but had taken off his tie and utility belt and unbuttoned his collar.

His grin flashed briefly, dazzling white against his olive skin. "Ready for dinner?"

"Sure." Skye gulped. "Come on in." His smile was irresistible. "Go ahead into the sunroom. I'll get the silverware and plates."

He strolled into the foyer. "Sounds good."

"What do you want to drink?"

"Got any beer?"

"Budweiser okay?" Skye asked. It was the brand her father drank, and the only one she kept in the house.

Wally nodded, but Skye noted a slight curl to his lip. What kind did he usually drink? She couldn't remember ever seeing him with a bottle in his hand.

As she went into the kitchen, she thought to herself, *That lack of basic personal infor-*

294

mation goes to prove that I'm right; we really don't know each other well enough yet. We need to take things slow, no matter how strong the physical attraction.

When Skye entered the sunroom, she found Wally sprawled on the wicker settee, TV remote in hand, watching the Weather Channel. She put the tray she was carrying on the glass-topped coffee table and asked, "Expecting a storm?"

Wally clicked off the television, his expression sheepish. "No. I just find the music on that station relaxing. It helps me shut off my mind after a long day."

"Oh. You know, I have some relaxation tapes I use with the kids, if you ever want to borrow them." Skye took a seat in the armchair next to the sofa and started to arrange silverware, napkins, and drinks on the table. "Unfortunately, I haven't found anything that helps me turn off my thoughts."

"That sounds like a challenge." Wally's tone was light but held a hint of seduction.

His teasing excited her, despite her best intentions to maintain a casual atmosphere. She took a deep breath and tried to get the evening back on track. "So, what did you get for supper?"

Wally reached into the bag and drew out

a round cardboard container. Steam rose as he pried off the lid and handed it to her. "Hot and sour, your favorite, right?"

Skye nodded, inhaling the heady scent of the spices before dipping her spoon into the rich brown liquid. How had he known she loved that soup?

Between spoonfuls, Skye told Wally about her conversations with Jess Larson and Joy Kessler. As she finished the last tidbit of silky tofu, she said, "So, do you think Priscilla Van Horn was being blackmailed by Beau, too?"

"That would explain the sense of fear I got from her when I interviewed her yesterday." Wally's hand disappeared into the plastic sack and pulled out a waxed paper packet that he handed to Skye. "I got egg rolls since they were so good, and the restaurant didn't have pot stickers. Hope that's okay?"

She had already bitten into the crispy appetizer, so she could only nod.

"I'll have to go back and talk to Priscilla again, but I don't think she or the other dissatisfied customers are our killers."

Skye swallowed. "Why?"

"Both Jess Larson and Joy Kessler indicated they weren't currently being extorted by Hamilton, which makes it sound as if he didn't try to keep getting money from his victims — one score and he moved on to another mark."

Skye nodded. "True, both made it sound like it was only a onetime deal — because he had messed up on the work he was doing for them, and didn't want to either give their money back or have them tell other potential clients what a screwup he was."

"Which probably means that if Larson, Kessler, or Van Horn wanted to kill him, they would have done it when he first shook them down." Wally extracted two white cartons from the second plastic bag. "Empress chicken, and shredded pork with plum sauce. I know you like them both, so do you want to share?"

"Mmm. Yes, please." Skye scooped a portion of each onto a plate and pushed the containers back to Wally, who did the same. "I wonder who else he was blackmailing."

"I'll take a look at his business records and talk to anyone else whose job he didn't complete, but you were his most current client. Did he try holding anything over on you?"

"Nope." Skye considered sharing her theory about Bingo's disappearance, but she was afraid Wally would think she had gone over the edge. Instead she said, "That reminds me, did you or the sheriff search Beau's place?"

"We both did." Wally stabbed a baby corn with his fork.

"Only his house? Did he have an office or someplace he did business out of?"

"Nothing on record. Why?"

"Anything interesting at his house?"

"There was a desk and filing cabinet, which we emptied, but it was all business records, nothing personal. Other than that, just the usual bachelor stuff. Pizza cartons and beer cans piled everywhere, porno magazines and videos, and lots of unwashed clothes and dishes."

"No drugs?"

"Nope."

Skye drew her brows together. "Doesn't that indicate he wasn't using or selling?"

"To me, yes. To Peterson? No."

"Any indication he had a pet?" She tried to slip that question in under Wally's radar.

"No." He shot her a sharp look. "Only the two-legged variety. His black book was crammed full of names like Bambi, Kat, and even a Fifi."

"Why am I not surprised?" Skye was silent as she savored the last bite of shredded pork. She could just picture the parade of poodle-perfect women in and out of Beau's life. "Did you check out all the girlfriends?"

"I sent Quirk to talk to the women listed in Hamilton's address book, and I talked to the ones Alana's boyfriend indicated were Hamilton's most recent conquests."

"Did either of you come up with anything?" There was something she had wanted to ask Wally about Beau's girlfriends. What was it?

"No, both Nikki Price and Yolanda Doozier had ironclad alibis. Nikki was in the hospital getting her breasts enlarged, and Yolanda was in court all afternoon testifying at her brother's DUI trial. After that, the whole clan went to Chili's for supper, and the serving staff vouched for them. Said they were unforgettable."

Skye grinned. "I'll bet they did." The Doozier family was a legend in Scumble River — colorful and boisterous didn't begin to describe them. She could certainly believe that they would be well remembered wherever they went.

Wally grinned back, having had his share of encounters with the Dooziers, too.

There was still something she couldn't put her finger on. What was it? No. It wouldn't come to her. Hoping to trigger her memory, she asked, "Wasn't there a third girlfriend you mentioned before?"

Wally handed her a fortune cookie. "Yeah, but she claims she wasn't dating Beau, she had only met with him to do some work on the house she just bought. She only relocated here in June."

Skye had started to tear open the cellophane on her cookie, but froze when Wally mentioned the woman moving into town only a few months ago. "Was her name Raette Craughwell?"

"Yes. Why?"

"I met her today." That was what had been bothering her. Wally had mentioned Raette the night Beau had been killed. "She registered her daughter for school."

Wally frowned. "But if they've been here since June, why didn't the girl start school a month ago?"

"Her mom was homeschooling her. She . . ." Skye started to explain about the girl's troubled past, but stopped herself just in time. She couldn't share confidential information with Wally, but she had to say something. He was staring at her, waiting for her to continue. "Uh, so, do you believe Raette's story — that she was only seeing Beau for home repair?"

"I guess so. Shouldn't I?"

Skye was torn. She needed to think before she answered him. Spotting his empty beer bottle, she grabbed it and stood up. "Let me get you another Bud. I'll be right back. Keep that thought."

Wally narrowed his eyes, but let her go without commenting on her odd behavior.

She hurried to the kitchen, trying to get her thoughts in order. First, Raette was somehow involved with Beau. Maybe she really was a prospective client, but maybe not. The whole situation didn't feel right to Skye.

Second, Raette's daughter wanted to move to Scumble River. Since there was nothing in the town to attract a teenager, Skye was betting Xenia had somehow found out who her dad was and that he lived in the area. Considering her plan for the other girls to commit patricide, the teen plainly had father issues.

Third, Beau had been murdered. Could Xenia have been his killer?

Skye bit her lip and paced. What should she do? She could only break confidentiality if the girl was a danger to herself or others. Was she a danger? If she had already killed Beau, she had been a danger, but wasn't now. Shoot! What was the right thing to do?

Before doing anything irrevocable, Skye had to find out for sure who Xenia's father was. If it was Beau, then she'd decide what her next step should be, but for now she'd keep her mouth shut. She needed some real evidence before she took such a big step.

Having sorted out what she would do, Skye grabbed a beer for Wally and rejoined him in the sunroom.

He raised an eyebrow. "Did you decide to tell me or not?"

"Not." She handed him the bottle and headed back to her chair. "At least not now."

Wally captured her hand as she edged past him, and pulled her down next to him. "Why wait?"

Skye tried to put some distance between them, but the settee was built for two, with no room left over. "Because I'm not sure, and before I break confidentiality I need to be positive."

"I understand." Wally's thumb made circles in her palm. "I don't like it, but I understand."

"Thank you." She was intensely aware of his seductive touch. "I promise to tell you as soon as I can."

"I trust you." His arms encircled her. "And I hope you know you can trust me."

Was he talking about the case or her heart? She wasn't thinking clearly enough to sort it out, but she made one last stab at putting the brakes on her desire. "Actually, I'm sort of surprised that you've told me so much. Don't police have to keep information confidential, too?"

"It's not part of our ethical code of conduct, if that's what you mean." Wally hugged her tighter. "We swear to get the guilty off the street and protect the innocent. We're free to use any legal methods to do that. So if I think going over the case with you will help me catch the bad guy, I'm free to do so."

"Oh." She relaxed against him; her head fit perfectly in the hollow between his shoulder and neck. "Good."

His hands crept under her sweater, caressing the planes of her back. A small voice was trying to tell her to stop him, but she shivered at the pleasure of his touch, and the voice became fainter.

His lips came coaxingly down on hers and she drank in the sweetness of his mouth, forgetting Simon, forgetting her resolve to take this relationship step-by-step, forgetting her determination not to leap into the fire pit of temptation. She discovered she had no willpower when she was floating on cloud nineteen.

There was a dreamy intimacy to their kiss now, and caution had completely fled from Skye's thoughts. She undid the remaining buttons of his shirt and pressed her hands to the warm muscles of his chest.

As he paused to slip her sweater off, a loud thud resonated over their heads, followed by the sound of glass shattering.

"What the hell?" Wally leapt from the settee, his hand going automatically for the gun at his hip — the gun he wasn't wearing. Swearing, he leaned over, pulled up his pant leg, and released the pistol strapped to his ankle.

Skye pulled down her top and jumped up after him. "I think it came from the bedroom that's right above this room."

Wally nodded. "Stay here and I'll go check it out."

Skye shook her head. "I'm coming with you."

He sighed and handed her his cell phone. "If there's a problem, press nine and say, 'Officer needs assistance.' Keep behind me."

They proceeded silently out of the sunroom and up the stairs. The door was ajar on the bedroom she indicated and Wally eased it open with his foot, as he and Skye stood off to the side. He cautiously looked around the corner, then inched forward.

Skye followed. There was no one in the room, but a ceiling-high stack of boxes had fallen over onto a dresser, which had upended, shattering the attached mirror. Everything lay in a jumbled mess on the hardwood floor.

"Shit!" Skye's cry of frustration slipped out. "I worked all Sunday night sorting that stuff in those boxes."

Wally put a finger to his lips, but patted her shoulder sympathetically.

After searching the rest of the house and finding no evidence of an intruder, Wally said, "I'm glad your father decided to board up your windows."

"Yeah, like you didn't put that bug in Mom's ear."

He smiled innocently and didn't comment.

She had almost forgotten about her suspicions, but remembering made her decide not to tell him that she suspected someone could still get in through the exposed roof. He'd only insist she stay somewhere else, and that wasn't going to happen. Besides, another day or so and Dulci would have the roof done anyway.

They had returned to the room where they started and were looking at the mess when Wally said, "The boxes must not have been stacked evenly."

"I guess. But if that's the case, why did they fall at this particular time? It's not as if we had an earthquake or anything." It seemed that whenever she and Wally got past a certain point of intimacy, something happened to stop them. It was almost as if the house didn't want them to be together, or at least wanted them to take it slow. Skye shook her head. Now she really was being silly.

Wally shrugged. "Let's walk around the outside and see if we can spot anything." He took Skye by the hand and led her out the front door. As soon as they got past the threshold, his cell phone began to ring.

Pressing the button, he barked, "Boyd here." He listened, then said, "No, my phone's been on. I must have been in a dead zone. Okay. I'll be there as soon as I can. Tell Quirk not to notify the sheriff's department." He clicked off and turned to Skye. "Alana Lowe is being taken to Laurel Hospital. It looks as if she tried to commit suicide."

CHAPTER 20
20/20 HINDSIGHT

"What happened?" Skye demanded, running after Wally as he hurried toward his squad car.

"A neighbor found her lying unconscious on the couch with an empty bottle of prescription sedatives on the floor next to her."

"Was there a note?"

"No." Wally flung open the cruiser's door.

"Maybe I should go with you, so Alana won't be alone when she wakes up."

"Neville's been contacted and is meeting the ambulance at the hospital." Wally pressed a quick kiss on Skye's lips before she could say anything more, then got in the car. He rolled the window down and shouted as he started to pull away, "I'll call you as soon as I know more about Alana's condition."

Skye watched until the taillights disappeared, then went back into the house.

Should she have insisted on going with Wally to be with Alana? No. She and Alana weren't that kind of friends, and with Alana's boyfriend there, she really wasn't needed. Besides, Neville didn't strike Skye as the type who would want or appreciate her company.

As she swept up the pieces of shattered mirror and restacked the boxes that had fallen, her thoughts were fixed on Alana's suicide attempt. While emotionally fragile, the art teacher had never struck Skye as depressed, nor had she ever exhibited any self-destructive behavior. Why would Alana try to kill herself?

Skye was still trying to answer that question as she started to clean up the remains of the Chinese dinner. Putting the leftovers in the fridge, Skye wondered, *Could Alana's suicide attempt be motivated by guilt? Could she have had something to do with Beau's murder?*

No. She simply couldn't see Alana killing her brother. Not after that heartbreaking story Alana had shared with Skye about their mother's murder.

On her last trip to the sunroom to make sure nothing had been forgotten, Skye noticed her partially unwrapped fortune cookie under the table. She scooped it up and broke it open. Her fortune read: SEVEN BLIND MEN WILL ALL HAVE A DIFFERENT PICTURE OF AN ELEPHANT.

Skye considered the message, then looked around for Wally's cookie, but there was no sign of it. He must have taken it with him. What had his fortune been?

"Hello." Skye snatched up the telephone receiver, then glanced at the grandfather clock in the hall outside the living room. It was a little past one.

"Did I wake you?" Wally's tone was apologetic.

"No. I've been waiting for your call." She put the psychological report she had been writing down on the sofa and stretched. "Is Alana okay?"

"The doctors pumped her stomach, but she hasn't come to. They're guardedly optimistic that she'll recover."

"That doesn't sound too positive."

"They don't seem to know why she's still unconscious and I think that worries them." Wally's voice was gentle.

"How's Neville?"

"Raising hell," Wally said in disgust. "He's threatening lawsuits right and left."

"Why?"

"Since he's not a relative, they won't let

him stay in the room with Alana."

"Then I don't blame him." Skye rotated her head, trying to unkink her neck. "It's not as if there are a lot of relatives lined up to be with her."

"They let him see her, but not stay. The nurses have to follow the hospital rules."

"That's true. Every profession has a set of ethics they're bound to follow." Skye thought of her own current confidentiality issue. "I appreciate you calling. You must be exhausted." She stood up; she hadn't realized how tired she was, and tomorrow was a school day. "I'm pooped."

"I guess that means you don't want me coming back over tonight."

"That's right." Skye smiled into the phone. "I'll call you after school tomorrow."

"You're a cold, cold woman."

"And you're a pushy, pushy man." After placing the receiver into its cradle, she looked at it for a long moment. Even in the midst of her worry over Alana, hearing Wally's voice made her feel better. Had Simon been able to do that? She couldn't remember.

News of the art teacher's suicide attempt had raced through the high school, and Skye spent most of her time Tuesday talking to teens who ranged from curious to upset. It had not been the best day for Xenia to start, and Skye was grateful when Trixie said she would meet the girl when her mother dropped her off and keep an eye on her for the rest of the day.

At lunchtime Skye finally broke away from seeing kids and went to check on how Xenia was doing. As Skye approached the library her stomach tightened. What if the girl had turned on Trixie and hurt her? Automatically, Skye's footsteps quickened, and by the time she got to the entrance, she was nearly running.

She forced herself to slow down, then walked through the library door. When she rounded the circulation desk she blinked. Xenia would have been easy to identify even if Skye didn't already know all the other students in the room.

She was tall, probably at least five-ten, and well built. She wore an extremely short ruffled skirt with a pair of unlaced combat boots, along with two or three T-shirts, all ripped in various places and none reaching her waist. Over fishnet gloves she wore at least twenty bracelets on each arm, and her hair stood out as if she had put her finger in an electric socket. Her white skin and the magenta streak at her temple were the only contrasts to the unrelieved black of her clothing.

But it wasn't the girl's appearance that shocked Skye; it was what she seemed to be doing. Skye crept closer, hoping to go unnoticed as she observed.

Standing slightly behind one of the shelving units, she heard Justin say, "That would be a way cool article. Don't you think so, Mrs. Frayne?"

Trixie answered, "Sure would, Justin. Would you be willing to work on it, Xenia?"

"Sounds like fun," the girl said in a bored tone.

Skye couldn't stand it anymore. What in heaven's name would someone like Xenia want to write about that Trixie would approve? Surely how to kill your father in three easy steps wouldn't get an adult's okay.

Skye eased from her hiding spot, stepped forward, and said, "Hi. What are you all up to?"

Frannie looked up and said, "Ms. D, Xenia has a terrific idea for a piece for the paper."

Skye smiled at the new girl. "Hi, Xenia, I'm Ms. Denison, one of the newspaper's sponsors."

"Hi." Xenia gave her a cool look. "My mom told me you were the school shrink."

"Right, that's one of my jobs, too."

"So, do you think I'm crazy, like the guy at the other school did?"

"Not so far." Skye's expression remained neutral. "Do you think you are?"

"Maybe." Xenia shrugged.

"This probably isn't the place to discuss it, but if you ever want to talk to me, drop by my office."

Skye watched as Xenia checked out the other kids' reactions. When none seemed shocked, she looked a little disappointed, then shrugged again and said, "Sure."

"What's the great idea?" Skye changed the subject.

Justin spoke up. "Xenia suggested that we profile a different teacher each week."

"Oh." Skye couldn't quite see how that was such a *great* idea. A good one maybe, but not extraordinary.

"The twist is," Frannie broke in, "we concentrate on what they do when they're not at school. You know, present them as a person, not a teacher."

"Interesting." Skye wondered if the teachers would go along with that.

"Maybe we could start with you, Ms. D," Justin proposed. "You know, how you like to solve crimes."

"No." Skye barely stopped herself from

screaming. "We don't want the other teachers to be jealous. We'll do Mrs. Frayne and me after all the others." Skye would have to figure out some other hobby for them to concentrate on when it was her turn.

The newspaper staff agreed, and Skye excused herself since she had to get back to her counseling duties.

As she walked to her office, Skye wondered about the look on Xenia's face when Justin had announced that Skye solved crimes. Had the girl looked a little scared?

When the final bell rang that afternoon Skye was exhausted, but she had one more task to complete — calling Mrs. Craughwell. Skye waited half an hour, figuring that was a reasonable amount of time to return home after having picked up Xenia, then punched in the numbers.

After greetings had been exchanged, Skye said, "Before I forget, you need to bring in Xenia's birth certificate. It's missing from her file."

"Why do you need that?"

"It's proof of her date of birth." Skye wondered at the mother's hesitation. "It's something we require from all students."

"Oh." There was a brief silence; then Raette said, "You know we've just moved, so

I'm not sure I can put my hands on it right away."

"The district's policy is that within a week of the student starting school, his or her birth certificate needs to be on file."

"Okay. I understand."

"The other thing I'm calling about is to let you know Xenia had a good start."

"That's wonderful." Raette sounded relieved. "I thought about her all day."

"I figured you might, but considering we had a bit of a crisis here, and the other kids were upset, Xenia did quite well."

"A crisis?"

Skye explained about Alana, ending with, "Her brother, Beau Hamilton, was killed a few days ago, and she must not have been able to cope with the loss."

"He never told me he had a sister."

Gotcha! Skye smiled. "Then you knew Beau?"

Silence. Then Raette said, "I had talked to him about doing some home repairs for me."

"Really? It must be more than that. If you only met once or twice to discuss business, why *would* he have mentioned Alana?"

Raette's tone conveyed her unease. "Look, I told the police I was not dating Beau and that's the truth."

"Not dating him since you moved to Scumble River, right?" Skye chewed her lip. Should she press the matter? In for a penny, in for a pound. "But you did date him sixteen years ago, right? He's Xenia's father."

"How did you —" Raette cut herself off and slammed down the receiver, disconnecting them.

Skye leaned back in her office chair and stared at the ceiling tiles. Had Raette been about to say "How did you know," or "How did you ever jump to that conclusion?"

Wally wasn't at the police station or answering his cell. Skye left messages in both places, then got up to leave for the day. With Dulci and her crew on the job, Skye was actually looking forward to going home and seeing what progress they had made.

Skye played a game with herself on the way home. If she guessed correctly how many more windows Dulci and her crew had installed since yesterday, Skye could invite Wally over for supper when he returned her calls.

Her bet was five — no, four. Okay, five if they didn't do the finish work, four if they did. She mentally shook hands on her wager as she turned into her driveway, before coming to a screeching stop.

At first she couldn't comprehend what she was seeing. She closed her eyes, but an instant later they snapped open and the scene hadn't changed. It was like a bad summer action movie. A mutant bulldozer was chasing Luella Calhoun, one of Dulci's crew, back and forth in front of Skye's house. The dozer had already torn up the gravel drive, several bushes lay uprooted, and a compact car had been turned on its side.

Luella was a big woman, tall and brawny; regrettably, she was not fleet of foot. While it looked as if given a chance she might be able to bench-press the dozer, she was having trouble outrunning it.

Her fellow workers were yelling and chasing after the grotesque vehicle as it careened in a circle, its movements abrupt and unpredictable.

Only the worn treads and the rusty, pockmarked blade were visible. Some sort of gray metal box had been welded onto the top of the machine, and a small slit where the driver could peer out was the only observable opening. Why would anyone armor-plate a bulldozer?

Skye briefly considered throwing the Bel Air into REVERSE and hightailing it out of there. Regrettably, she had a strong feeling that she could run, but she couldn't hide — at least not for long.

Still, she had no idea what to do. After a second or two, when no inspiration came, she decided she'd simply have to leap into the fray and ask questions later.

She backed up a few feet, parked her car by the downed wrought iron gates, climbed out, and sprinted down the driveway. At least she had worn slacks and flat shoes to work that day. Skye imagined herself trying to navigate the gravel surface in a skirt and high heels, and shuddered.

Off to the side, Skye spotted Dulci near her purple pickup. The contractor had reached into the open window and was extracting a shotgun from the rack mounted behind the driver's seat. Making an abrupt turn, Skye darted toward the truck.

She skidded to a stop and panted, "What the devil is going on here?"

Dulci looked up from loading the gun. "Some freak is trying to kill my crew, and I'm going to stop him."

"Why?" Skye instinctively reached for the gun, but Dulci swung it out of her reach. "Why is someone trying to kill your crew?"

"These women all come from abusive situations." Dulci stepped around Skye and pumped the shotgun. "It could be any one of their exes."

Skye recoiled. She had read enough professional literature about what an abuser could and would do if he felt "his property" was getting away from him. She must remember to thank her good friend Loretta, if she lived through this. Sure, no police or Mafia had shown up — only a crazed husband or lunatic boyfriend driving a monstermobile.

Dulci had begun a flanking maneuver on the dozer, and Skye ran after her. "Have you called the police?"

"Someone probably did." Dulci shrugged. "But he might kill someone before they bother to show up. Sheriff Peterson is not big on protecting women from domestic violence."

Skye wondered if she could wrestle the gun from Dulci, but decided she didn't have a chance in hell of overpowering the muscular contractor. What else could she do? She had to stop this before shots were fired. After that happened, all bets were off.

She zigged away from Dulci toward the front of the hulking bulldozer. Always one to believe in the power of words, she managed to get near the right front tread and yell, "Stop! You are trespassing on private property. The police have been called."

The dozer slowed to a crawl, and several moments later a familiar voice shouted from behind the metal box, "Miz Skye, I come to rescue you."

She peered into the slit. "Earl? Earl Doozier, what are you doing in my driveway trying to crush an innocent construction worker?"

Earl was the patriarch of the Red Raggers, an extended family of misfits who always seemed to be around whenever there was a troublesome situation. They didn't usually make the first move, but they never missed a chance to be in the thick of the fighting.

The Dooziers were tough to describe to anyone who hadn't grown up with the legend of the Red Raggers. The best Skye could come up with was that Dooziers didn't invest in mutual funds — they invested in Elvis memorabilia. They didn't have a 401(k) — they had the gambling boat. They didn't have a landscaping crew — they had a parking attendant for all the junked cars and crashed trucks that occupied their front lawn.

She had established a good relationship with Earl through working with his many children, sisters, brothers, nieces, and nephews, in her job as a school psychologist. Also, Earl and his kin had managed to save Skye on a few occasions, which meant they now treated her like their pet hound: with casual affection unless someone bothered her; then it was all-out war.

The bulldozer ground to a halt, and the hull squeaked open. Earl popped up like a life-sized jack-in-the-box and was instantly surrounded by a mob of angry women brandishing nail guns, sledgehammers, pickaxes, and various other makeshift weapons.

Earl quickly sat down and tried to lower the metal box back over himself. It stuck halfway, and he bawled, "Save me, Miz Skye! Save me!"

Skye shouted to the female army gathered around the bulldozer, "Hold your fire. I know this man. He's not all there." She pointed to her forehead and twirled her finger. "He's missing a few buttons on his remote control, if you get my drift."

Earl whined, "That ain't a nice thing to say about a friend trying to help you, Miz Skye."

"Shut up, Earl." Skye looked nervously from face to face. If these women were all abuse victims, they wouldn't be too trusting of what a man had to say. She turned to them and said, "Ladies, how about if you all go over to Dulci's truck and let me figure this out."

No one moved. Skye met Dulci's gaze and the contractor raised an eyebrow.

"Ladies, I promise you this man isn't dangerous. His receiver is just off the hook."

"Miz Skye!" Earl bleated.

She ignored him. "Listen, you all still have the gun. If he tries anything, you can shoot him."

"Shush, Miz Skye! What are you sayin'?"

The women whispered among themselves, then moved off toward the pickup. Before Skye could move, an ancient Buick Regal came rattling into the driveway and the queen of the Red Raggers burst out of the driver's side.

Skye moaned. She hadn't thought it possible, but things had just gotten worse. Earl's wife Glenda had arrived. She had do-it-yourself dyed-blond hair, a Dolly Parton bust, and the personality of a wolverine. Ignoring everyone else, she glared at her husband and screamed, "If you know what's good for you, Earl Doozier —"

Earl, taking his life in his own hands, cut her off, saying, "Aw, ain't that sweet? She's worried about my health."

"Get out of that thing right now." Glenda

put her hands on her hips and narrowed her eyes.

"But, honey pie, Miz Skye needs me —"

"Don't make me break a nail by comin' in after you."

Everyone's gaze was drawn to the bright red talons on the ends of Glenda's fingertips.

"You get home." Earl didn't move, a stubborn expression on his usually slack-jawed face. "This is man's work."

"I'm countin' to three." Glenda crushed out her cigarette under a scarlet stiletto-shod foot. "And you better have your skinny butt out of that there contraption or I'm comin' in to get you."

Skye seized the moment to climb up into the dozer and grab Earl by the shirt. "Move it or lose it."

Tugging at the crotch of her spandex shorts, her halter top exposing a large expanse of chalk white skin, Glenda glowered at Skye. "What are you doing with my man?"

Skye kept a firm grip on Earl, but said placatingly, "I promise I'll send him home as soon as he tells me what he was doing and why."

Earl looked from his wife to Skye and back. "I'll be right home, baby, I promise."

For the first time, Glenda seemed to notice the armed women surrounding her. Several shouted that Earl wasn't going anywhere until they got an explanation.

Not quite as thick as her husband, Glenda nodded her agreement, then bawled at Earl, "Ok, mister. You stay here and tell the ladies what was on your puny little mind when you tried to run them over with that thing." She turned to leave, but swung back, facing her husband. "I told you that guy was more full of crap than an outhouse. Miz La-di-da Skye don't need your help."

"What guy?" Skye asked.

Glenda ignored her and continued to lecture her husband. "So you stay, but you better not be comin' home half drunk."

Earl scratched his head. "What if I run out of money?"

"Don't be stupider than you already are." Glenda whacked him upside the head and got in her car. "You best be home in half an hour, or don't bother comin' home at all."

After Glenda roared away, Earl meekly followed Skye into the house, where she sat him on a Queen Anne chair in the parlor. When she got a good look at the skinny little man dressed in desert fatigues and a combat helmet, sitting on the delicate antique chair, she sniggered. Earl almost looked like a ten-year-old boy playing army, until you noticed the dense tattoos up and down his forearms and exposed by his half-buttoned shirt.

He immediately started to whine. "Why'd you go do that, Miz Skye? I had them on the run."

"Why, Earl?" Skye collapsed down on the sofa and eased off her loafers. Blisters were forming on both heels. "Why did you want them on the run?"

"I heard that your contractor was cheatin' you and messin' up your fancy new house."

Fancy? Skye let her head flop back. "That was my *old* contractor, Beau Hamilton. Didn't you hear he was murdered last Friday?"

"This guy only told me yesterday about you bein' taken advantage of."

"What guy?"

Earl shrugged. "Just some guy who stopped by the house to admire the Doozier Dozer."

"And why did you have an armor-plated bulldozer hanging around your front yard?"

"I'm getting ready for the end of the world." Earl took off his camo-colored helmet, revealing muddy brown hair that formed a horseshoe around a bald spot the size of a cantaloupe. "Haven't you been watching Reverend Alphonse on TV? The godless hordes are about to attack us any day."

"Okay, at least now I sort of understand why you had the dozer." Skye would have loved to explore Earl's latest whim further, but she had a feeling that Dulci and her crew would be growing restless real soon. "But why didn't you call me and ask me if I needed help?"

"What kind of friend would I be if I expected you to ask for help?"

"I see." Skye realized she wasn't getting anywhere with this conversation. "So, do you promise to never bother these women again? No matter *what* anyone tells you?"

"I does, Miz Skye. I surely does."

"What did this guy who told you I needed help look like?" Skye tried again to make sense of what had happened.

Earl blew his lips in and out before finally saying, "Rich. Rich and important." Earl stood and put his helmet back on. "I'll just skee-daddle out the back way, and come over later for the Doozier Dozer." Over his shoulder he added, "You tell those ladies I'll fix anything I broke."

"Terrific." Skye waved him down the hallway toward the kitchen, then walked to the front door, leaned out, and yelled, "You all want to come in now? Everything's settled."

Once Dulci and her crew were inside and seated, Skye asked, "So what happened?" She'd heard Earl's story; now she wanted to hear the other side's.

"I called a break at three thirty and the crew scattered," Dulci explained. "Some headed for the bathroom, others to their vehicles for some privacy to make phone calls, and I went to get the cooler from the back of the truck."

"Then what?" It was a huge leap from women going on break to being chased by a mad dozer.

"As I reached for the tailgate, I heard a rumbling. I looked up and this mutant machine came barreling through your gates."

"Luella, how did you end up being chased?"

The powerfully built brunette leaned against the doorjamb, having flicked a derisive glance over the delicate antique sofa and chairs. "I had climbed into the bed of my pickup to stretch out and take a nap, when that moron came through the gates. I jumped up when I heard the noise, then when that fool lurched by, I jumped on top of the hull. I figured if I could get to the driver, I could stop him before he did any damage." She straightened and flexed her arm. "I've been working out since I left that no-good husband of mine. No man will ever hurt me again."

"I see. Very impressive." Skye nodded encouragingly. "Did you slip off the bull-dozer?"

"Yeah. I bounced like a basketball. From the way the thing looked, I thought it was armor-plated and would hold me, but it was some cheap lightweight metal. For armor-plating you need two sheets of half-inch steel with a layer of concrete between them."

Skye raised an eyebrow. How did Luella know that? *Why* did Luella know that?

"What does all this matter? It's not what *we* did, it's what *he* did." Dulci had plainly had enough. She had been pacing up and down the center of the room, but now she stopped in front of Skye and put her hands on her hips. "Who was the goon in the dozer, and why did he attack us? Did one of our exes send him?"

After Skye finished explaining Earl's origins and his motivation, she looked up at Dulci and said, "So he acted completely on his own." As soon as the words were out of her mouth, something tickled the back of her mind and she wondered if she'd spoken the truth. Why would some rich guy tell Earl she needed help?

Before she could pursue that thought, Dulci turned to her crew and asked, "Are you all okay with that explanation?"

The workers responded with nods and "yeahs."

Skye beamed at the women. "Earl said he'll make restitution for anything he damaged. Give me a list and I'll pass it on to him. Didn't I see a car he had overturned?"

A delicate woman with long strawberry curls down her back said, "That was my VW. The girls helped me put it right side up, and it's fine."

"Anyone with any claims?"

They all shook their heads and Dulci said, "The only thing he harmed was your landscaping."

Skye nodded. "I'm so sorry this happened. I sure hope you won't quit on me."

Dulci looked at her crew, then back to Skye. "No. We'll stick with you."

After the women left, Skye moved her car into the garage, then went upstairs to change. As she was taking off her school clothes, she wondered again who had told Earl her contractor was giving her a problem. Was it an innocent comment, or had someone goaded Earl to act? The Dooziers weren't a family that others casually gossiped with. It looked as if the man had deliberately sought out Earl to tell him about Skye's supposed contractor problem.

Chapter 21
Twenty-One
Gun Salute

Skye surveyed the damage done by Earl and his Doozier Dozer. What a mess! The front lawn's sod had been peeled back like a banana skin and the bushes that had bordered the front sidewalk were uprooted and flung into the yard like croutons on a salad.

It was a miracle he hadn't flattened the steps leading up to the porch as well. Luckily, the two oak trees that stood on either side of the front of the house were huge. Earl had only managed to clip off a few low-growing branches.

She had been hoping to put off the cost of landscaping until the spring, but now she wasn't sure she could. Skye squinted, trying to picture the minimum that would have to be done. There was no way she could charge Earl for his destruction — not when he thought he was rescuing her. But maybe if she had him haul away all the uprooted shrubbery and sheered-off tree limbs, and roll the turf back into place, she might be able to live with the result until April.

As she considered her options, a sheriff's car pulled into her driveway and parked by the front steps. Deputy McCabe, who bore an unfortunate resemblance to Barney Fife from the old *Andy Griffith Show,* leisurely exited the vehicle.

Skye knew him from several previous encounters, starting with her first week back in Scumble River when she had found the body of a TV celebrity, Mrs. Gumtree. Sad to say, but if stupid were a talent, he'd be considered gifted.

He sauntered over to Skye, hand on his gun, and drawled, "Got a report that some crazy man on a bulldozer was chasing a bunch of ladies around your yard."

Skye raised an eyebrow. "So you're told several women are in danger, and it took you how long to get here?" Dulci's crew must have called the sheriff by three forty-five, four at the latest. Skye glanced at her watch. It was now past five o'clock.

McCabe hitched up his pants and bristled. "It's a big county. I suppose you want me to run over little children so I could be here faster."

Skye shook her head, tempted to point out that there was supposed to be a deputy patrolling each twenty-mile sector of the county, and that even if McCabe had been in Laurel, the farthest point from Scumble River, it shouldn't have taken him more than forty-five minutes, tops. But she knew that showing him the errors in his statement would get her nowhere, so she remained silent.

McCabe waited a few seconds for her to speak, and when she didn't, he tugged at the collar of his uniform shirt. "Well, I'm here now. Where's the galldarn emergency?"

"You're too late. It's all been settled."

"Settled?" McCabe took off his hat and hit the side of his leg with it. "You mean I came all the way over here for nothing?"

"It looks that way."

"Who owns that bulldozer parked over there?" McCabe pointed to his left. "That's an illegal vehicle. I could give you a ticket for it."

"Not me — Earl Doozier. He was under the impression I needed saving, but when he learned everything was okay, he left peacefully."

"Doozier." McCabe paled and his Adam's apple bobbed like it was caught in a Slinky. He'd had many run-ins with the Doozier clan and had yet to win one. In fact, he usually ended up being made a fool of. "Uh, you don't want me to go talk to him or nothing, right?" His tone had swung from pompous to pleading.

"Well . . ." Skye realized she had the deputy over a barrel. "Since no one was hurt . . ."

"Right. No need to involve the long arm of the law." McCabe backed toward his patrol car.

"Right. We need to save you for the really dangerous cases. So, if you answer my questions, and since Earl's promised to restore whatever he damaged, I could let this go."

McCabe froze. "What questions?"

"About Beau Hamilton."

"That case is closed. We have a confession."

"So I heard. But I was wondering if, before the confession, the sheriff was looking at someone else for the murder."

A crafty expression took over McCabe's face. "Besides you?"

"Right."

"Well, we were sort of thinking it had to be someone who lived along the river or had private access. It looked as if the killer arrived by boat."

Skye stopped herself from rolling her eyes. "Had you narrowed it down any more than that?" Since Beau had been found in a boat, the fact that his killer had river access wasn't exactly a quantum leap.

"Let's see, there's that guy that owns the liquor store in town. It's right on the river and he had a set-to with Beau."

"Jess Larson."

"Right, and then there's one of Beau's girlfriends."

"Which one?" Skye asked.

"She's new around these parts. Bought a place on the river in June."

"Raette Craughwell?"

"Yep." McCabe had made it to his cruiser and opened the door. "And of course the sister lives not too far down the river from you."

Skye hadn't realized Alana lived nearby. Of course proximity on the river and closeness via the road were two different things. Still, it was odd that when Skye inherited the Griggs house, Alana had never mentioned that they were practically neighbors.

"Anything else?" McCabe was now inside the vehicle. He rolled down his window a couple of inches and his pointy nose stuck out. "I can't spend all day here."

"Was there any indication that Beau had a pet?"

"I can't say I heard of any." He turned on the motor. "Can I go now?"

"Just one more question. Did the sheriff's department search Beau's storage building?"

"Hamilton didn't have a storage building." With that he put the squad car in DRIVE and sped away.

Skye watched the taillights as McCabe turned out of her driveway. She remembered Wally saying they had searched Hamilton's house, but that was it. It looked as if neither the sheriff nor the police knew about the building on the back of Alana's property. She'd better let Wally know right away. It could be important.

Thinking about the other suspects McCabe had named, Skye went inside and changed clothes. She still didn't feel Jess was Beau's killer. Nor did she believe Alana had killed her own brother, unless she was a better actress than Katharine Hepburn. Skye would swear that Beau's sister had really been attacked and was truly distraught over his death.

That left Raette Craughwell. Her name certainly kept popping up. Skye was ninety percent sure Beau had been Xenia's father, but that ten percent was keeping her from breaking confidentiality and telling Wally. She chewed her thumbnail; she had already tried to brazen it out with Raette, and another confrontation would probably be useless.

She'd have to figure out a way to point Wally in Raette and Xenia's direction without actually telling him anything she knew from reading the teen's file or from meeting with the mother. Maybe she could suggest to him that he try and find out if Beau had ever fathered a child. As long as she didn't mention Xenia's name, she was pretty sure that would be ethically okay.

In the meantime, she had a mess to clean up. Skye grabbed a box of trash bags and went outside. She started by picking up the smaller pieces of debris, and when she had filled two sacks, she took them around back to the Dumpster. As she slung the bags into the receptacle, the momentum forced her to take a step backward, and she felt a sudden pain in her ankle.

At first she thought it was a branch poking into her skin, but when she looked down, she gazed into the malevolent yellow eyes of the moose head she had thrown off her balcony. Its gaping jaws were around her ankle and the teeth were digging into her flesh.

Gingerly, she worked her foot free of the moose's mouth, then bent and struggled to pick up the offending stuffed head. "Okay, Bullwinkle, you've had your last bite of me. Into the Dumpster you go."

Grunting, she heaved the trophy over the side, then grimaced when she heard the sound of plastic tearing. Putting her hands on the rim, she peeked over the edge. Bullwinkle's antler had torn open a black plastic trash bag.

For an instant, Skye considered leaving things the way they were, but the fear of scavenging animals made her fetch a stepladder and crawl over the side.

As she descended into the Dumpster, she thanked goodness that the majority of its contents was construction material, nothing too squishy or smelly. She had been putting her trash there, but had made sure it was double-bagged and closed tight.

Carrying a fresh sack, she worked her way to the torn bag and squatted down. Her objective was to insert the torn bag into the intact one without losing any contents. The transfer was going well until a field mouse scuttled across Skye's foot. She screamed and jerked upward, spilling the remainder of the torn sack's contents.

Swearing, she bent to retrieve the items that had escaped. What was a book doing in the trash? Oh, yeah, she had found a ruined library book in one of her searches for Bingo.

Skye picked it up and examined it again. She hadn't noticed before, but a page had been dog-eared. Flipping the book open to the marked place revealed a fine art painting of a distraught woman lying on a bed. Skye stared at it for a long time. Where had she seen a painting like that before?

The memory teased her as she finished bagging the rest of the trash, tucked the book under her arm, and climbed out of the Dumpster.

It was too bad the printing under the photo was so water-damaged. Maybe she'd bring the book for Alana to look at when Skye went to visit her in the hospital, and the art teacher could help identify the painting — once she regained consciousness, that is.

Skye felt a flicker of anxiety. She'd been repressing the possibility, but what if Alana didn't recover? Should Skye have done more, been a better friend? The thought of the bright, talented woman dead made her feel as if she had been punched in the stomach.

She leaned against the side of the metal container and took a steadying breath. Tomorrow after school she would go to the hospital to see Alana, even if she was still not awake. Skye knew that friends and relatives were encouraged to talk to patients who were unconscious in the hopes of rousing them.

Having a plan made Skye feel somewhat better. After putting the book in the sunroom, she continued clearing up the Doozier damage. As soon as she finished, she planned to call Wally. She assured herself it was only to see how Alana was doing, not because she wanted to hear his voice or have him come over.

She hoped she wasn't lying to herself, but she suspected that if she looked in a mirror right then her nose would have grown an inch or so.

As planned, Skye had called Wally's cell as soon as she got in the house. When he didn't pick up, she'd left another message, then tried calling the hospital, but they wouldn't give her any information about Alana's condition.

She was washing her hands when she heard knocking. She took a second to comb her hair, then ran downstairs. She looked through the peephole and wasn't surprised to see Wally standing on her front porch.

Tonight he had changed out of his uniform

and wore black jeans and a crisp white polo shirt. His hair was damp and he was freshly shaved. He held out a takeout bag.

She smiled to herself, wondering if Wally was afraid he wouldn't be welcome without food. "Come on in." She could smell the aroma of fried chicken and corn fritters. "You went all the way to White Fence Farm?" The restaurant was in Lemont, a good forty-five or fifty-minute drive.

"I had business up that way." He started down the hall, asking over his shoulder, "Sunroom?"

"Sure. Beer?"

He nodded and Skye followed him, detouring into the kitchen for plates, napkins, etc. As she assembled the tray, she realized his visits were becoming a habit.

Entering the sunroom, she still hadn't decided if that was a good thing or not. When she saw he was once again sprawled on the wicker settee, this time watching an old Marx Brothers' movie, she was ready to vote not.

She hated the Marx Brothers. Their brand of humor left her cold. She narrowed her eyes. Simon liked the Marx Brothers, too. Was this some sort of sign, that Wally wasn't right for her either?

As soon as Wally spotted her, he turned

off the TV and gave her a dazzling smile. "I could get used to seeing you across the dinner table every night."

Skye's worries about Wally's taste in comedy vanished. He really was a sweet, handsome, thoughtful guy. And the fact that he was incredibly sexy didn't hurt either.

"You might change your mind if you tasted my cooking," she teased.

"Not a problem. I love to cook."

Skye smiled, but thought to herself, *How could I not know that?*

Before going on, Wally put the white cardboard box of chicken in the middle of the table. "Besides, it's not as if I ever thought you were the housewife type."

"That's a relief," Skye said, then frowned. What did he mean by that? Her house was clean — well, as clean as possible considering the circumstances. And in reality she could cook — not as well as her mother, but pretty well. She made a face at herself. What was the matter with her? Was she trying to find something wrong with the guy?

"I got your message, but decided to come over rather than return your call."

"Oh." Skye pried the plastic lid from the round Styrofoam containers of mashed potatoes, gravy, and coleslaw. "I wanted to know if you'd heard how Alana's doing. Has she regained consciousness yet?"

"No. I checked with Quirk and she was still out, but the docs say they can't figure out why. The tests show that everything is fine."

"Mmm." Skye thought about what she knew about the art teacher, and wondered if her comalike state was more psychological than physical. Another good reason to go see her tomorrow.

"Quirk said her boyfriend hasn't left the building. When he's not allowed to be with her, he sits and watches her door."

"Now that's devotion." Skye squeezed the lime wedge into her Diet Coke. "The other reason I called is to ask if you know about Beau's storage building."

"No. There's no record of one."

"My new contractor figured out he had one when she was looking for the windows for my house. I didn't realize until today that you might not know about it."

Wally leaned forward. "What happened today?"

Skye told Wally about the Doozier Dozer and McCabe's statement that the sheriff wasn't aware of the building. She finished her tale with, "So, do you think it's important? Are you going to search it?"

"It might be. Legally, the building probably belongs to Alana, so that might make getting a warrant trickier."

Skye nodded, glad he hadn't mentioned the fact that Dulci probably shouldn't have retrieved Skye's windows from the building without Alana's permission. She decided to change the subject before he thought of it. "So, why were you up north?"

"After your question last night, I decided to do a little investigation into Raette Craughwell's past, and the last address she gave us was in Lemont." Wally opened the paper bag holding the fritters and popped one into his mouth.

"Find anything out?" Skye carefully selected a chicken breast, then filled her plate from the rest of the cartons.

"Plenty, but I doubt it's anything you don't already know." Wally looked intently at Skye.

"Maybe." She bit into a fritter. As she crunched through the outer layer she tasted the sweetness of the powdered sugar, then the fluffy cornmeal center. "Hey, these are still warm."

"I stopped at my house to change clothes before coming here, and I put everything into the oven while I showered."

"How sweet." He really was a nice guy, much more so than she would have guessed.

So, why was she so attracted to him if she hadn't previously thought he was considerate?

Wally looked at her, waiting for her to say more, and when she didn't he continued. "Anyway, when I went over my notes, I realized that even in this mobile society, Raette moved around a lot." He took a swig of beer, swallowed, then said, "I'm sure you already know why she moves so much, and it's what you couldn't share with me the other night."

"Probably," Skye answered tentatively, not wanting to let anything slip before she was sure Wally had found out about Raette's daughter on his own.

"The police in Lemont were happy to tell me the story of Xenia Craughwell and how she corrupted the town daughters." Wally finished a chicken leg and wiped his fingers on a napkin. "They also revealed that this wasn't the first time the girl had been in trouble, just the most serious incident."

"So you see why I was concerned that Raette and Xenia might be a part of the whole Beau situation."

"Do you think the girl might have killed Beau?" Wally didn't beat around the bush.

Skye pushed her half-finished plate away. She had lost her appetite. "I hope not." The idea of a teenager as the murderer made her nauseous. "I met her today, and even though she has a great deal of anger bottled up inside, there's a hint of something that makes me think maybe she could still be okay if the adults around her do the right thing."

Wally nodded, then said, "Anyway, what motive would she have for killing him? Do you think he came on to her? There's no history of him going after girls that young."

Skye debated with herself. Very little had changed. Wally might know about Xenia's father fixation, but he had no idea that Beau might be her father, and Skye still didn't feel she could tell him. Skye knew she was walking a tight line ethically, and prayed she was making the right decision. "No. I don't think he'd come on to her."

"Was she defending her mother?"

"I doubt it."

"Then what?" It was apparent that Wally's patience was wearing thin.

"All I can say is that if I were you, I would look into Beau's past. Maybe his and the Craughwells' intersected at some point."

"You can't just tell me?"

"Honestly, I don't know anything." Skye started to clean up their mess. "I have some guesses, but I truly don't *know* anything."

CHAPTER 22
CATCH-22

Skye climbed into bed alone, stretched out between the cool crisp sheets, and stared into the darkness.

It had been a close call tonight. She didn't know if she would have had the willpower to push Wally out the door instead of inviting him upstairs, if fate hadn't intervened once again. Either his charm was getting stronger or her resolve was getting weaker. Lucky for her — at least she guessed it was a good thing — once more the house itself had forced them apart.

They had been close to the point of no return when the space heater in the sunroom exploded as if someone had dropped it into a bucket of water. Sparks flew and flames shot upward.

Wally and Skye sprang apart. He grabbed the afghan from the back of the settee and tried to smother the blaze. She ran to the kitchen, grabbed the fire extinguisher she kept underneath the sink, raced back, and sprayed the heater until the extinguisher ran dry.

By the time they'd checked to make sure there were no other embers ready to ignite in another part of the room and cleaned up the mess, the mood had been shattered. Wally had given her a rueful kiss good-bye and gone home.

Now, as Skye tried to fall asleep, her thoughts seesawed between her growing feelings for Wally and Beau Hamilton's murder. She knew she was overlooking something in both situations, but what?

She idly reached out to stroke Bingo. As her fingers encountered thin air, his absence hit her once again and she swallowed a tear. Was it stupid to believe he was still alive? He'd been gone for over a week.

If Beau had kidnapped him, where was he now? The police hadn't seen any evidence of an animal in Beau's apartment. He wouldn't have dared keep the cat in his truck, for fear someone would spot it and recognize it as the feline whose picture was on all the missing-pet posters around town.

Beau didn't have an office, so where else would he stash the cat? While she tried to think, Skye let her gaze wander around the room. The newly replaced window caught her attention and she wrinkled her brow.

Hadn't Dulci said they would install all the downstairs windows first? Why had she done the one in the bedroom? Skye gave a mental shrug. It *was* an odd size, so maybe it had been in front at the storage building.

Dulci had mentioned that the building had been stuffed with construction materials and machinery. She had told Skye that if her windows hadn't been right at the door they would never have been able to find them.

Skye sat straight up in bed. The storage building! That was where Beau had put Bingo. Dulci and her crew wouldn't have seen him among all the clutter, and it hadn't been searched, since at the time of Beau's death the authorities didn't even know the building existed.

It had been nearly five days since Beau's murder, which meant the cat hadn't been fed in all that time. As Skye threw on jeans, sweatshirt, and sneakers, she hoped that Bingo had been able to catch some mice.

She was halfway down the stairs when it dawned on her that perhaps rushing alone into a deserted building in the dark was not the best decision she had ever made.

Skye sank down onto the step. She couldn't leave Bingo hungry, thirsty, and terrified for another night, so what were her other options?

Wally? No, he had said he would need a search warrant, and if he did agree to go and they were discovered, it could ruin his career. She couldn't put him in that position.

Trixie would go in a flash, but Owen wouldn't like it, and their relationship was only now getting back to being good after a major bad patch. Skye couldn't ask her friend to risk her marriage.

She could no longer turn to Simon, and her parents were certainly out of the question. She wasn't speaking to her mother, and her father was in the same spot Trixie was, only recently getting back into his spouse's good graces.

That left Uncle Charlie or Vince. The choice was plain. She couldn't see dragging a seventy-four-year-old man out in the middle of the night and asking him to climb over who knew what.

Vince it was. He owed her, and he was used to existing on very little sleep. After all, a drummer in a rock band didn't exactly go to bed at ten o'clock every night.

Having made her choice, she ran down the rest of the stairs, stopping briefly in the foyer to get a backpack from the hall closet.

Then she went into the kitchen and loaded the pack with a flashlight and a box of dry cat food. She grabbed her car keys from their hook, then raced to the garage.

The Bel Air's engine roared to life and its tires sent up a shower of pebbles as Skye stomped down on the accelerator. Five minutes later she pulled into the parking lot of Vince's apartment building. The halogen light was out, and the moon was under a cloud. She could barely make out the shadows of the other cars. A good night for breaking and entering.

Thumbing on her flashlight, she walked up to Vince's door, thankful that he lived in a ground-floor unit. She rang the bell and waited. Nothing. Maybe he wasn't home. She rang again, this time leaning on the bell.

A few seconds later the door was yanked open and her usually mild-mannered brother, dressed only in a pair of plaid boxer shorts, bellowed, "There better be a fire, or I'm going to rip you a new one!"

Skye stifled a smile. Vince's hair was standing on end, one side of his face was creased from being pressed into a pillow, and his eyes were bloodshot. She had never seen him look this bad before. She always thought he woke up looking as gorgeous as he did all day.

"Skye?" He squinted. "What are you do-ing here at two in the morning?"

"I've figured out where Bingo is, and I need you to help me go find him."

"Now?" Vince shoved a hand through his hair, not improving its appearance.

"Now. He's been without food or water for days and days." Skye's voice broke as she explained how she had deduced Bingo's whereabouts.

"Okay." Vince scrubbed his eyes with his fists. "Uh, let me throw on some clothes."

He started to close the door, but Skye asked, "Can't I wait inside?"

"Uh." Vince glanced behind him. "It's, uh, you know, I have to get dressed and this is a studio and all."

"Forgetting the fact that I'm your sister, can't you change in the bathroom?"

"Uh . . . it's just that the place is such a mess."

"Yeah, like I'm the housekeeping police." While Vince struggled to explain himself, Skye pushed past him and strode over the threshold toward the light coming from the lamp on an end table.

She took two steps, then turned to see why Vince wasn't following. He was staring over her head at the center of the room, a look of consternation and helplessness on his handsome features.

Following his gaze, which was fastened on the unfolded sleeper sofa, Skye noticed a distinct lump under the covers. Suddenly she understood her brother's reticence. This must be his new girlfriend — the one who was such a big secret he had denied her very existence.

Skye put a hand to her mouth and started to back out of the apartment, but before she completed her first reverse step, she noticed a leg sticking out of the sheets. She stopped her retreat and studied the appendage. Not only was it the color of rich, dark chocolate, but the thin gold chain encircling the shapely ankle looked mighty familiar.

Moving closer, she focused on the charm attached to the bracelet. Yes, as she suspected, it was a tiny scale of justice. So that's how Loretta had known about Beau's murder. She must have spent Friday night at Vince's and heard the news on the local radio station.

Vince had come out of his trance and moved between Skye and the bed. He reached down and pulled the sheet over the object of her attention, then said, "Okay, you caught me with a lady friend. Now, will you wait outside?"

Skye debated with herself. Should she

pretend she didn't know who was in Vince's bed, or bring it all out into the open?

"Please just wait in the car." Vince eyed her warily.

Skye could tell he was trying to gauge whether she knew his bedmate's identity. Abruptly, she came to a decision. It was silly to pretend ignorance. In a small town like Scumble River, Vince couldn't keep his affair quiet for long, so he might as well get used to people knowing. She knew what he was afraid of, but if this relationship was his choice, he had to stand behind it.

"I'll only be a couple of minutes, then we can go find Bingo," Vince cajoled.

"Great." Skye stood her ground. "Go get dressed while Loretta and I chat."

Vince groaned, but picked up a pair of jeans that had been flung over the back of a chair and a shirt draped across his drum set, and trudged into the bathroom.

When the latch clicked closed, Skye's dear friend and sorority sister Loretta Steiner sat up, clutching the blanket to her breasts. "Nancy Drew, I presume?" Loretta snapped. "You really should get a job on that TV show *Unsolved Mysteries*."

"What?" Why was her friend so mad? It wasn't as if Skye had lain in wait and sprung a trap on her.

"I knew you'd never be happy until you figured out who your brother was dating."

Skye moved a lacy red bra from the seat of the chair and sat down. "I had no idea anyone was here with Vince. The only reason I came is to ask for his help in finding Bingo." This was incredibly awkward, and Loretta's ill-concealed anger wasn't helping matters.

"Sure!" Loretta glared at her. "Then you're not going to tell anyone?"

"No, I won't. But there's only so long until the gossip mill gets ahold of the news."

"Shit! Shit! Shit!" Loretta pounded the mattress. "I hate small towns."

"I don't understand why your relationship is such a big secret, anyway."

"Oh, please. Here's a little tip for you, Ms. Psychologist. When you're at a loss for the right word — try silence."

"Huh?"

"In case you haven't noticed, your little community isn't exactly diversified. In fact, I'm pretty sure that Scumble Rathole is lily-white."

Skye opened her mouth to defend her town, but Loretta was right; there were very few shades of Jesse Jackson's Rainbow Coalition in Scumble River.

Loretta wrapped her arms around her

bent legs and laid her head on top of her knees. "I told Vince this would never work out."

Skye moved over to the bed and put her arm around her friend's shoulder. "Give us a chance. We might not exactly be a model town for the NAACP, but I really don't think many people will have a problem with you and Vince dating." *Except maybe my parents* — but Skye kept that thought to herself.

Before Loretta answered, Vince charged out of the bathroom, ignored Loretta, and said to Skye, "Okay, I'm ready. Let's get going."

Loretta shook off Skye's arm and, wrapping the sheet around herself, leapt from the bed. She strode past Vince into the bathroom and slammed the door.

Vince looked between Skye and the closed door. He took a step toward the bathroom, then shrugged, took Skye's arm, and tugged her toward the front door, saying, "Let's get this over with."

"Shouldn't you stay and talk to Loretta? I can go alone."

"Look," Vince snarled, "you came here in the middle of the night for my help. Which is fine. I'm your brother and that's what brothers are for. But then you had to force your way inside, and now that you've created a mess, you want me to let you go break into a murdered man's building alone?"

Skye didn't have an answer. She knew she needed Vince to go with her, but she hated to see him sacrifice his relationship with Loretta to help her.

She allowed herself to be pulled out of the apartment and into Vince's Jeep. As they were driving out of the parking lot she finally said, "I'm sorry I pushed my way in, but you know that you couldn't keep this a secret for long."

Vince shrugged. "Maybe, but it should have been our choice, not yours."

"You're right." Skye swallowed painfully, guilt settling heavily on her chest. "But now that I know, I can help."

"How?" Vince shot her a speculative glance. "Will you tell Mom and Dad for me?"

Skye gulped. She hadn't been thinking of that sort of help. On the other hand, she owed him. "Okay, I'll tell them."

Vince nodded, a small smile on his lips, then quickly frowned. "Might as well wait a while. After tonight, Loretta probably won't be speaking to either of us."

They were both silent until a few minutes

later, when Vince turned into the narrow dirt path that ran alongside Alana Lowe's property. The shed was well camouflaged by the landscape, and if Dulci hadn't told Skye of its existence, she would never have spotted it.

The windows of Alana's house were dark, and no lights went on as the Jeep drove by, its engine revving as Vince changed gears. Skye nodded to herself. She had been counting on Neville still being at the hospital with Alana. If he were home, at a minimum he would stop them and demand an explanation, but probably he would just call the cops. She shuddered, picturing Wally catching her trespassing, or even worse, Sheriff Peterson. She wasn't sure whose territory Alana's property fell into.

The lane ended at the back of Alana's acreage where a massive building hunkered near the river. The moon had come out from behind the clouds that had hid it earlier, and the metal structure reflected the glow.

As Vince parked in front of the immense sliding doors, Skye said, "I wonder why Beau built his storage shed back here. Ground this close to the water is too sandy to be stable. Not to mention the possibility of flooding from too much rain."

"His sister probably offered the land, and since it was free he took a chance." Vince shrugged. "We haven't had a flood in twenty years. People forget."

Skye nodded and opened the Jeep's door, jumping to the ground. People did indeed seem to have short memories. How else could you account for the continued existence of trailer parks all along Tornado Alley?

Vince followed her as she moved to the doors and asked, "What if they're locked?"

"My new contractor said they weren't."

"How did she know?"

Skye explained while she tugged on the door. It was so heavy, at first she thought maybe someone had bolted it since Dulci had been there. But when Vince reached over her and yanked, the door slid open, creaking in protest. Maintenance had obviously not been high on Beau's to-do list.

There were no windows, and the interior was pitch black. Skye stepped across the threshold, turned on her flashlight, and swept the wall for an ON/OFF switch.

Vince, right behind her, said, "I'll bet there's no electricity. I didn't see any utility poles or lines out to here. It's almost as if Beau wanted to keep this place under the radar of any government agencies."

"Great." Skye arced the flashlight's beam around the cavernous space. "How can we find a black cat in the dark?"

Vince scratched his head, then said, "Wait a minute." He ran out to his Jeep, started it up, and pulled it inside the enormous building. He turned off the motor but left the headlights on. Before returning to Skye, he grabbed a flashlight from the glove compartment.

Skye smiled at him. "Good idea." The high beams illuminated the front half of the storage area. "Let's split up. You go to the right and I'll take the left, and we'll meet in the back."

Vince nodded and walked away calling, "Here kitty, kitty. It's Uncle Vince. I've got supper."

Skye went in the opposite direction, shaking the box of dry cat food she had taken from her backpack. At first it looked as if the wood, drywall, and shingles were stacked haphazardly on the concrete floor, but after a while Skye detected a certain pattern and started to plot a route as if she were in a maze.

From time to time she could hear Vince's voice, but for the most part the rattle of the dry cat food was the only sound. It was slow going, stopping every few feet to check out a hidey-hole or climb up to look on top of a pile.

By the time Skye had made it halfway through the labyrinth she was sweating. Even though the inside of the building was cold, the air was clammy. The dank, musty smell triggered her sinuses and brought on a violent bout of sneezing. She paused to catch her breath and was wiping her damp forehead with her sleeve when she heard a noise. Was it Vince?

No. It was a clicking sound. Where had she heard that before? It came to her in a flash. She had heard it the day she had moved into the Griggs house and Bingo had gotten into the basement. It was the sound of his back claws on the concrete floor. Excitedly, she shook the box and called, "Here kitty, kitty."

"Meow."

Bingo! "Here, boy, come to mama." Excitedly, she wound her way through the warren of supplies and machinery.

Following the sound of the meowing, she edged past a mountain of pink insulation rolls and was abruptly at the back of the building in an area roughly the size of a small office.

It had been left empty except for a beat-up desk and a new-looking, closet-sized cabinet which marked the inner boundary. A door in the corner and the metal walls of the structure formed the three outer edges.

A four-foot by four-foot wire cage occupied the center. Pacing the length of the pen like the panther he resembled was Bingo. As Skye ran toward him, she yelled to Vince that she had found the cat.

When Skye got closer to the cage, she noted a roasting pan in one corner containing an inch or so of water and an overflowing litter box in another. An empty food dish had been knocked over, but when she opened the cage door and scooped Bingo into her arms he didn't feel as if he had lost weight.

She looked around and saw that someone had left a twenty-pound bag of dry cat food leaning against the pen. Bingo had chewed a hole in it and had been dining alfresco.

The big black cat purred loudly and rubbed his head against Skye's cheek and chin. All of a sudden, the relief of having found Bingo alive and unharmed got to Skye, and her legs started to tremble. She stumbled over to the desk and collapsed onto the chair.

After several minutes of petting and scratching, Skye's gaze wandered to the desktop. Following a short, internal debate on right and wrong, she swiftly leafed through the papers on the top. They were mostly invoices and contracts — nothing interesting. Next she pulled open the center drawer. Pens, pencils, stapler, but again nothing out of the ordinary.

Bingo was getting restless; he'd had enough affection and wanted to go home. Holding the squirming feline in one arm, she opened the desk's side drawer. It was empty. That was odd. She got up and tried the cabinet. The doors were ajar, and when she opened them fully, those shelves were empty, too.

Someone must've been here before her. Had Alana cleared things out or had Beau's killer been searching for something? While she had been thinking, Bingo had gone beyond wriggly and leapt from her arms. He ran toward the desk and into the knee-hole.

Skye pulled out the chair and crawled in after him. As she grabbed him, she noticed he had a crumpled ball of paper in his mouth.

Afraid Bingo would get hurt if he escaped her hold again, Skye stowed him in her backpack. Gently prying the paper from his teeth, she threw it into the bottom of the pack, then laced the opening so that only his head was free. As he yowled in her ear, she turned to make her way out of the building, wondering why Vince had never showed up.

When she reentered the storage area maze, she heard footsteps. Thinking Vince had finally found her, she called out, "Over here. I've got Bingo."

A moment later, a figure draped in a sheet appeared in front of her holding a gun.

CHAPTER 23
TWENTY-THREE
SKIDDOO

Skye couldn't tell who it was, or even if it was a man or a woman, but she instinctively aimed the flashlight beam at the eyeholes cut into the sheet. The enshrouded figure flinched, throwing up an arm to shield its eyes. She immediately thumbed off the light and ran back the way she had come.

A gunshot ricocheted off a metal ladder a split second after Skye had passed it. Breathing hard, she flung herself at the door she had previously noticed and fumbled with the knob. It wouldn't budge.

Scanning the area for a weapon, Skye briefly considered trying to hide, but Bingo's yowls made discovery a sure thing. Instead she quickly moved beside the hulking cabinet, put the backpack containing the feline behind her feet to protect him, and braced herself.

Her attacker would be passing by the massive piece of furniture any second. She could hear the footsteps nearing, and as the pseudo-ghost stepped into her line of sight, she shoved the cabinet with all her strength. It teetered, and immediately she rammed her shoulder into it.

After a heart-stopping instant, it toppled with a loud clatter, the metal ringing off the concrete floor. Her aim had been good. The cabinet had landed on top of the pretend poltergeist, and only a shiny wingtip shoe protruded.

Skye knew she was losing it as a vision of the Wicked Witch of the West crushed by Dorothy's farmhouse flashed through her mind, and a giggle bubbled forth. Giving herself a mental slap, she refocused, grabbed the backpack containing Bingo, stepped around the downed spirit, and ran toward the front.

Vince met her near the door as he came rushing from the other side of the building. "I heard a gunshot."

"Where have you been?" Skye panted. "I've been calling and calling for you."

"I caught my foot in a pile of lumber. I only got it free a minute ago."

"Are you okay?"

When he nodded, she said, "We have to get out of here, now."

"Bingo." He reached over to pat the

feline's head, but she grabbed his arm and tugged him toward the Jeep.

"Get in." Skye shoved him toward the driver's side, then sprinted around the hood and jumped into the passenger seat. She held the backpack tightly in her lap, and as soon as Vince was inside she ordered, "Lock the doors and get us out of here."

He complied, then threw the vehicle into REVERSE. As he got the Jeep turned around, Skye saw the phony phantom running out of the storage building, sheet flapping around its ankles. Vince stomped on the accelerator, and they flew down the lane followed by the sound of gunshots.

Phew! That had been close. Too close. Skye'd had a hard time persuading Vince to let her go home alone. Only when she had pointed out that Loretta's car was still in his apartment parking lot, and he might have a chance at sweet-talking himself back into the attorney's good graces, did he agree to let Skye go. Vince's libido nearly always won over his common sense.

Driving home, she tried to decide what to do about the pistol-packing poltergeist. Should she report what had happened? Obviously she couldn't admit to breaking and entering, but she had to tell someone that she'd been shot at.

As Skye passed the only pay phone in town — the one at the gas station across from Vince's hair salon — she made an abrupt decision and pulled up to the booth. She rolled down her window and called the police department. Disguising her voice, Skye anonymously reported hearing gunshots at Alana's address. The dispatcher was still asking questions when Skye hung up and drove away. She had done the best she could without incriminating herself. She just hoped it was enough.

Skye spent the rest of the night locked in her bathroom with Bingo and her shotgun. She dozed for a few minutes at a time, only to be jerked awake by dreams she couldn't remember.

At five a.m. Skye gave up attempting to sleep, showered and dressed. She was eating a bowl of raisin bran when she remembered the ball of paper Bingo had carried with him into the backpack.

The pack was by the front door where she had flung it after freeing the cat from its confines. She hurried over and grabbed the backpack, scooped out the crumpled wad and flattened it. She frowned. It was a newspaper page. On one side were listings for movies at theaters in Chicago and the suburbs; on the other side was a picture of a painting that looked familiar. In fact, it looked a lot like the one marked in the discarded library book.

She took the newspaper page into the kitchen, grabbing the library art book from the sunroom on her way, and spread them both out on the table. The paintings were unquestionably done by the same artist. The caption under the painting pictured on the newspaper page read KAHLO'S FRIDA AND THE MISCARRIAGE LITHOGRAPH ON PAPER SOLD AT AUCTION FOR $107,216.

Skye gasped. That was definitely the kind of money for which someone would kill. Still, none of this made sense. How would Beau get hold of an expensive painting? And who would know he had it, know it was valuable, and be willing to commit murder to get it?

She chewed her thumbnail. Had it been a payoff from one of his blackmail victims? But none of the people that Skye knew of could afford that kind of artwork. She was getting nowhere with this line of thinking. She needed to approach it from another angle.

Okay. Who knew about art, was trusted by Beau, and would be willing to take a life for money? Alana fit the first two criteria, but would she kill her own brother?

Skye rubbed her temples, trying to make herself think clearly. Alana certainly couldn't be the ghost who had shot at her and Vince at the storage building. And she couldn't be the person who stirred up Earl Doozier. Earl had said it was a man who told him about Skye's troubles, and she was pretty sure whoever got Earl going did so for a reason connected to Beau's death.

Besides, Skye prided herself on being a good judge of character, and she would swear Alana loved her brother and would never kill him. However, Skye had been wrong before, and maybe Alana was a better actress than Skye was a psychologist.

One way or the other, it was time to visit the art teacher in the hospital.

Skye checked her appointment book. She had a Pupil Personnel Service meeting at seven thirty at the elementary school, but nothing afterward that she couldn't put off until Thursday. She'd take an emergency day and leave right after the PPS meeting.

The smell of disinfectant and flowers combined into an eye-watering aroma in the hospital corridor. Skye checked the numbers beside the doorways as she hurried down the sterile hallway. She had been surprised to be directed to a regular hospital room when she asked for Alana. She hoped that meant the art teacher was conscious and doing better.

Three twenty-six. Skye paused and knocked on the partially closed door. There was no sign of Neville, and no answer even after she called out. Skye took a half step inside to see if it was the right room.

It was. Alana lay motionless on the bed. Skye fully entered the room and moved closer to the still figure. She said softly, "Alana, it's me, Skye. I've brought something to show you."

An eyelid flickered, and then Alana's index finger curled slightly, seeming to beckon Skye closer. Skye obeyed, stepping right next to the bed, and bending down to the reclining woman's level.

"Is he still here?" Alana breathed, her voice rusty from disuse and softer than a whisper.

"Who?" Skye asked, looking around. "I don't see anyone else."

"Bathroom?" Alana asked in an undertone.

Skye checked and came back. "No one."

Suddenly Alana sat up and clutched Skye's arm. "You have to save me. When I figured out he had murdered Beau, he tried to kill me and make it look like suicide."

"Who?"

A voice from behind her answered, "Me."

Skye whirled around. Neville Jeffreys walked into the room, closing and locking the door behind him. In his right hand he held a gun with a silencer attached to the muzzle.

"Why?" Skye tried to back away from the advancing gun, but she was trapped between Jeffreys and Alana's hospital bed.

"Why did I kill Hamilton? He double-crossed me. He welshed on a deal."

Skye forced herself to think. "How did he do that?" There had to be a way out of this.

"He refused to hand over the painting he stole from you. He said he found a higher bidder, but my buyer isn't someone you can get away with doing that to."

The call button! Skye inched her hand down on the mattress near Alana, who once again appeared to be unconscious. "I don't have any valuable artwork." If she could find the button, she could signal the nurse. When the nurse came to see what Alana needed and found the door locked, she'd get help.

"He found it when he was nosing around looking for something to blackmail you over. That old pack rat who left the house to you must have bought it from the artist herself back in the thirties. No one's known where that painting has been since then."

Skye's fingers found the smooth plastic of the button and she started to press it frantically, wishing she knew Morse code. "That explains the art book and the newspaper clipping. Beau must have seen the painting at my house, then read the article in the paper. He must have gotten the art book to check and see what else that artist had painted." She kept talking, hoping the nurse would be quick to answer the summons.

Jeffreys nodded at Skye's deductions. "Right, then he showed it to me and asked me to sell it for him."

"How did you know you'd do something illegal?"

"She" — Jeffreys used the gun to point to Alana — "always refused to admit that I dealt in stolen artwork, but Beau had no trouble accepting what I did."

"He wouldn't, considering his own propensity for criminal activity."

"Exactly. And as to why I'm going to kill her — she's an ungrateful bitch. I've been supporting her for years with my ill-gotten gains, and then she gets all self-righteous and says she can't close her eyes to the fact that I killed her brother. Stealing is one thing, murder, apparently, is another."

Skye held her breath. Was that someone in the hall trying to open the door? "So you bought her all those designer clothes, her trips to New York, and her BMW with dishonest money." She had to keep him distracted.

"Yes, not to mention buying her that house." He took a step closer. "Now, the reason I'm going to kill you is because you're too nosy to live. All you had to do was mind your own business. I did you a favor getting rid of Hamilton. He would have sucked you dry."

Skye looked into Jeffreys's eyes. Unlike her previous experience with murderers, his gaze was cold and sane. She could feel panic starting to bubble up inside of her. There was no room to maneuver. Her only hope was to keep him talking. "You killed Beau before finding out where he hid the painting, didn't you? You were the one breaking into my house trying to find where he stashed it, weren't you?"

"Yes. First through the window — then when you boarded them up, through the hole in the roof Hamilton made when he attempted to tear off your shingles." Jeffreys gave a humorless laugh. "I've even been there when your cop boyfriend stopped by. He almost caught me the other night when

I accidentally knocked over that stack of boxes and broke that mirror."

"Did you do something to my space heater and faucet, too?"

"No, that wasn't me." Jeffreys moved even closer to Skye, standing mere inches from her with his left side nearly pressing against Alana's bed.

"But you were the person dressed as a ghost at the storage building?" Skye kept pressing the nurse's call button. "Everyone said you never left the hospital."

"I slipped away that night to take a shower, and I was just in time to see your headlights turn in. I thought maybe you'd stumble on the painting, even though I'd already searched there, so I followed you."

"So you haven't found it yet?"

"No. You went and hired a real contractor on me. Once she finishes with your roof, it will be a lot harder to get in. Unless, of course" — he pointed the gun at Skye's head — "you're gone. She'll stop working and no one will be living there." A sudden pounding on the door made him look behind him.

At that moment Alana's right leg swung up and arced down on Neville's wrist. The gun clattered to the floor.

From the hallway they heard a male voice

order, "Get the keys from the nurses' station." Then the hammering got louder and the same voice shouted through the door, "Security. Open up in there."

Without thinking, Skye jumped on the startled art thief and he toppled backward. Alana leapt off the bed, frantically searching the floor for the gun.

Skye had managed to grab Neville's wrists, and her weight pinned him to the ground, but she knew she couldn't hold on long. She shouted to Alana, "Forget the gun! Unlock the door!"

Alana raced to the door, flipped open the dead bolt, and flung it open. Pointing, she said, "That's him. That's the man who killed my brother."

Two large men dressed in dark blue security uniforms ran past her. Between the two of them, they separated Skye from the murderer, but before they could secure Jeffreys, he scooped the gun from beneath him, pointed it at the guards, and edged toward the door. "I'll shoot the first person who moves."

As Jeffreys backed across the threshold, the senior guard yelled, "Doug, don't let him get away."

Doug, the security man stationed in the hall, shoved a wheelchair into the escaping murderer's path. Jeffreys fell backward, plopping into the chair, and his gun dropped to the floor. Doug, a strapping young man who no doubt had played high school football, tackled him, and instantly the other security guards rushed out of the room and secured him. Jeffreys's curses trailed down the hall as they dragged him away.

While hospital personnel swarmed around Alana and Skye to see if they were okay, Skye looked at Alana and said, "You're a lot stronger than I thought."

Alana appeared dazed. "I'm a lot stronger than I thought, too."

A commotion by the door drew Skye's attention. She turned back to Alana and took the other woman's hand. "It looks like we'll both need to be strong for a little longer."

Before Alana could ask why, they heard shouting, and Buck Peterson pushed his way into the room.

He strutted up to Skye and poked her in the chest with his index finger. "I shoulda known I'd find you here. Anytime there's a ruckus, you're always in the middle of it."

"You're welcome." Skye stepped out of range of his jabbing finger. "Glad I could help you catch the *real* killer."

Ignoring Skye's comment, he turned to Alana. "And you. Don't think for a minute that this puts you in the clear, missy. Your part in all this will come out real soon. My men will have your boyfriend singing like Robinson Caruso."

Skye and Alana looked at each other. Alana was biting her lip and Skye felt a gurgle of laughter trying to escape. Suddenly, the stress of the last week slammed into her, and Skye lost control. She looked down her nose at the sheriff and said, "If you mean Robinson Crusoe, that would imply that Neville will be performing on a desert island. And if you mean Enrico Caruso, that's impossible. Caruso was a tenor and Neville is distinctly a baritone."

Peterson narrowed his eyes, then without warning backhanded Skye. She swayed from the vicious blow and the coppery taste of blood filled her mouth. Instinctively, she stepped forward and jerked her knee up into his groin with as much force as she could muster. The sheriff squealed like a rubber bath toy and grabbed his nightstick from his belt.

As he raised the weapon in Skye's direction, Alana launched herself at him. He flung her away like she was a piece of lint on his uniform and she landed hard, hitting her head against the wall.

Peterson smiled meanly at the injured

women while fingering the bleeding scratch on his cheek. "Both your asses are mine. Assaulting a police officer is a felony."

Before either of them could reply, a voice from the door said, "I don't think so, Peterson. I saw the whole incident, and I'll be glad to testify at their civil trial when they sue you for police brutality if you try to bring charges against either of them." A man wearing a Laurel city police chief's uniform stood a few inches inside the room, his hand resting on his gun. "Now move away from the women, and go process a real criminal for a change."

EPILOGUE

"Ms. D, thank you so much for letting us have the party at your house." Frannie Ryan rushed up to Skye and hugged her from behind.

Skye had considered canceling the celebration after Jeffreys's arrest, but decided to go through with it. After all, his crime had nothing to do with the kids, and they deserved their reward for all the hard work they had put into the newspaper.

After freeing herself from the teen's embrace, Skye turned to face the girl. "You all earned it. Winning the Blevins Award took a lot of talent." Skye had been sitting at the kitchen table with the other adults, but now she stood. "I only wish the house was in better shape."

"But it's the coolest." Frannie turned to Xenia, who had been standing silently in the doorway. Today she wore black jeans with a humongous black sweatshirt that fell to her knees. "Xenia says she can feel a presence in this house. Later on we'll have a séance and see if she can summon it."

Not quite knowing how to react to Frannie's last statement, Skye responded to her first one. "The house will be even cooler once my contractor finishes fixing it up. I'm just relieved the windows are in and my new roof is on." It was Saturday afternoon, and Dulci's crew had finished installing the last pane of glass and shingle that morning.

Justin sauntered into the room and up to Frannie. He whispered something in her ear, then led the giggling girl away. Xenia raised a sardonic eyebrow in Skye's direction, then followed the other two teens.

"Should we see what they're up to?" Skye looked at Trixie. "It worries me a little that Xenia has become so tight with Frannie."

"They'll be fine. Frannie's a leader, not a follower. She won't let Xenia get her into any trouble." Her friend waved away Skye's concern. "Besides, you were about to fill us in on the details of the Case of the Bumbling Art Thief."

Skye nodded, but resolved to check up on the teens in a little while. For now, she looked around the table. Everyone was supposedly there to help chaperone, but what they really came for was to hear what had happened to Neville Jeffreys. For the past few days, Skye had avoided discussing the matter.

May sat silently next to Jed, a pleading expression aimed toward Skye. Skye hadn't talked to her mother since being locked in the bowling alley basement with Simon.

Vince and Loretta were also there, although not openly as a couple, and Vince had made it obvious that he expected Skye to fulfill her promise to tell their parents about his relationship with the attorney.

Uncle Charlie knew the least, not having been involved in the situation. This was an unusual position for him and he didn't like it. A semipermanent scowl had settled on his face.

Skye knew she had postponed this moment for as long as possible. She braced herself and began her story. "Beau had made it a habit to look around the houses he was renovating in search of something to hold over the owner's head in case they didn't like his work, which was usually the case.

"When Beau was searching my house, he found a small painting that looked familiar to him. He had seen a similar one in the *Chicago Tribune* that had sold for over a hundred thousand dollars. Beau knew that his sister's boyfriend dealt in stolen art, so he showed Neville the painting. Neville not only told Beau it was authentic, but that he had a buyer for it."

Uncle Charlie tilted his chair back, unconcerned when the old wood groaned under his weight, and commented, "Then Hamilton got greedy, right?"

"Sort of. He somehow found a buyer on his own. We're not sure how. Alana thinks maybe one of the online sites." Skye stepped into the hallway, listened to make sure the teens were okay, then came back into the kitchen. "Anyway, in order to be discreet, Neville came by boat the day he was supposed to pick up the painting. Beau met him at the dock and told Neville he was selling it on his own. They struggled and Neville shot him."

May piped in, "Okay, we know the part after that. You found Beau and tried to save him, but it was too late."

Skye felt a twinge of guilt. If only she had come directly home that day. "Neville killed Beau before he found out where Hamilton had stashed the painting. He searched Beau's truck, his house, his storage building, everywhere, but no painting. Finally, he decided Beau must have left it somewhere in my house."

Vince spoke up. "So he was the one who kept breaking in, moving things around, and making you think you had a ghost."

"Sort of. He did break in, and he was the one who shoved the boxes into the dresser and kidnapped Alana, but he claims he didn't turn the kitchen faucet into a geyser, and he had nothing to do with the space heater blowing up the other night."

"Gotta expect that with an old house," Jed commented.

Skye nodded, but wasn't completely convinced. It still seemed odd to her that those things only happened when she and Wally were getting intimate. "Then on Monday night, Alana overheard a conversation between Neville and his buyer, and realized Neville was always away when something bad happened. She put two and two together and concluded that Neville was her brother's killer. Foolishly, she confronted him. He convinced her she was mistaken, but then decided he had to get rid of her before she changed her mind and went to the police. He got her drunk, then gave her a margarita with an overdose of sedatives crushed into it.

"When Alana's neighbor found her, and the doctors saved her, he couldn't risk her telling the police about him. That's why he stayed with her at the hospital. He was trying to find a time to finish killing her, but there was always staff nearby. She faked being unconscious, waiting for him to leave, but she could never be sure he was really gone, not merely sitting outside her door."

"Then you showed up." Loretta crossed her arms.

"Did you know Neville was the murderer?" May asked.

"No, but I had figured out Beau was killed over a painting." Skye explained how she'd found the art book and the newspaper clipping.

"How did the art book get thrown in the ditch?" Charlie questioned.

"We know Beau checked it out of the library using Alana's card, because she got an overdue notice for it. We think Neville threw it out of the truck window when he drove off after killing Beau — probably to get rid of anything connecting Beau to the painting."

"Why didn't Jeffreys put Beau's truck in a deeper lake?" Vince asked.

"Neville had been to the Recreation Club with Beau and Alana. He was a champion rower, or whatever you call it, so he knew to use Beau's key to get in. But not being local, he didn't know that particular lake was so shallow. By the time he realized the truck wouldn't sink, it was stuck, and he couldn't move it.

"Excuse me for a minute." Skye went to check again on the kids. While sorting through Mrs. Griggs's belongings, Skye had found an old trunk full of board games from the forties and fifties. She had put it out for the teens to explore. Currently they were engaged in a wild game of Monopoly.

Skye smiled and went back to the kitchen, continuing her story. "The wet patches the police discovered in Alana's trunk after her car was found at the Rec Club were from the inflatable raft Neville had been using to get back and forth from Alana's house to mine. He must have deflated it and carried it away with him when he walked back to her place."

Loretta took a sip of her wine, then said, "I'm guessing Neville was the guy who stirred up Earl Doozier and got him to try to scare Dulci away."

"Yep. Alana had told Neville some Doozier stories, especially the ones about how they've adopted me, so he figured Earl was the perfect stooge to rile things up." Skye shook her head. "Dulci was too good a contractor, and she was getting things done too fast. Neville was afraid that, since I had changed the locks, he wouldn't be able to get inside the house anymore once the windows were in and the roof fixed."

"So what happened after Neville was arrested?" Trixie asked.

"I was lucky on two counts. First, Loretta wasn't far away so she got there quickly to represent me." Skye didn't mention that the attorney was nearby because she was at Vince's. "And second, the hospital was within Laurel's city limits. Laurel's police chief is a reasonable man, and between him and Loretta, Sheriff Peterson couldn't be too awful to me." Skye resisted the urge to touch her bruised cheekbone. She had decided not to tell anyone that Peterson had hit her, afraid that Charlie, Jed, or even Vince might feel they had to even the score with the sheriff.

"Still, the police kept you an awful long time," Trixie commented.

"That's because I had to give my statement about a hundred times Wednesday night. That's why I didn't want to talk about it for a while, and put you all off until now."

Charlie took a swig of beer, allowed a soft burp to escape his lips, then said, "From what I hear, come the election, we won't have to worry about Bucky Peterson anymore. My sources say that the people are fed up with him after he tried to blame Hamilton's murder on his being a drug pusher. Everyone knows we don't have none of that nonsense here in Scumble River."

"Yep." Jed nodded. "Peterson cackles a lot, but I ain't seen no eggs yet."

Skye refrained from reminding everyone of the meth lab that had been discovered last February.

"Are you getting back the money that you gave Beau for a deposit?" May asked, cutting to the important issue.

"Alana has promised to give it to me as soon as she gets his estate settled. Minus the materials that my new contractor managed to get ahold of."

"How about the painting? Did you find it? Are you rich?" Trixie demanded.

This was the one thing she couldn't tell them, especially with Xenia in the next room. "All I can say is the painting has been located. It turns out it belongs to someone else, so no, I won't be rich." Skye looked around. "Any more questions? No? Good, because I have some for you guys."

The others at the table squirmed as Skye pinned them all with a stare. "First, Dad, how did you get Simon's cell phone number?"

"Ah." Jed looked nervously at May. "He

gave it to me in case of emergency when I was working on his mom's car."

"Oh." Skye moved on. "Who called the sheriff that day I found Beau dying?"

"The EMT from the ambulance that picked Beau up the night he was shot is Buck's nephew," May offered. "I bet he phoned his uncle when he got the radio call to come out here."

Skye turned to Loretta. "Why does Dulci need work? She's a fantastic contractor and should be booked months ahead."

"I'm only telling you this because she said I could," Loretta prefaced her answer. "Due to some events in Dulci's past, she'll only work for women, and there are not that many women-only jobs out there."

Skye looked at Vince and asked, "Now?"

"As soon as we leave." Vince got up, took Loretta's hand, and tugged her to her feet. "We've got to go. Bye, everyone."

When Skye heard the front door close, she turned to her parents and said, "Now for some good news."

May's gaze immediately shot to Skye's left hand.

"Not about me, about Vince."

"What?" May demanded. "If it's good news, why didn't he tell us himself before he left?"

Skye crossed her fingers, hoping her parents would understand that what she was telling them was a positive. "Vince wanted me to tell you that he's dating Loretta." She waited for a reaction. When none came, she added, "It looks pretty serious." Still no comment from her folks. Finally, she asked, "Are you two okay with that?"

"Well, we've never had one of those people in the family before." May frowned. "But she seems real nice."

Skye counted to ten. She had been hoping Loretta's race wouldn't be an issue.

Before Skye could figure out what to say, May continued. "Of course, I suppose not all lawyers are evil, bloodsucking leeches."

"No." Skye grinned. "Not all of them."

"And considering Vince's usual taste, the possibility of a serious relationship with a non-bimbo is a step in the right direction for him." May looked at Jed, who dipped his head in agreement. "Do you know if she wants children?"

"I'm sure she does." Skye crossed her fingers again. Having a baby was not a subject she had ever discussed with her friend, but she'd worry about that if her brother and Loretta lasted as a couple for more than a month.

Later on, May got Skye aside and said,

"Are you still mad at me for locking you in with Simon?"

"Yes. And if you do anything like that again, I swear I truly will move."

"I'm sorry." May looked down. "I really thought he was the one for you. I was afraid you were throwing away your chance at happiness."

"I know, Mom. For a while I thought he was the one, too."

"But he isn't?"

"It doesn't look that way."

May nodded sadly.

Skye was silent for a moment, then said, "Hey, one thing. How did you and Bunny ever work together to pull off getting Simon and me locked in the basement?"

"I just gritted my teeth and was nice to her." May hugged Skye. "You know I'd do anything for you."

Skye hugged her mom back. "I know, Mom. But I can handle anything that life throws at me. I may not be able to handle it well, or gracefully, or the way you think I should, but I will handle it."

"How was the party?" Wally asked from his usual spot on the sunroom settee.

"Good. The kids all seemed to have fun." Skye put a plate of leftover sub sandwiches, relishes, and chips on the table in front of him. "Though I was a bit worried when Xenia found an Ouija set. Luckily, before any spirits could respond to her summons the old board crumbled into a thousand pieces, and they had to give up."

"Good. That girl doesn't need any more power than she already has." Wally patted the cushion next to him, silently inviting Skye to sit down. "Did you answer everyone's questions?"

"Pretty much." Skye took a seat in the chair, ignoring Wally's invitation. Tonight she wouldn't let him distract her with his kisses. "You know, there are some answers I don't have, and some that aren't mine to share."

"You never did figure out what Jess Larson was being blackmailed about?"

"No, and I didn't try. He's been open with me on several occasions and his secret is none of my business." Skye popped an olive into her mouth.

Wally nodded. "Priscilla's secret is safe, too. Since Jeffreys confessed to Hamilton's murder, there's no need to investigate her further."

"Was that fingerprint they found on the boat Neville's?"

"Yes. He's never been arrested before, so

we had nothing to match it to until he was processed after trying to kill you and Alana."

"That's good. It's always handy to have a piece of physical evidence."

"You never did tell me how you got Bingo back." Wally reached down and stroked the feline in question, who was rubbing against his legs and purring.

Skye bit her lip. She still hadn't decided what to tell Wally about Bingo's reappearance. Would her actions in rescuing the cat ruin their budding relationship? Finally she told him the whole story, ending with, "I couldn't leave him there another day without food and water." If she and Wally were going to be together, he had to be able to accept her as she was.

He nodded slowly. "I see your point."

When he didn't comment further, Skye breathed a sigh of relief and changed the subject. "I'm glad Raette Craughwell came forward and told you that Beau was Xenia's father, and that he had given her the painting to sell for his daughter's education."

"Me, too. Because I know I would have never gotten the information from you."

Skye ignored his jibe and went on, almost talking to herself. "I've been consulting with Raette quite a bit this week. I finally convinced her to talk to Xenia about Beau —

both his life and his death." Skye's voice thickened. "As I suspected, Xenia had figured out Beau was her father, which is why she wanted to move to Scumble River. Once she was here, Xenia followed Beau around, even managed to 'bump' into him a few times, but never told him who she was."

Wally said, "That's what Raette told me, too."

"Did she tell you she finally contacted him, and told him she and his daughter were in town?" When Wally nodded, Skye went on, "At first he turned his back on the situation, but finally he came around, which is when he gave Raette the painting and told her to sell it and use the money for his daughter. But before they could set up a meeting between Beau and Xenia, he was killed. After his death, Xenia became even more angry and hostile."

"Sounds like they'll need to use a good chunk of that money for therapy for the girl," Wally commented.

"I sure hope they do." Skye brushed a tear away. "It's so sad that Beau never got the chance to change. He might have become a better man. It seemed like he was going to step up and be a father to Xenia. Granted, giving her dirty money wasn't the best way, but it was a move in the right direction.

Neville stole that chance from both of them."

"Jeffreys might be glad he's going to prison. Xenia's revenge might be worse than jail time." Wally took a swig of beer before asking, "After everything you've been through, are you sure you want to let Raette keep the money from the painting?"

Skye thought about her decision, then said, "Yes. The painting was never mine to begin with. Who knows what Mrs. Griggs would have done if she knew it was so valuable. She probably would have left it to a museum or something."

"But that's not your real reason." Wally leaned toward her and took her chin in his hand.

"No." She looked into his warm brown eyes and risked exposing her inner self to him. "The truth is, I like to think of this as Beau's chance for redemption, and Xenia's chance to recover from her father abandoning her. I hope Xenia will see the money from the painting as an expression of his love and forgive him, which will free her from the world of hatred she's been living in."

Wally kissed her gently on the lips. "Do you really think you can make things right — make sure people get what they deserve?"

"Sometimes."

Wally tried to take her in his arms, but Skye scooted back in her chair. "Hey, I have a question for you. How did you know all my favorite foods and all that other stuff about me?"

"I've worked with your mother for ten years." Wally stood up and took Skye's hands in his, drawing her up beside him. "I've listened when she talks about you. Doesn't that prove I know you well enough for us to get involved?"

"But I don't know those kinds of details about you." Skye took a step away from him. "We need to take it slow until I do."

"How can you ignore the physical attraction between us?" Wally moved behind her, rubbing her shoulders.

Skye gulped, then said in a breathy voice, "Regardless of how hot and steamy a relationship is at first, the passion fades, and there had better be something to take its place. I don't want to rush into things."

"You can't rush into love." Wally kissed her neck. "It's either there or it isn't."

Skye felt herself melting, but tried again to put the brakes on. "I just don't know. I don't want to be hurt again."

Wally turned her around and put his arms around her, leaning his forehead against hers. "Life may not always turn out the way we want it to, but we might as well grab for the good times that are offered."

Skye looked past him to a book lying on the coffee table. It was a rare edition of *Little Women* signed by the illustrator, and had been delivered that morning. The card contained a single word: "Sorry." There hadn't been a signature, but she recognized the handwriting.

ABOUT THE AUTHOR

Denise Swanson worked as a school psychologist for more than twenty-two years. She lives in Illinois with her husband, Dave, who is a classical music composer, and their cool black cat, Boomerang. For more information, visit her Web site at www.deniseswanson.com.

The employees of Thorndike Press hope you have enjoyed this Large Print book. All our Thorndike and Wheeler Large Print titles are designed for easy reading, and all our books are made to last. Other Thorndike Press Large Print books are available at your library, through selected bookstores, or directly from us.

For information about titles, please call:
    (800) 223-1244

or visit our Web site at:
    www.gale.com/thorndike
    www.gale.com/wheeler

To share your comments, please write:
    Publisher
    Thorndike Press
    295 Kennedy Memorial Drive
    Waterville, ME 04901